I0760669

SECOND CHANCES

For permission requests, write to the publisher, addressed "Attention: Permissions Coordinator," at the address below

THE PUBLISHING CIRCLE
Regarding: Miriam McGuirk
4615 NE 25th Court
Vancouver, WA 98663
USA
or
admin@ThePublishingCircle.com

SECOND CHANCES is a work of fiction. Names, characters, businesses, organizations, places, events, and incidents are products of the author's imagination or are used fictitiously. Any resemblance to actual persons, living or dead, or actual events is entirely coincidental.

SECOND CHANCES / MIRIAM McGUIRK
FIRST EDITION
ISBN 978-1-955018-27-2 (EBOOK)
978-1-955018-25-8 (SOFTCOVER)
978-1-955018-29-6 (LARGE PRINT)
978-1-955018-28-9 (HARDCASE)

Book design by Michele Uplinger

A NOVEL

MIRIAM McGUIRK

DEDICATION

I dedicate *Second Chances* to
Breast Cancer Now—Someone Like Me
And the NHS Cancer Surgeons, Oncologists,
and Nursing Staff, UK

ACKNOWLEDGEMENTS

Thanks to Linda Stirling of The Publishing Circle agreeing to sign me, I have walked into my novel adventure. Linda took me under her wing and continues to show me the important tools to dig deep and develop my craft. Thanks to her skilled approach and vast experience, this novel has come to life. I thank her for the time she has given me and her never-ending patience and wisdom.

To Laura Steward, a US podcaster, keynote speaker, author, and radio host of It's All about the Questions. Thank you for making a life-changing introduction to Linda Stirling.

Thank you to Linda's superb design team for this captivating book cover. I love it and think of Molly as a kind of Mary Poppins, balancing on the tightrope of life while reaching out and supporting her community.

Thank you, Liz White, of Think Wild Media for your feedback. You have been my supporter and cheerleader since 2013.

Thank you to Ollie Reece-Jones for the conversation we shared. Over mugs of coffee in my garden, we discussed the feelings and emotions of young adults that gave me more insight to write Jamie's character.

To Jessie Cahalin, @booksinhandbag who has supported me these last years. Passionate about writing, she reaches out to other authors. Thank you for your kind heart and knowledge.

To my core family, friends, writing colleagues, subscribers to my newsletter, and followers on social media, I truly appreciate your support and the special bond we continue to develop.

And to my brother-in-law. Thanks to him owning a vintage Morgan, I named Florence's Morgan, Millie. Waiting for that drive out and wind in my hair feeling, David!

To you, dear early readers and reviewers, along with my loyal readers, some I know, and others I look forward to meeting and getting to know. A great big thank you.

Finally, to my constant love, my husband, Chris. His support and help are immeasurable. He continues to be my superhero. Perhaps it's time I ordered him a flowing red cape for him to show off his superpowers.

TESTIMONIALS

The chance to slip into other worlds where you as the author show us redemption, caring, second chances, gentleness, and happy new beginnings is a gift for which your readers—including me—will thank you. You manage to weave stories together beautifully, paint word pictures of exotic places and times, and keep readers engaged and caring.

Ricki Baker

I truly loved each page. Heart-warming, positive, encouraging. I was charmed by each character and the world you created for them. A warm and caring read with some good truths. This will be a favorite for many readers. Reminded me of a Maeve Binchy book.

Jena C. Henry

I loved how each character was not only described, but also brought to life in such detail, at times I felt I could go outside and meet them in person. And the nostalgia, I am a big fan of nostalgic memories and love to read the back stories of people in books. The author did a superb job in placements of her characters nostalgic memories, that it did not take away from the plot or story line as I continued reading. From India, London and a coastal town called Little Shore, the adventures throughout this story is heart-warming, breath-taking, wonderfully written and beautifully told.

Catherine Mellon

The writing is beautiful and at times poetic, conjuring up descriptions that transport the reader through time and place, into the world of your characters, so perfectly that I felt I was there, with them, on every step of their journey. What's more, the visualisations remain with you, long after you read that final page. The knowledge and beauty of India was perfectly conveyed, and I fell in love with Boudie and her guest house – what a wonderful woman to give young Kit/Jamie a second chance.

Elly Redding
AUTHOR OF *IN TOO DEEP*

Congratulations on such a wonderful story, the mysteries of the characters back stories which eventually came full circle were really enjoyable. It had the right mixture of surprise, joy and sadness. I wonder whether there will be a sequel?

Jemma Fairclough

A beautiful book—a delightful story. A nice mix of characters and back stories. Not too many that I got confused by complicated threads. Enjoyed the unexpected plot twists. Some lovely touches of humour which made me smile. Chapter 20 with Florence's letters was poignant; one of my favourites.

Traci Ferguson

I enjoyed the story. It became my friend in troubled times. My favourite characters without doubt, were Florence and Boudie. What a pair! They were both intriguing but for different reasons, the type of people I'd liked to meet in real life.

Lisa Settle

A beautiful and mindful book. There is, intrigue, love, community, and Bryce's strong character jumps off the page. Relaxed and yet full of mystery. Describing a book as a page turner is usually a compliment but I would say this is a 'page re-player' because you want to relive the gentility, heart break and feisty characters over and over. The flow is just the right pace. I love the book. Others will love the book.

Liz White

The idea of 'second chances' is well and truly front and centre in this book. Second chances at love, at family, at work, with friends, with hobbies, with yourself, and with life itself. Even after I'd finished, I kept thinking I had to go back to it, because I enjoyed it so much. It's a beautiful, heart-warming, tender story.

Victoria Bucknell

BOOKSBYYOURBEDSIDE.ORG

CHAPTER 1

RACING UP THE STAIRS TWO STEPS AT A time, she pushed open the door to Jamie's bedroom. His bed lay bare. She turned and snapped open the double wardrobe doors. Cleared out. Not even a pair of muddy trainers or an old, frayed T-shirt littered the floor of the closet. She ran back down the stairs and out into the garden. In the winter silence, her breath puffed out as she spun around, calling out his name. She shivered and tore back into the house. Her mobile sat on the carpeted floor in the living room. Yanking it from its charger, she scrolled to Jamie's number and pressed it, only to hear a recorded message.

"Hey, Jamie, where are you?" she said after the beep, doing her best to keep from sounding pleading. "We have plans, remember? Today is the day, and we promised to share a last breakfast at the house. Hurry home." She hung up. Could he have gone to buy breakfast to surprise her?

Her normal calmness, acquired through practicing and teaching yoga, disappeared. Over the next hour, she checked the phone repeatedly and finally convinced herself that checking it nonstop couldn't force it to ring, so she shoved it into her trouser pocket. Thoughts jumbled through her brain. Had she been selfish in her wish to move and change her life?

Okay, so Jamie initially was not keen to move, she reasoned, but they had discussed it. She'd pacified him with a promise, saying if he continued to have misgivings, they would look for a flat-share or other digs for him. If he'd changed his mind, why would he not tell her? Was he afraid he might cause her more hurt after the pain of her separation from his father?

Unable to help herself, she once again pulled the phone from her pocket and pressed the redial button, but it went straight to message. Without thinking, she called Rory. When that call, too, went to voicemail, she dropped the phone onto the carpet. She pressed her eyes closed and leaned against the living room door.

A shrill buzzing startled her. She bent down and picked up the mobile from the carpet and saw Brandon O'Neill's name flash up. At the same time, the doorbell rang, reverberating around the house. After a few moments, an irate voice called through the letterbox. "Hey, Molly, it's Brandon. Where are you? Time is pressing. We need to get a handle on the day. Open the door."

"Jamie, Jamie, where have you gone?" she whispered. Were the bridges of her future about to crumble?

CHAPTER 2

KIT GRAPPLED WITH THE KEY IN THE LOCK of the front door. He staggered into the hallway of his friend's flat when the door suddenly swung open. Bending down, he tried to remove his knee-high boots, lost his balance, keeled over, and the side of his face slapped the rough floorboards. "*Ouch*", he muttered. His cheekbone stung. The roughness of the wooden floor reminded him of the spikes from the pygmy hedgehog he owned as a child, causing him to laugh a crazy kind of laugh.

"Shh, shh . . ." he whispered into the darkness. Gliding the other hand across his face, it came away greasy, unlike the stickiness of blood. *At least one part of my mind is still functioning*, he congratulated himself, realising the grease came from the caked theatre makeup he hadn't bothered to remove before heading to the pub earlier. Nor had he taken off his jewellery or costume. Lifting himself up, he leaned against the wall near the staircase and finally managed to pull one boot off.

Groping in the dark for the handrail, he hobbled up the stairs, each rickety step creaking, sending a screechingly painful message to his brain. At last, he reached the landing and tumbled into the spare room his co-actor friend had offered. The shape of an unmade bed swam into view. His mother would give him one of her lectures about it. He realised through his muddled mind, that was his past. He'd changed from Jamie to become Kit without her the wiser. Through his drunken state, that made him even more miserable.

Unable to care about the blasted boot remaining on his foot, he flung himself into the centre of the bed and drifted toward sleep. Images of performing on stage followed him towards oblivion.

• • •

From beneath the covers, a piercing sound spooked him awake. Some part of him recognised the sound as his phone. Rolling over with a groan when the phone continued to ring, he reached down to the baggy trousers he still wore and pulled out his mobile. Blinking his sleepy eyes, he squinted at the screen. He swiped the *accept* icon.

"Good morning, Kit. It's Boudie. Rise and shine. It's six thirty. Hope you are up, showered, and dressed. Remember, you made a promise to collect Florence and drive her to The Belleview?"

Irritated by Boudie's cheery intrusion, he wanted to scream, "Leave me alone!" He put one hand to the side of his face, finding it still sensitive. Navigating logic to connect with his voice, he begged for some semblance of focus.

He imagined Boudie's foot tapping as she waited for

his reply. Boudie eventually broke the silence and calmly called out her sister's address. It dawned on him that she had already painstakingly written it on a piece of paper five days before and handed it to him. He'd stuffed it into his bag, forgot about it, and immediately drove to Rochester in Kent. The opportunity to perform for three nights in a theatrical romp with his fellow actors had been a lucky break. He'd hoped being part of this touring festival would give him more kudos.

He cursed his fuzzy thoughts. Why, oh why, did he have to collect Boudie's sister and drive her back to Little Shore?

"Oops, I'd almost forgotten it was today," he said into the phone. His eyelids heavy, he shook his head from side to side.

"For heaven's sake, Kit. Florence is looking forward to her away-day. Please don't let her down. We're counting on you, and I expect you to wear a clean shirt when you collect her. Drive safely, darling boy. Have to dash. I've got a handful of guests who need feeding." Boudie rang off.

He stared at the mobile screen. How could he get out of this one? He pulled the sheet over his throbbing head.

• • •

Scrambled reflections from the night before, the grand finale of their production of a spoof on the film *The Pirates of the Caribbean,* came spilling out. At a theatre near Rochester, he'd performed in the lead role as Captain Jack Sparrow, a swashbuckling hero. Following a sparkling review of the production in the What's On section of *The Kent Chronicle,* the cast threw an impromptu wrap party by heading to the nearest Irish pub. He could not remember much, but alcoholic chasers had been involved. He recalled stomping in his knee-high boots on top of a table and singing with a pint of beer in one hand and a tequila shot in the other. The bemused locals had joined in with him and the other raucous actors as they clinked glasses.

Drumming hands on tables, the troop's drunken voices had reached a deafening pitch when the publican finally stepped in and calmly told them, "Now lads, you've had your fill of drink and your fun. It's time to leave in an orderly fashion."

He checked his watch; already seven. He needed to get a wiggle on, or he would have to listen to a further telling off from Boudie.

Feeling as sick as the ragged yellow and green parrot stitched to the shoulder of his black and gold embroidered pirate's costume, with the theme music of *Pirates* spinning around in his head like an earworm, a helplessness crept over him.

He remembered Boudie describing her sister as "a woman with more of a country look about her, older than I, with a personality that matches her untamed hair." That provided a half-decent clue, he decided, envisioning a woman of certain years standing by her gate in the wintry morning light, awaiting his arrival. She was probably like his grandparents, another older person who was a stickler for time, didn't sleep much, and filled the days with all kinds of to-do lists. There couldn't be too many pallid old women with wild hair standing on the curb at this unholy hour in freezing temperatures. This thought threw a heavy weight across his chest.

He pushed himself up and sat on the side of the bed, the springs squeaking as he moved. His unsavoury breath flowed out into the dingy, parquet-floored room. He looked around at the cluttered mess. What a far cry from the relaxed comfort of Boudie's Boutique B&B. He had surprised himself at how long he'd remained enmeshed in Boudie's life and work. The Belleview had allowed him space, providing a comfortable refuge these last years.

Sliding from the bed, standing tall, and stretching his arms high above his head, he headed into the bathroom. He sat on the loo. Tiny daggers of pain struck across his brow and chewed at the side of his temple. He pulled the stubborn boot from his left foot. On removing the pirate costume, he tried not to suck in the stench of alcohol and stale sweat. Where had he left his pirate hat? If he didn't find it, he would be called upon to pay for another to be made. Hand on his forehead, his thoughts still fizzed.

He stood and studied the tiny walk-in shower, cringing at the sight. The thought of allowing his feet to touch its slimy floor nearly caused him to back away, never mind the sight of the dirty brown stain that rose halfway up from the drain and spread across one side of the tiles. A small square of dried soap stuck to a rusty soap holder. He would have no option but to use it to wash his body. Stepping in, he turned on the tap. Icy droplets hit his pounding head. He almost cried out. After a few minutes, warmer bursts sprinkled onto his body. It dawned on him he would not be able to remove his pirate's wig. The glue solvent was more than likely back in the theatre dressing room or packed away in one of the other actor's bags. So, hitching the mass of dreadlocks above his head, he leaned back, allowing the water to run down his recently waxed chest and the length of his torso. He twisted his body around so the warmer jets could soothe his aching shoulders. He prayed the headache would release itself.

The flow of hot water suddenly died. Frustrated, he turned off the tap and grabbed the lone towel from the rail. Boudie would be appalled over the state of the bathroom, never mind the blasted towel that was scarcely bigger than an old gentleman's handkerchief. Doing his best to dry off with the skimpy towel, he refused to think about how long it had been there, or where it came from. He picked up the boot and baggy trousers from the bathroom floor and padded into the chill of the bedroom. The cold air clung to his body, and the heat drained away.

Unhappy about the promise he'd made to Boudie, he nonetheless scrunched up his eyes and searched the makeshift bedroom for his kit bag. Kneeling, he looked under the bed and felt around the dusty corners to no avail.

Damn, I have no fresh clothes. And where the hell is my crisp white shirt? Suppressing his irritation, he stood up, exhaled, pulled on the creased trousers and the single knee-high boot. He had no choice but to wear the stage jacket that reeked of alcohol.

He spun around, spotting a metal clothes rack crammed with theatrical costumes. He walked over to it and rifled through the hangers. How tempting to change into one of the period outfits. But best not draw more attention to his already dishevelled state. At one end of the rack, a cracked mirror hung from a piece of string. He gazed at his sketchy reflection: red veins created paths across the whites of his eyes, and his right eye revealed an inky black-and-blue circle. He considered it for a few seconds. Could it be a bruise from his fall a few hours before in the hallway, or the aftereffect of the smudged kohl pencil he'd used to exaggerate the look of a cold and menacing pirate? Whatever the cause, red veins took precedence over the usual deep shade of blue. His mother had once described his eyes as "young and bright; eyes that would light up long summer days and nights." She wouldn't say that if she saw him now.

A stretchy love-and-peace bracelet rested on his wrist. He undid the twisted band and wound it into the matted wig to form a ponytail. He shivered as remaining squiggles of water trailed down his back onto the worn, stained parquet floor.

Snatching the car keys from the side table by the unmade bed, he patted both pockets of his trousers. Mobile and wallet in place, he trod down the warped steps of the staircase.

Still with only one boot on his foot, he limped his way into the kitchen and switched on an overhead light. He couldn't remember when he had last eaten. Opening the fridge door, a queasiness lodged at the back of his throat; blue and grey mould lined the empty shelves. In the fridge door, two open cartons of sour milk made his stomach lurch. "Bloody hell, that smell would make the dead rise again." He scrunched up his nose in disgust and slammed the door, turned to the kitchen sink, and ran the tap. He reached for a glass on the draining board and noticed lipstick marks. Grimacing, he filled the tumbler with water. It smelt of chlorine. The taste nauseated him. *Best not throw up*, he thought.

He snuck out to the hall and found his right boot. Hopping on one foot, he pulled it on, unable to do anything about the creaking floorboards. Quickly, he opened the front door and left.

He stumbled down the pavement, wondering where he had parked Boudie's car. First things first. He needed food. Passers-by wore heavy overcoats, their heads covered in warm hats, hands protected with leather gloves and necks enveloped in thick wool scarves. They stared at him in what appeared to be bemused wonder.

He spied the main street on his left, and a corner café that flashed with a blue neon sign—The Morning Light.

Crossing the street, he stepped inside and took in the crowded room. Hit by the smells of bacon fat, and the banging and clanking sounds from a coffee and expresso machine, his insides, hollow with hunger, made him want to shout, "Feed me, feed me now." Kit willed the chef to acknowledge him. "Here is a young man of theatre fame who needs to eat. Stand aside everyone while we prepare food for this thespian." Of course, in his imagination the customers graciously did as the chef requested.

Back in the real world, he caught sight of the beefy, six-foot-something chef and saw beads of sweat drip from his brow. Teeth clenched, he barked at one of his juniors, "For pity's sake, get a move on."

Kit felt empathy for the harried kitchen worker and remained silent. He stepped into the queue and waited his turn like the other customers.

Every table seemed occupied with men in either well-worn navy-blue suits or paint-splashed overalls. Others wore rough leather boots covered in blobs of dry cement.

These men knew their way around a full plate of food. He watched as they eagerly tucked into eggs, bacon, side orders of hot buttered toast, and pint mugs of Builder's Tea, their heads stuck in their morning papers. Those who weren't reading chatted in between mouthfuls of food, and some traded with each other for a sausage or another piece of bacon.

Moisture-ridden windows faced the street. The sound of Johnny Cash's *I Walk the Line* belted from an overhead speaker. A television sat on a shelf in a corner. The anchor woman had not a hell's chance of sharing her morning news above the music and din of the cafe.

He craved carbs and a few hits of caffeine. Smells of richly roasted coffee continued to fill his nostrils. Smoked fat from the pans of fried food curled up toward the ventilation system. A Scandinavian-looking girl, the only female in the café, stood at the till and took his order. She had perfect skin and kissable lips.

"Two takeout double espressos; two bacon, egg and sausage sandwiches; and two cans of Red Bull," he called out.

Within minutes, the pretty girl handed over the hot food and drinks. She smiled at him. "Going anywhere nice today?" she asked.

"Oh, just my usual flight to the Caribbean to be a pirate," he replied.

She looked him up and down and gave him a smirk. "Well, you look the part, but the black eye and the makeup on those sharp cheekbones need a bit of adjusting." She winked at him and held his gaze for a few more seconds. "Hope you come back soon. Enjoy the trip. Next, please. Who ordered the almond pastry and skinny latte?"

He toyed with the idea of hanging around. With a seat at one of the floral plastic-covered tables, he could have worked up the energy to chat up this gorgeous girl and explain the ridiculous costume and smudged makeup. But time pressed on, and he could not let Boudie down. He handed over the money, picked up the paper bag, and hurried out of The Morning Light.

He walked up and down the street, searching for Boudie's blue estate car. Eventually, he found it under some barren trees, although he had no recollection of leaving it there. He unlocked the passenger's side door, opened it, and carefully laid out his breakfast on the car's seat. He then opened the trunk. Relief washed over him. He retrieved the missing kit bag. As he slammed the trunk, he saw his crisp white shirt on a hanger on a hook in the back seat.

Desperate for a strong blast of coffee and some greasy food before the drive ahead, he moved around to the driver's side and quickly scrambled behind the wheel. Pushing the seat back, he settled in and flipped the lid off one of the cups of coffee and put it to his lips. Feeling a sharp burn on his tongue, caffeine lashed through his bloodstream. Reaching for a bottle of water on the floor, unscrewing the cap, he threw the liquid into his mouth and tore open one of the paper bags containing the sandwiches. He bit into one. *Manna.* Egg yolk dribbled out from the two thick slices of bread and ran down his chin. Grabbing some paper napkins the pretty Scandinavian had added to the bag he wiped the yellow stains away. On one napkin, scrawled in bold pen, she'd written her name, a mobile number, and a message:

Hey, Mr Pirate Man, I think you are so cute.
Call me.

Tyra

P.S. Have added a handful of facial wipes. Can't have Mr Pirate Man looking like Clown Man!

His face relaxed into a smile, and he placed the paper napkin in the centre pocket of the car. One day soon he would present himself as himself to Tyra.

He continued to eat until only crusts and fatty edges from the rinds of bacon remained. He wiped his mouth again and flicked the oily bag with the leftover food onto the floor. Later, he'd remove the evidence when he cleaned and vacuumed Boudie's car.

Refuelled, he sat for a few minutes, then unfolded the facial wipes and rubbed at his face, massaging his scratched cheekbone. On checking the results in the rear-view mirror, puffy eyes and dark circles that made him look like a raccoon reflected back at him.

"No more wallowing," he declared, speaking loudly at the vision in the mirror.

He snapped open the tab and gulped from one of the cans of Red Bull. In the middle pocket of the car, he found painkillers and a pair of oversized vintage shades. Peeling off two tablets from the blister pack of foil, he pushed them into his mouth and slugged more Red Bull.

On checking the clock on the dashboard, his thoughts wandered to Boudie's sister. She was probably frozen to her spot on the ground by now. He knew he would be late, but he stepped out of the car and removed the pirate's jacket with the stuck-on parrot. Naked from the waist up in the freezing air, he unhooked the clean shirt from its hanger and hastily put it on. Shaking, he got back in the car, threw the jacket onto the back seat, and turned the heat to full blast. He tried on the sunglasses. His head still hurt, but at least the intense light no longer dowsed his eyeballs in splinters of pain.

Looking a mess, there was no time to tidy himself up. Would Boudie's sister be a forgiving soul and allow him to make amends later? Without a magic fairy to sweep him any faster to his destination, he placed the key in the ignition, started the engine, and put the car in drive.

Even the anticipation of fresh sheets on a clean bed and a few hours of kip after taking Boudie's sister to Little Shore did not stop his mind from twitching with uncertainty.

What possessed me to get into such a state? Of course, he knew the answer. It was a thorny subject and not one he could afford to focus on today.

Accelerating, he drove onto the main road.

CHAPTER 3

Colonel Bryce Beckwith's mornings started not with the assault of an alarm clock but with a cacophony of sounds from next door—another red-brick house much the same as his own. Footsteps descended wooden stairs; doors opened, then slammed shut. The day had begun.

He found comfort in the racket his neighbour created.

This morning, Florence clattered around earlier than usual. Her voice boomed through the walls as she instructed her beloved dog, saying, "Come along, Lulabelle, into the garden. Go do your business."

He wondered if Florence had an early appointment.

An architect of time and ritual, at the start of every day, he picked up a glass picture frame from his bedside table and pressed his lips against the faded photograph of a young boy holding hands with a skinny girl who looked taller than him in the image of them laughing as they perched on two swings.

After kissing the photo, he looked directly across the bedroom to a small bookcase. A gilt-framed photograph faced outward. Diane Beckwith, his deceased wife, stared back.

She'd appeared unexpectedly in his life, for his parents had chosen her. They insisted he marry a woman of standing. "A future legacy," they said, uniting two business families, an alliance that would lead to a notable rise among the higher echelons of ex-pat society.

Romantic notions for the skinny young girl swinging happily in the photograph had to be dismissed. Other framed memories of the past graced the tables scattered throughout the house. Many showed a blissful childhood entwined with his best friend, Florence.

Over dinner one evening after Diane had agreed to the marriage, she casually said, "I have known since the beginning of this courtship, I am not *the one*. So, let's make the best of the arrangement, shall we, for our parents' sake?"

After taking solemn vows on the day of the wedding, Diane informed him she could not have children and insisted he must not get his hopes up.

Resigned to the marriage, he adapted, determined to lead a happy life with her. They accepted each other's habits and settled into a quiet companionship. After Diane passed, alone and unsure where his life would guide him, something led him to find Florence again. Even the prickly hedge that had divided them for nearly ten years could not quench his romantic dream of someday becoming more than a next-door neighbour and friend.

He walked through to his stark kitchen. His stomach rumbled as he set a table for one. Nestled on the window ledge among flowering potted plants sat his vintage

Bush radio. He turned the switch to BBC radio four, his soundtrack for the day.

Plucking three oranges from the fruit basket, he peeled them and dropped them one by one into the juicer, then poured the liquid into a tall glass.

The previous night, he'd soaked a small bowl of oats in milk. He threw them into a pan and stirred furiously once the liquid came to the boil and the oats swelled. After serving the steaming porridge into a warmed dish and allowing it to cool, he took his uniform of blue overalls and a beaten-up bowler hat from a hook on the kitchen door. Once he'd placed the overalls across a chair, he sat at the table, ready to eat.

He closed his eyes and tasted the first spoon of heavenly creaminess, his thoughts spinning back through time to India. In his memories, he felt a glow of heat caress his face. The vividness of his childhood, one filled with whistling thrushes, the buzz of bees, tastes of tropical fruit and sunshine enveloped him.

He recalled his nanny's wisdom. "If you eat well, you will do well," she'd say when he'd been a little boy sitting on a veranda alongside her, eating his porridge with a fresh chopped banana that had been picked earlier. His nanny always added a dollop of Indian honey. He ate quickly, eager to rush off to play and swim with his friend Florence.

The memory vanished as quickly as it had appeared. He carried on eating and sipped his tea, always Darjeeling.

Once replete, he tidied the kitchen and slipped the overalls over his neatly pressed trousers and a crisp white shirt. With his bowler hat in place, he gathered a jangle of keys from a drawer near the kitchen sink. Using a looped rope, he secured them around his waist, reached for the Old Spice aftershave he stored in the same drawer, splashed some on his face, and left by the kitchen door. He walked down the pebbled path to the bottom of the garden and through an open wooden gate. Underfoot, crisp, frozen leaves broke the silence. He kept his stride brisk until he reached the narrow lane that led to his lock-up shed.

Untying one key from around his waist and inserting it into the perfectly oiled lock, he gave a quick turn and the door opened. He reached to pull a long black cord and the overhead strip light flickered on. The tools of his trade rested on hooks, and a sturdy wheelbarrow made of wood and steel leaned against one wall. Taking a pair of shiny shears from their hook, he then took a cloth from a pile stacked on a nearby shelf and delicately wiped the sharp blades. When finished, he ran one hand over the metal teeth of a fan-shaped rake and his other hand stroked the hard and soft-bristled brooms. Whistling, he wheeled out the vintage wheelbarrow, and his past flashed before him again. An image came to him of himself and the wild-haired Florence sitting on top of a pile of rough grass clippings as the gardener pushed them in that same wheelbarrow, their legs dangling over the side as they giggled and sang nursery rhymes.

He set out the garden tools, ready to create miracles in his neighbours' gardens.

On Sundays, his routine changed. Before church, two boiled eggs and freshly brewed coffee were his pleasures, and like always, he ate his breakfast while holding a vision of Florence and himself engaged in animated conversation at his kitchen table. Later, hand in hand, they would walk to St. Johns church.

In real life, he regularly invited Florence to join him, but she would bluntly reply, "Bryce, I admire your deep devotion to Sunday church, but it is not for me. I think of myself as more of a free spirit. And I rather enjoy being alone first thing in the morning."

Bruised by Florence's refusal and lack of tact, he routinely swallowed his disappointment.

Every Sunday, without fail, he entered the church, grateful for the peace that washed over him. Mesmerised by the ethereal patterns on the stained-glass high above the altar, he listened to Reverend Horatio Jones' sermon. Once the service finished, he always crossed to a quiet corner and ceremoniously lit candles. Their steady flame of yellow cast their spell and lifted his spirits. Remembering the people within his community, he also prayed for a miracle of rekindled love.

Outside, he would shake hands with Reverend Horatio Jones and his wife, who always stood close to her husband's side. The name Gabriella seemed exotic to him, and he felt beguiled by the type of composed beauty she exhibited. An ex-flamenco dancer turned portrait painter, Gabriella never failed to kiss him on both cheeks. If the truth were to be revealed, the affection shown to him by this lovely lady made his Sundays more special.

• • •

Whatever the season, Florence kept the door of her kitchen open. Inhaling the fresh air that blew in, she kept an eye on the ageing Lulabelle. The dog's current whim appeared to be digging random holes in the pristine garden.

Many years before, she told Colonel Bryce Beckwith, "I know I am impatient with people and plants, so don't ask me about flora or fauna, for that is your domain."

Without hesitation, he planted sweet-smelling roses around the curved corners of her grassy lawn. And each season after that, he waved his magic fingers over her garden. Even the kitchen sill rendered pots of healthy, blooming cyclamen. He lived in hope of hearing her mention how the rose perfume swept fleetingly into her kitchen and the delicate fragrance perhaps lifted her mood . . . but she never commented.

• • •

Rita and Stanley Cornell resided across the road from Colonel Bryce Beckwith. Stanley, infirm for some years, spent his days in a wheelchair. With house maintenance neglected and the garden a tangle of weeds that fought for space amongst the nettles, the couple despaired. Added to their garden woes, ancient trees that once bore the juiciest of apples and pears now lay fruitless.

Their daughter, Cassie, would rush without warning through their front door, pull a blunt pair of shears from a Hessian sack, and head into the garden. Hacking and slashing for an hour or more, she'd attack the dried stalks from the rosemary and lavender hedges. Carnage followed at the edges of the weed-ridden lawn and her clumsy efforts failed to ever create form or structure.

Colonel Bryce Beckwith often received telephone calls from Stanley following Cassie's visits. He would hear Mrs Cornell sobbing, and Stanley pleaded with him to wave his magic. Promptly, Bryce would appear like a garden genie.

Happy to assist other neighbours with his gardening skills, one of which was neighbour Molly Mulligan, who lived next door to Mr and Mrs Cornell.

Young Molly had come to live on the street three years ago. He thought of her as an earth angel who spread her smile and kindness in great measure. A sensitive man, one not given to expressing his deep-rooted feelings, Colonel Beckwith recognised the haunted look of sadness in her eyes and the unspoken words of grief and heartache. But he never pried. Compelled to help in some silent fashion, he lit another of the fat beeswax candles after every Sunday service and always reflected for some minutes on the rays of hope that shone from the golden hues of light.

CHAPTER 4

THROUGHOUT THE NIGHT, MOLLY TOSSED AND turned, consumed by a vivid nightmare. A hazy figure at the bottom of the bed whispered, "I never left you."

She wanted to call out, "Jamie," but her mouth felt stuffed with wads of cotton wool and the sound of her words twisted at the back of her throat.

She awakened, and a familiar fretfulness ran through her. Yet again, she soul-searched, asking herself, "how did I fail my son?" Wearily, she sat up in bed, reaching for a glass of water that rested on the bedside table. She sipped the cold liquid, chastising herself for feeling vulnerable. She waited for the feeling to pass. Hugging her body, she reminded herself of the home she moved into three years ago and felt a surge of gratitude for the neighbours who'd embraced her.

She climbed out of bed, allowing her feet to find the floor before she headed to the bathroom. Once showered, she dressed, headed to the kitchen, and made breakfast. She inhaled the comforting aroma, then drank two cups of strong tea and ate two pieces of toast.

An hour later, she slipped out of her apartment into the deserted street. Standing in the grim whispers of dawn, she rolled up the collar of her blue tweed coat and vowed to shed her dark dreams. She tugged at her thickly knitted red scarf and wrapped it twice around her neck.

The leaf-strewn path, icy in patches, crackled under the heels of the inch-high heels of her cowboy boots. She hummed an uplifting song from the line-dancing class she'd taught the night before but stopped when she heard a twig snap, followed by a crunching sound of uneven footsteps behind her. Puffs of chilled air skimmed across her face as she turned and saw Florence striding up the path behind her. Florence reached Molly's side, her stern face towering over Molly's.

A striking woman at six-foot and a bit, Florence lived across the road from her. Seemingly having sworn off smiling for years, Florence pushed strands of windswept grey hair from her lined face. Her pewter-coloured giant dog, Lulabelle, stood at her side. The dog's imposing size did not marry well with the sight of its tail tucked between its legs.

Florence's eyes darted this way and that. Hunching forward, Florence moved in close enough that Molly could feel her breath.

"Have you seen a blue car pass by, or heard a young man ask for directions to my house?"

Florence's tone might sound brusque to others, but not to Molly. She had accepted Florence's gruff and odd ways because she'd seen how kind she was at her core.

"Good morning. You're up early." Molly smiled with affection at the odd twosome.

"And good morning to you. 'Tis a bit of a cold one."

Florence pulled her luminous raincoat around her body. "I forgot the time. My sister suggested her adopted grandson collect me from my house and drive me to her place. Remember Boudie? "You've heard me speak of The Belleview Boutique Guest House she runs." Florence fidgeted with Lulabelle's lead. A long pause followed. "To be honest, I'm not sure if I want to make the trip."

Molly noticed dark circles under Florence's eyes, betraying distress across her neighbour's already crinkled face.

"The ghosts of this winter's morning have not appeared. Nor has anyone stopped to ask where you live."

Florence stared at the ground. Eventually, she sucked in a few breaths through her teeth. "Sorry. Remiss of me not to ask how you are on this bitter day." Florence linked Molly's arm in hers. "Anyway, where are you heading?"

Molly pointed to her parked car a few hundred feet away.

With Lulabelle tagging along, they walked past the church and stopped once they reached the car. Molly wanted to curse when she spotted the bird poop splattered across the windscreen. "Look at what the birds have done!" she said. "My mother still says bird poop on your car is for luck, but I'm not convinced." She grinned at Florence, but her words whipped straight past her neighbour into the squally morning air.

"The thing is," said Florence, apparently not having heard anything Molly said, "I've never met this lad and I can't abide tardiness." She continued on, muttering about how her aching bones rattled after seventy years. "Travelling to see Boudie could be a chore. Such a distance. Then there's Lulabelle. Poor dear will have to stay at home. That is, if the lad decides to show up."

Lulabelle's ears drooped. She looked up to her mistress, her doleful eyes appearing to plead, *Please don't leave me.*

Florence rambled on, speaking of Boudie's allergic reaction to dog hair that began as a child in India and how Boudie's guests might not take kindly to a long-haired canine monster. "I've not thought to discuss Lulabelle with Boudie, but it will need consideration." She bent down and stroked Lulabelle's ears and patted her head, but Lulabelle stared back in what appeared to be wretched sorrow.

"But we know, don't we, that my Lulu is no monster. She's like the inside of a tough crab shell, delicate and a softie inside once you know how to handle her."

Molly did not want to further upset Florence, but she needed to get on with her day. She moved to the boot of the car, opened it, and retrieved a sponge and a spray bottle of water. She rubbed at the bird poo on the windscreen.

Florence stepped back. "It's probably best if Lulabelle and I sit in the window seat and wait. I hope this boy—name escapes me—arrives soon."

Florence went to walk away, but Molly placed a hand on her elbow.

"I am sure the boy will be along soon, and I am here for whatever help you need with feeding or walking Lulabelle. Now, no more worrying. Everything will get sorted. Think happy thoughts about the reunion you shall have with your sister."

"Thank you. I am grateful for your kindness. And what good fortune that you came to live on this street. How long has it been?" Florence asked.

Tears threatened to engulf Molly as she recalled the day her life changed, the day her only son left without reason. Willing herself to stay composed, she said, "Three years; three years today as it so happens."

"Well, I say, 'twas a damn fine day when you made this your new home." Florence walked away, bellowing her thanks through a light gust of wind. Her brown waterproof coat flapped around her legs. Lulabelle, tail drooping, padded close to Florence's side.

Florence turned back towards Molly. "Are we still on for yoga and heavy breathing on Thursday?"

Molly beamed at Florence and gave her a thumbs-up. "Sure thing."

"Hope you don't mind if I bring Lulabelle and her sofa bed. She can lie in a corner and spy on us as we set about stretching our decrepit bodies. Not you, of course, Molly. You're a young bit of a thing. What we oldies would give to have your bendiness. You're a catch for any single man, dear." She waved, turned back around, and stomped down the street.

Molly watched her disappear through her gate. She admired Florence and how she blustered through life. If the gods were on her side, Molly wished her neighbour to blossom with a good man's love.

Molly continued wiping at the stained windscreen. Once she finished with the chore, she opened the driver's door and pressed the wiper switch. *Splish, splash, splish, splash*, back and forth they went, the greyish-white streaks marking the glass. Throwing the sponge and spray bottle back into the boot, she swung her shoulder bag into the passenger's side of the car. Standing by the driver's door, she looked across to the gardens of the church. Branches stuck out from the old chestnut and oak trees, causing them to resemble haunted scarecrows. She could see through the high stained-glass windows that someone had switched on the church lights. As she raised her eyes to the inky skyline, a sharp wind swept around her and invaded the heavy wool of her coat. Hardly visible overhead, a lone seagull beat its wings. Brazenly, it settled on top of the carved steel dove atop the church's pinnacle.

Molly shivered. Allowing her mind to drift towards spring, she pictured birds singing amongst green leafy trees and elegant pear and cherry tree blossoms. They would form a perfect arch across the street once the growing season took hold.

The lamenting melody of *The Secret Garden* playing on the church's piano interrupted her reflection on warmer days. The voice of an angel streamed out. *It's Grace*, she thought. Reverend Horatio Jones' and his wife's Gabriella's only daughter. At twenty-two, Grace would be the same age as Molly's handsome blue-eyed son. The power of the song weaved its way into her heart. She pressed her body against the car door and closed her eyes, compelled to listen. Putting her face in her hands, she felt the rawness of the day—the third anniversary of her son disappearing from her life.

She murmured, "Absolutely, no way will I be miserable, for I have come too far with changing the fabric of my life."

CHAPTER 5

MOLLY LIFTED HER HEAD AND GAZED AT the stained-glass windows. Grace's voice continued to fill the silence. She hadn't a clue how long she'd stood frozen to the spot like the ancient statues inside the church.

Pulling herself back to the present, Molly got into the car and sat behind the wheel. Cold air enveloped her. Wiping at her eyes, she willed a tightness around her chest to disappear and let her mind focus on Florence.

The woman wore baggy, insipid clothing. Molly realised Florence never wished to draw attention to herself. She'd often wondered how Florence's young life in India, and later in Tamshire with her father, affected her. Sometimes, when Florence and Molly were alone, Florence dropped her mask and shared stories about her childhood. During those times, she spoke to Molly about her father's years in India when he served in the army. Florence was the eldest of two sisters born in India to "cultured parents" as Florence liked to call them.

After Partition, her father had returned to England and inherited acres of farmland from his aged parents. Once he'd settled, he sent for young Florence and introduced her to the ways of agriculture.

In the cold depths of Tamshire, Florence lived a desolated life that necessitated wearing robust layers of clothing. Florence laughed at the idea of wearing her father's faded denim dungarees over knitted tights beneath baggy jumpers, but protection remained key against tough weather. Florence told her the Indian climate remained "the grandmother of bright and uplifting colours. Tamshire," she'd always add, "is a far cry from the sunny, humid days of my beloved birthplace."

Florence became wistful about her childhood during these times of sharing. She spoke of wearing cotton and linen, describing them as light as butterfly wings skimming across her skin. She told Molly that following the years of her hard work on the farm, she'd given up any notion of wearing clothes to flatter her growing and lanky figure. Now in her twilight years, she critically called herself a frumpy, grey lump of a woman.

"Don't know where my parents found me," she often said. "I am the opposite of both my ladylike mother and younger sister. Perhaps that is why I remained single? The opposite sex didn't find me, or my clothes, in the slightest way appealing. I was always just their tomboy friend."

"Now look here, Florence, I'll not have you chastise yourself in this way. You are a warrior, considering your tale of survival."

She believed she knew Florence well, but never liked to ask if Florence had ever had her heart broken. Did she know what it felt like to live with frayed emotions lurking below the surface? Had she felt true loss?

For three years, Molly had held onto the closely guarded secret of her son's disappearance. She had decided she would not muddy the waters in her new life. But today she wanted to scream and shout and finally share her grief.

"Please show me what to do," Molly hollered into the emptiness of the car, thinking about her father's wisdom. "Life is full of twists and turns," he would say. "We are often thrown down a path we never expected to tread on. Don't let fear remove your wonderful smile, Moll. Promise you'll never lose your sense of fun and your wish to reach out to others. Trust me, humour will see you through."

His wisdom had always kept her on track. "And I have to ensure it will today," she said into the coolness of her car.

• • •

Colonel Bryce Beckwith pushed the red wheelbarrow down the lane and around the corner. Against the snappy wind, he headed towards the church and pulled his bowler hat further forward onto his forehead.

From the high stained-glass windows, a sound like that of a nightingale escaped. The song was a sorrowful song at the best of times, but his face lit up. He realised Grace would sing at the service the following Sunday. A few feet from the church gates, he spotted a familiar car with a figure sitting in the driver's seat. He quickened his pace, set the wheelbarrow down, and moved closer to the stationary vehicle.

Through the misted windows, he recognised Molly from across the road. She sat bolt upright with her eyes tightly shut.

He bent down and peeked through the window at Molly. She appeared lost in some other world. After a few moments, he watched as she almost physically yanked herself out of some trance. He gently tapped on the glass. Molly fidgeted and wriggled in the seat, pulled a handkerchief from her coat pocket, and blew her nose. Only then did she press the window button to turn and meet his gaze, smiling at him.

"Good morning. I think we gave each other a bit of a jolt. How are you?" Colonel Bryce Beckwith asked.

He didn't want to pry, but in his opinion, Molly's smile seemed to express sadness today. Most unlike her, he thought. She looked ruffled. The light had dimmed from her topaz eyes, so he assumed something had upset her. Embarrassed, he stepped back. A blast of wind shifted his bowler hat to one side of his head. Silence hung like the chilled air around him.

"My dearest Molly, sorry if I alarmed you, I'm simply checking to see if everything is in order." He leaned in through the open window to get a clearer look at her. He couldn't remember ever seeing her look vulnerable, and he recognised distress in her bloodshot eyes. Tempted to reach out and hug her as a father might comfort a troubled child, he stalled. Perhaps that would be improper. He waited for Molly to find her voice.

"I'm grand. Really. Just taking a few quiet moments before I set off," she eventually stuttered.

"The music coming from the church would urge anyone to stop and listen for a while," Colonel Bryce Beckwith said, trying to sound upbeat. "So pleased Grace is back home." He scrutinised Molly's face again, watching her blink several times. It pulled at his heart to see her look wretched. He desperately wanted to understand, but didn't know how he could console her. Unsure of what to do, he said, "It's probably time I let you head off."

She turned, gave him another one of her smiles, and pressed the window closed. He watched her pull away from the curb.

Colonel Bryce Beckwith waved at Molly and remained standing on the same spot long after the car drove away. He put a hand to his chin and stroked it. What troubled this woman? He resolved to pay more attention to the angel who helped change the lives of oldies like himself.

Agonising over how to assist Molly, he pushed the bowler hat firmly back onto the centre of his head. In a crisp white shirt, burgundy-and-cream chequered tie, over which hung French blue dungarees, Colonel Bryce Beckwith took hold of the handles of the red wheelbarrow. He walked through the open gates of the church. His highly polished lace-up brogues shone despite the grim morning light.

• • •

Gabriella, the reverend's wife, had telephoned Colonel Bryce Beckwith the day before and informed him of a few split kneeling rests. They would need replacing along with new carpet pieces. "Could you help us as soon as you can?" she'd asked.

Armed with fresh wood, strips of carpet, a screwdriver, some screws, a saw, and glue, he looked forward to applying his carpentry skills.

Gabriella stood waiting by the church doors, ready to greet him. Her task of polishing the glass completed, she gave him a smile of welcome.

He admired Gabriella's natural poise, a certain style that came with being a trained dancer. Her coiffed hair was pulled back from perfectly defined cheekbones, and she'd stained her full lips red. He noted the colour lifted her pale complexion. Dressed from head to toe in black, the jersey dress held a ruffle at the hem that swished around her.

"Aw, Colonel, it's good of you to come so promptly." Gabriella gave him an unexpected hug.

She led the way into the central nave, a most sacred area, the sound of her shoes echoing across the paved stone floor. He always enjoyed Reverend Horatio Jones's enthusiastic Sunday sermons, the use of honed good humour, and Grace's musical talent that encouraged the reverend's depleting flock to remain loyal. Stepping into the nave brought that all to the forefront of his thoughts.

Gabriella stopped until Colonel Bryce Beckwith came to stand by her side. She linked his arm in hers. "Before you begin, please join Grace and me for tea. She's already been practising on the piano for Sunday's service. And you must taste the lemon and almond cake we baked for you."

Together, they stepped into a makeshift kitchen, behind a pillar at one side of the church. He heard a kettle boiling and saw Gabriela's daughter, Grace, preparing tea and setting a tiny circular table with plates, cups, and saucers.

"Good to see you're back with us for a while. Heard you practising earlier," Colonel Bryce Beckwith addressed Grace.

Grace stretched out a slender hand and shook Colonel Bryce Beckwith's. Her skin felt soft.

"It's always good to come home and to know I have at least one fan for Sunday," she said, then laughed.

One by one, she lifted three chairs that sat in a corner of the small space, unfolded them, and beckoned both her mother and him to take a seat. She poured tea from a fine china pot and cut into her baking efforts. For the next half hour, they chatted, drank tea, and enjoyed the lemon and almond cake. Relaxed in their company, Colonel Bryce Beckwith did his best to let go of his earlier concerns for Molly.

CHAPTER 6

MOLLY NORMALLY WENT TO THE LIBRARY on Wednesdays. Today, driving away from the church, she felt lost in sadness and guilt as she admonished herself for being unable to engage with Colonel Bryce Beckwith. She had wanted to share her unhappiness, unlock her secret with him. But no, not yet, she told herself. She put a smile on her face and determined she'd ensure today was well spent.

She drove down the street. To her right, she spied her neighbour, Mrs Rita Cornell. Rita and her husband, Stanley, lived next door to her. Mrs Cornell stood feebly at her gate, leaning on a wood and metal stick that had an angry-looking snake's head adorning the top.

Molly parked, shifted herself out of the car, and walked across the road to where Mrs Cornell stood. She watched her neighbour's thin hair catch in the wind as if it had a mind of its own. Her automatic impulse to care for others kicked in. She'd been a devoted caretaker—her profession for over twenty years. After Rory left, she'd changed her career and took a leap of faith by travelling to Goa to become a yoga and meditation teacher. That followed with new gusto and a move to live in Kent.

She saw Mrs Cornell wore an oversized, zippered track-suit top and what appeared to be a child's flared track bottoms that sat well above her ankles. Her skinny chicken legs stuck out beneath the pants. Molly noticed the frayed plimsolls, tied up with coloured string, and Mrs Cornell's bare feet, branded with patches of red. The woman's glasses sat perched precariously on the end of her nose and Molly observed how cloudy Mrs Cornell's eyes looked through them. Stanley, Mrs Cornell's husband, once shared with Molly that his wife suffered with cataracts. He'd confided that she sometimes didn't recognise people's faces, had no idea of distance, and often lost her sense of time.

"What are you doing standing outside on this winter's morning? You'll catch a chill," Molly said. She touched the woman's shoulder. Mrs Cornell flinched.

"Ah, Molly, is that you? I've stood here, must be nearly an hour, waiting for my daughter to show up. Going to the hospital for blood tests. Been fasting since last night. Feel wobbly." Mrs Cornell's teeth chattered. "Thought it best to stand by the gate. My Cassie doesn't like to be kept waiting. Constantly rushing about, she is." Mrs Cornell's false teeth moved in her mouth and her face contorted. A strange cackling sound spouted out. She clicked her tongue several times, her face set with a determination. Eventually, she continued.

"You see, my Cassie lives on a farm, dedicated to her animals and there's no time for anything else, so she tells me. And don't get me started on them ailing chickens and birds with broken wings she fosters. Neighbours and strangers alike appear at her front door with their injured animals and fowl." Mrs Cornell sniffled. "And she's a vegetarian, eating seeds like them rescued birds and chickens she feeds. Scrawny bits of things they are, with big clawed feet. Won't sell or kill 'em for food."

Mrs Cornell carried on talking about her wayward daughter.

"The folk in her village call her The Animal Whisperer. To be honest, me and my Stanley believe she'd rather be in the company of animals than humans. Hides away, she does, and never brought a man to our house." Mrs Cornell peered over her thick-lensed glasses and glanced anxiously up and down the street.

"Look, Mrs Cornell, why don't you go back inside and sit with Stanley? I'll stay here and give you the nod when your daughter arrives. First, let me get you a bottle of water."

"I've got a bottle of Cherry Coke in me pocket. That will put some spark into me after they've taken blood at the hospital." Mrs Cornell looked down at the cloth bag hanging from the ugly snake's head atop her cane. "Got me sandwiches of sliced yellow cheese, too, and a boiled egg and pickle."

Molly's attention was drawn to the pink plaster peeking out from the sleeve of Mrs Cornell's oversized tracksuit top. Supported in a sling, the woman's arthritic fingers looked bruised and crooked. Molly gazed in sympathy at Mrs Cornell's arm.

"Now there's a story. Fell as I came out of the house," her neighbour explained.

"Ah, I'm sorry. Wish I'd known. I could have helped," Molly replied.

Clouds dropped like dark blankets, releasing a cloak of fine rain that splattered onto Mrs Cornell's head. The mist attached itself to her lenses.

Mrs Cornell and Molly heard a car braking and the screech of tyres. Through the biting wind and web of rain, a blue Volvo Estate drove at full speed down the street. The driver swung the car from the left-hand side of the road and suddenly stopped near Molly and Mrs Cornell. The wheels hit the curb, and the driver hit the nearby telegraph pole, finally parking the Volvo. A metal sign that stated the hours of free parking fell to the ground with a sharp clang.

Molly reached out and put her arm around Mrs Cornell's tiny waist. "Don't tell me we have a joy rider at this hour."

Unperturbed, Mrs Cornell explained in a perfectly calm voice, "That will be Cassie. Mustn't keep her waiting." Mrs Cornell scrunched up her eyes and scanned into the distance. The car remained by the pole, and the driver seemed motionless.

"I've burdened you. Didn't mean to," Mrs Cornell said.

"Let me assist you," Molly continued to support her neighbour, but Mrs Cornell insisted she could take the few steps to the parked Volvo. Leaning on her stick and dragging her feet in their flimsy plimsolls, she slowly manoeuvred her frail body from side to side, huffing and puffing as she walked. Mrs Cornell reached the passenger door, yet her daughter remained solidly behind the wheel.

Shouldn't she be assisting her mother? Molly wondered. Opening the passenger's side door and rolling the car window down, Molly guided Mrs Cornell into her seat, taking her stick to place it by her left side. Once Molly had clicked the safety belt in position, she closed the door and continued to hold on to the handle. She bent down to eye level, wishing to acknowledge Mrs Cornell's daughter.

"Hi. Are you okay?" Mrs Cornell's daughter didn't reply. The woman's long black hair fell forward, obscuring her face.

The oddly dressed scarecrows her father kept on his allotment came to mind, and Molly stifled a fit of giggles. Oversized shades, jangly hooped earrings, smudged black kohl-lined eyes, and a white shirt were surely not the dress code for a farmer. But then, Mrs Cornell often described her daughter as kooky.

"Keep me posted," Molly said.

Mrs Cornell nodded.

Even though Molly's hand still gripped the handle of the car door, Cassie revved the engine, her foot heavy on the accelerator. She started to drive away, almost dragging Molly along with the car. Just as Molly released her hand, Mrs Cornell cried out, "Ahh, the pain, the pain." She watched as Mrs Cornell's head was thrown back, bouncing against the headrest. "I'm in plaster with me broken arm . . . mind me shoulder for heaven's sake, Cassie. You're driving like some bank robber making a hasty escape. Take it easy, will you!" Mrs Cornell shouted.

Left standing in the middle of the deserted street, Molly did not know whether to laugh or cry at the disturbance she had just witnessed. She spotted a plastic box on the road, stooped to pick up what appeared to be sandwiches, and walked to the back of her car. She turned and saw Stanley wave from his usual place in the window. Had he seen his daughter's erratic arrival and her graceless departure with his poor wife?

Molly placed the sealed sandwiches in the boot. Why had Cassie shown her mother so little respect? She planned to drop by to check on Stanley and Mrs Cornell later.

Walking around to the driver's side of her car, she

opened the door and got behind the wheel. She heard herself let out a whopper of a sigh as she caught sight of her knuckles. Her fingers had turned a shade of blue. She switched on the heater and prayed for warmth to blow through. Leaning across to open the compartment in front of the passenger seat, she rummaged for her fur-lined driving gloves. Pamphlets and photos in black and white tumbled from a blue folder and scattered into the footwell. She felt drawn to one headshot with a bold heading: **Missing.**

The young man's stare and his composed face caught her off guard. Her blond-haired boy—the spitting image of his father. "Where did you go?" she asked aloud. She opened the car window and rubbed her face. After a few slow, deep breaths, she did her best to ignore how she really felt. Pulling down the sun visor above the windscreen, she stared into the mirror. "I've become some crazy woman by having too many conversations with myself. That's what happens when you live alone." She shook her head in disapproval.

Doing her best to raise a smile, she closed the window and, after checking the rear-view mirror, finally escaped the deserted street. Turning onto the main road, she drove to her local library.

• • •

Frustrated, Kit sat in traffic that moved at a snail's pace. He looked across at the dozing passenger next to him. He cringed at his earlier behaviour. The sound when the car hit the pole would have drawn everyone's attention. He'd completely lost it when he saw the woman on the path speaking to the woman he assumed must be Boudie's sister. Remorse washed over him. Why had he sat like a mummy and let Boudie's sister struggle to get into the passenger's side of the car? Then, in sheer panic, like some formidable madman, taken off again at top speed?

The face, those sharp eyes, framed by her dancing mane of red hair, left his heart thumping in his chest. He'd immediately recognised his ma, and her so damn close he could have almost touched her.

Why had he not reached across, taken her hand tightly in his, and said, "I am so sorry. Can you forgive me?" But any courage disappeared. Had she sussed him out? He hoped his costume had kept his secret intact.

How had she filled the years since her move to Kent? He'd never bothered to write down her address, nor had he been to her apartment, but she obviously lived around here.

A powerful urge beckoned him to turn the car around, drive back, park safely, and allow his body to sink into her comforting arms. His hands grew clammy, and a warm sweat trickled down the back of his neck. How could he begin to explain? All thoughts of reuniting with his mother evaporated. He could find no words to redeem himself. Anyway, he thought, she wouldn't have recognised the Volvo.

As for the damage to Boudie's pride and joy, he dared not check. He dreaded her reaction. Her voice of disapproval resounded in his brain.

He snatched another look at the woman who sat next to him, her face cold as a slab of grey stone. He could not recall her name. The fragile woman bore no resemblance to Boudie. Even with his hangover, he could not see a connection between the bright and bubbly Boudie and his sickly-looking passenger.

• • •

Mrs Cornell tried to settle in her seat and prayed her

daughter would drive safely to the hospital. Once her blood tests were complete, she could drink her Cherry Coke. Disappointed that the box of sandwiches had fallen out of the car, she would insist Cassie buy her a sandwich and a pastry at the hospital café. Oh, and a pot of tea, too. The thought cheered her up.

Mrs Cornell already knew that once Cassie dropped her home, she would make excuses about why she could not stay and cook lunch for her and Stanley. Her thoughts on her daughter lingered. How could Cassie have driven as if she were driving a getaway car? And she'd taken off without uttering a word to her or Molly.

Mrs Cornell tut-tutted to herself, but she dared not share such thoughts aloud. It wouldn't do to create a fuss. If she commented, her daughter would seethe with rage, and Cassie's raised voice would pollute the atmosphere. Downright rude is what she was. Mrs Cornell felt most disheartened.

A drowsiness overcame her. She closed her eyes and drifted in and out of sleep. She dreamt of Molly, a priceless treasure to her and Stanley. A beautiful and clever woman who fed the yoga group one Friday a month with her home-cooked meals. Mrs Cornell tried to remember the name of the event. Oh yes, Frolics, Food, and Fun.

Once they'd eaten and drank their fill, they always jived and waltzed for hours. A happy Stanley would turn around and around in his wheelchair, making himself and the others dizzy.

In this dream state, Mrs Cornell saw herself on a polished springy floor in the arms of a dark-haired man. Under a shimmering ball of silver, casting glittering shadows, the man danced with grace. Wearing an evening dress of pink and pale grey, a corsage of pleated flowers hanging from her left shoulder, she saw Stanley, her new husband, in his black tuxedo with its shiny lapels. The whiteness of his shirt glowed against his olive skin. He complemented her corsage by wearing a pink bowtie. In the dream, Stanley's eyes glinted as they met hers. They almost floated from one end of the ballroom to the other, holding each other close.

CHAPTER 7

After Molly's separation from Rory, suddenly thrust into a single life, and still raising her only son, Molly's self-esteem flagged, along with her confidence.

One morning Molly's best friend, the excitable Bonnie, knocked on Molly's door. Armed with a computer bag and her usual bubble of positivity, she kissed Molly on both cheeks and caught her hand. "Come on, what do you say we travel somewhere far away? Maybe nirvana awaits us. Let's shake things up. Go find us some love and a new life."

Bonnie made straight for the living room, sat on the sofa, pulled out her laptop, and started to tap on the keyboard. Molly, her spirit roused, followed Bonnie. She sat opposite her. "There's simply no time to waste," Bonnie said as she tapped away.

After that, they met up daily at Molly's, drinking copious cups of Irish Barry's Tea and sharing each other's dreams for a new beginning.

One day, again in Molly's living room, Bonnie gushed, "I have put a plan in place. You and I are going on an adventure that is going to change us forever." She told Molly she had spoken to a travel specialist. With that, Bonnie jumped up and wrapped her arms so tightly around Molly that Molly could hardly breathe.

"The wonders of Goa await us. It's all booked. There's no going back. For three months we shall learn the life of a true yogi," Bonnie said.

Molly thought, *Perhaps this is a chance to step away from my life since the old life doesn't work.*

Over the years of their friendship, Molly had experienced Bonnie's love of high drama and adventure. Her friend had a certain charisma that people enjoyed being around, herself included. Molly so wanted to believe this trip could remove the emotional knots she still felt tangled in. A new beginning lay before her. Could she take this leap of faith and trust Bonnie? She committed to travel to Goa and paid her share. With loads to plan, Molly shifted into too much thinking, and delved into an anxiousness for her son. Jamie, at eighteen, already in his first year of study at the College of Performing Arts, seemed keen about the trip and encouraged his mother to travel.

He'd told her, "Ma, I'm grand. You have been in a rut for too long. It's time for you to try something different. I'll always be your cheerleader."

She'd been upset when Jamie refused to have any contact with his dad. She'd watched Jamie build a mental wall of blame, and sometimes his outbursts were directed at her. Shaking off any concerns, she decided to grab the opportunity for change.

With only a month until Bonnie's and her departure, she received a text from Bonnie.

Hate to do this, but I have to cancel.

Can't go to Goa.

Got me a dream contract.

Bonnie's Bespoke Bakes and Cakes has been offered a three-year contract with a five-star hotel in London.

Have to seize this chance to develop my business.

Another time, eh?

Hope you understand.

Sorry.
Bonnie

Reeling from the text message, any excitement or anticipation Molly had felt drained away, and anger wormed its way in. How could Bonnie, who'd got her all fired-up for this mid-life trip, break her promise? She rang her friend, imploring, "If the company values you and your product, surely they could wait three months? I can't believe your flippancy." Molly fumed.

But Bonnie would not budge. She cancelled her trip and left Molly to make her own decision.

Molly argued back and forth with herself. "Do I travel alone or cancel? What's my heart telling me?" She knew she did not want to become one of those women who, later in life, regaled their sorry tale of a missed chance, saying, "Well, you know I could have, but I didn't." Finally, she made up her mind. To hell with fear of the unknown! She would damn well travel solo to Goa.

Molly's parents, on hearing of her plans, could not understand why she insisted on travelling to India, a country they considered a strange and foreign land.

"It's not safe for a woman to be on her own," her mother warned.

On Skype one evening, her father, normally a placid man, raised his voice in what Molly decided could only be concern for her. "Me darlin' girl, remember, you are still in the same body and mind and no amount of running away will change that. You're stuck with *you* until the day you are called to the next life. Do you really believe that travelling to Goa will help you work through losing Rory?"

She would not allow her past to define her and a fierceness for change propelled her, regardless of her parents' concerns.

She left London for three-hundred hours of training in meditation and Yin Yoga.

Once she reached Goa, she amazed herself, finding it easy to settle in with a small community of students. She lived in a hut made of bamboo and wood. Her days began with a dawn-kissed sunrise on a sandy beach with rolling waves. In the shade of coconut trees, she attended classes in yoga, meditation, and Indian head massage. She found a sense of tranquillity in these surroundings. Peeling away the hurt that had pinched her heart and mind following Rory's departure, clouds of loneliness dissipated. She embraced this simple life.

At the end of three inspiring months of learning, her energy returned. With renewed faith, she felt ready to make alternative choices.

Once back on English soil, Molly set about selling the family home and suggested that Jamie join her in Kent. He said he would, but he had conditions.

"Ma, I'll go. As long as you understand I need the freedom to soak up the creative hotspots for my craft. Right now, London is where I belong."

Molly accepted that in between Jamie's coursework, parties, and girls, he would live part time at their new home.

But, on the morning of the move, her carefully planned future had disintegrated. Her only son had scribbled a few words on a piece of card, packed up, and walked out of her life. That had hit her hard.

Guilt overcame her. She relived their last evening together, asking herself repeatedly, *why had Jamie excluded her from his plans?* Had she missed signs of his unhappiness, or had he never intended to follow her to Kent? She tried to settle into the new apartment and befriend her neighbours, Colonel Bryce Beckwith and Florence Scott Thomas. They reached out in welcome. Smiling for the outside world, she tucked her secret of loss away. Unknown to anyone, Molly sometimes pursued the search for Jamie, longing for the silent pain to disappear.

As time passed, she realised she could not carry on drifting. She'd taken early redundancy from her care-work career, but that would not support her for much longer. Since she'd invested time, money, and training in yoga and meditation, she concluded she'd act in that direction. Could she pass on the gift of flexibility and agility to the neighbours within the community? Would they benefit from classes? Then it came to her . . . companionship, togetherness, fun, laughter, and exercise. Everyone needed that, including herself. She would set up a weekly class and call it Karma and Calmer Yoga.

On a new mission, she designed posters and photos showing bendy women of a certain age, stretching and smiling in various yoga positions. Molly wished to show her potential students they could take a yoga class with ease.

Find Your Inner Balance and Energy
At The Karma and Calmer Yoga Class.

Join me,
10.30 am-12 noon each Thursday
at
St. John's church hall
Classes: - £5.00
(OAP's £3.50)
Pay at the door.
Everyone is welcome.
I look forward to teaching you.

Namaste,
Molly Mulligan

Reverend Horatio Jones—the vicar—and his wife Gabriella (of flamenco fame), approved her idea. They insisted she take over the yellow-bricked hall with its red tin roof at the side of the church. Shop managers and the women who ran the local laundry and bakery displayed the posters in their front windows. She knocked on neighbours' doors and explained in simple terms how she wanted yoga classes to become part of the community's activities.

The day of the first yoga class arrived. Inside the hall, Molly arranged chairs, yoga mats, and headrests. Against the brick wall outside and near the entrance to the hall, she placed a stand-up blackboard with a large handwritten sign. She played relaxing music and wondered if anyone would show up. Would the community be interested in learning how to build a connection with their minds, hearts, and souls?

Before the hand of the clock that rested on the wall opposite the main doors struck ten-thirty, seven ladies and two men shyly appeared in the doorway.

In bare feet, dressed in purple yoga bottoms and a vest top to match, Molly almost ran, opening her arms to welcome each student. She guided them to choose a mat within the haven of calm she'd created. Incense of jasmine drifted in swirls towards the curved ceiling. Placing her feet firmly on her mat, she stood in front of the group. "Good morning everyone. Today is the first of our Karma and Calmer Yoga classes." From a nearby table, Molly picked up two interlaced bells. The vibrating sound resonated through the room. "Let us slow everything down and begin. I would like you to stand in the middle of your mat, face me, and place your hands by your side. Close your eyes and breathe in through your nose."

Already befriended by Mrs Cornell and her wheelchair-bound husband, Stanley, Molly sought to assure them. "I am aware you both need to sit for this class. Just follow what I do and keep your eyes open for now. Right, dear students, time for us to start. Together we can build a steady flow of simple yoga positions." The tranquil music continued to play.

Transported along with her students, her first class began.

Following the unexpected enthusiasm, the Karma and Calmer Yoga class grew into two packed sessions on Thursday mornings.

Uplifted by the positive response of the community, Molly immediately sought to develop another social event to bring the young at heart more tightly together.

CHAPTER 8

MOLLY HAD COME UPON THE IDEA OF A Frolics, Food, and Fun Friday. On the first Friday of each month, her yoga students congregated around a rectangular table to enjoy a home-cooked meal that she had prepared in her small but functional kitchen and delivered to the church hall. Colonel Bryce Beckwith, her helper, and a dab hand at making puff pastry, baked sumptuous trays of chicken and mushroom vol-au-vent. To cheers of delight, he would often accompany the dish with French tarte tatin, served with lashings of freshly whipped cream.

Molly's heart always warmed when engaging with the group and hearing their animated chatter and bursts of laughter. Once replete with food, wine, and Cherry Coke for Mrs Cornell, the sprightlier ladies would gather around her.

"Come on, Molly, sing us a song from your homeland,"

they'd begged the last time they gathered.

Molly had waved a hand away. "Singing is not my forte. And, because I love you all, I dare not inflict my cat calls or cries of foxes squealing on you. I'll dance, I'll even hum in tune, but please don't ask me to sing."

"Well, in that case, you better show us some easy line-dancing steps. What about a shuffle? Or is it a pivot?" one of the ladies asked.

"I'll have to spin my Stanley's wheelchair and get him in the mood," Mrs Cornell had said, chuckling. But as her mouth opened, her false teeth dropped out, rolled along the floor, and went under the table. Colonel Bryce Beckwith got down on his hands and knees and scrambled under the folds of the tablecloth.

"Found them," he'd cried out. He stood up and, with a flourish, pulled a starched handkerchief from his top pocket, placed the discoloured false teeth on the fabric, and handed them back to Mrs Cornell.

At these Frolics, Food, and Fun Fridays, Molly noticed her neighbours always reminisced about their courting days and their first months of wedded bliss. They remembered the war years, spoke about husbands who'd passed, and occasionally sang songs from that time. One neighbour had said, "I had a man who, after being in the army, lost his way. That was enough for me." Another had joined in, saying, "I have been a widow for forty years. Independent is what I am. No hangers-on for me. Anyways, what would I be doing with a man in my bed at this time of life?" Someone else had commented, "How could we live with the guilt of a new beau after loving only one?"

Unable to share her past or innermost secrets, Molly had waited a few minutes before joining in with this heart-to-heart conversation. "I have no need for a man, or indeed a toy-boy. Rest assured, I will not be joining

Tinder anytime soon." But to herself she'd whispered, "I have one exception for including a male in my life—my son, Jamie, for I know he is out there somewhere and will return when he is ready."

Florence had chimed in, saying, "In my later years I thought I had a good 'un. But he upped and left in a hurry, with only a suitcase and a black eye. Said the case fell off the wardrobe before he had a chance to pack the damn thing. Lying so-and-so."

Everyone had laughed, but Florence fell silent.

Today, with renewed discussions of the past floating around the room, Molly observed Colonel Bryce Beckwith as he doodled with a pencil and paper. His face clouded over into what appeared to be a state of melancholy.

Much to Molly's surprise, Colonel Bryce Beckwith stood to attention, tapped his wine glass twice, looked around the table, and addressed everyone.

"I became a widower over ten years ago. I admit my late wife Diane wasn't the love of my life. You see, ladies and gentlemen, there's only ever been one love for me." He paused and wiped his eyes. "I was young and weak and unable to take a firm stand against my parents. So, I married Diane at their insistence." He sniffled. "Every day I wonder—could the woman I never stopped loving still hold a flame for me?" Colonel Bryce looked towards Florence. With his head bowed, he sat down. A silence like a cool draught moved through the room.

Molly, touched by this show of emotion from the stoic man she had come to know, went to him and wrapped her arms around him. Like others in the group, she knew about loss.

Stanley bellowed, "A round of applause for Colonel Bryce Beckwith for speaking his truth. That's a tough one, mate." Stanley put his hands together and clapped.

The others joined in with, "Here, here for the Colonel."

• • •

Florence didn't join in. She sat at the far end of the table, twisting uncomfortably in her chair. Not easily given to sentiments or weeping, she had listened to Colonel Bryce Beckwith's admission. She bit her bottom lip and felt a lump wedge at the back of her throat. Could the love embedded in her heart for as long as she could remember be ignited? And it wasn't for that fellow with the bruised eye.

Thinking back, she remembered her innocent, carefree days in India when she and Bryce were children. In her teenage years, she'd spent far too much time on her own. First, at the farm with her father and later when she worked in London. She admitted frustration and rejections in love had made her impatient. To the world, her indifference and bluntness pushed people away. Underneath all her bluster, she waded through anxiety and fear. She realised as a woman in her later years that if she did not join the hub of the community and talk about how she felt, life would remain one lonely path.

The chitter chatter around the room pulled Florence back to the present. Her mouth felt dry. She needed a hot drink. Almost stumbling over Lulabelle, who had been sleeping at her feet, she headed to the hot drinks table. She poured herself a cup of tea, added a touch of milk, and sipped the soothing liquid.

"It's okay for you, Molly Mulligan," Florence heard one of the women pipe up. She turned to see several women peeking over their refilled glasses of wine to stare at Molly.

"I say there's many a young man who'd be smitten

with a woman such as yourself, Molly," Mrs Cornell said, and gave another one of her unique giggles. "Look at you! Irish through and through, a natural wit, and yer the picture of a film star with locks of shiny red hair. You and Maureen O'Hara could be sisters, straight out of the film *The Silent Man*. "Your eyes are the colour of topaz. A man could easily take a fancy to them." Mrs Cornell looked around the room for a reaction. Everyone nodded in agreement.

Florence saw Molly's face flush like a ripened red fruit, and she caught a flickering fragility about Molly that she had not noticed before. She immediately jumped in protectively. "Well, I never knew you could be poetic," Florence said tersely to Mrs Cornell. Florence then moved to take up her seat at the table.

Another hush fell over the room.

Lulabelle stretched and yawned and padded over to sit by Molly. Molly patted the dog, picked up her glass of water, looked around the table, and noted the kindness being shown to her. She smiled and imagined herself humming, *Where Do You Go to My Lovely.*

• • •

After a few months of Colonel Bryce Beckwith assisting Molly with the event, one day he knocked on her door, wishing to discuss a matter he found upsetting.

Immediately, he addressed what was on his mind. "Rather than talk of sad old times and sorrowful memories, wouldn't it be rather marvellous to play some upbeat music? How about some dancing? You could teach us a few jive routines. Or, how about Gabriella showing us how to perform the flamenco?"

"You're right," Molly replied. "Our Fridays are supposed to be joyful, where we lift each other up and find that feel-good feeling. We certainly don't want our neighbours to wallow in doom and gloom. Let's find some up-tempo music and entice everyone to get on their feet and dance."

Once home, Colonel Bryce Beckwith climbed into the attic and retrieved his ancient Dansette record player. He found a box of cobwebbed LPs still in their original covers. Amongst his other hoardings, Glenn Miller and Frank Sinatra albums lay propped up in the same box that once sat in his parents' living room in India. He carried the LPs down to the kitchen, wrinkling his nose at the smell of must and mothballs. Using a fine soft brush for the stylus, and a fibre cloth for the records, he brought them back to life. The records played and sounded as good as new.

Time fell away while he listened to some favourites, *Come Fly with Me* by old blue eyes—Frank Sinatra—and *Chattanooga Choo-Choo* by Glen Miller. He tapped his fingers on the record player and travelled back to Florence's parents' home in India.

He fondly recalled guests dancing on the terrace and a skyline that looked like a canvas of crimson and spice. The descending, glittering sun set as cocktails were poured and music filled the air.

• • •

The next time the group met, following lunch and with their new plans in place, Molly and the Colonel pushed the long table against one wall in the hall. As soon as the music began to play, a buzz of excitement filled the room and neighbours were on their feet. Inhibitions disappeared as they twirled and danced in circles.

Colonel Bryce Beckwith glanced in Florence's direction, searching her face for some sign of enthusiasm.

But she remained seated. Her eyes were cast downwards while she tapped her foot to the beat. Disappointed and feeling rejected, he invited Molly to dance. She happily obliged, and they both encouraged others to shimmy across the floor to a quickstep, with *In the Mood* playing on the record player.

Stanley spun around and around in his wheelchair. Mrs Cornell followed him, holding on to her stick.

By five o'clock, everyone staggered home, exhausted and elated in equal measures. And Colonel Bryce Beckwith heard many of the group confirm they would add the next Friday's date to their calendars.

The event became known as FFF&F.

CHAPTER 9

KIT WONDERED, SHOULD HE REMAIN SILENT and allow the old woman beside him to doze, or should he introduce himself?

"Hi, my name is Kit. Sorry, but I can't remember yours. How are things with you and Boudie? I mean, how close are you two sisters?" No, that didn't sound right.

Maybe he could start the conversation and explain why he lived at Boudie's.

"Hey, would you like to hear my story? How I jumped out of my life three years ago? Opted-out is the phrase, I think. I wanted to reinvent myself. Yep, be anyone else but me. I arrived at your sister's place with little money, but she took me in, regardless. You could say Boudie saved me from flipping over the edge." He spoke these words aloud, as if performing on stage at one of his dress rehearsals.

He looked across at his human cargo. Poor dear.

He watched her head nod back and forth, lost in her oblivious sleep.

Distracted, he wondered, *Could I grab my old life back?* The question hung heavily on his shoulders. Could he reignite the close relationship he once shared with his mother, college friends, and his bestie, Matt?

Over the last three years, Kit and Boudie had forged a kind of love, an unspoken respect for each other that would normally be reserved within family ties. Whatever the reason, she understood him and allowed him the space he needed. He felt nurtured at The Belleview. Following the devastation of his father's leaving to become, his mother said, ensconced in some business in the South of France, he lost all interest in him. At least he told himself that.

Shoulders pressed down, he leaned back in the driver's seat. He imagined the dressing-down Boudie would give him for being late. Her tiny foot, dressed in a suede shoe with a kitten heel, would tap on the black-and-white tiled floor in the kitchen while she demanded answers.

"Really Kit, how could you present yourself in such a state?"

He envisioned her sparkling eyes blazing in disapproval.

Wired on caffeine and fizzy drinks, his thoughts spiralled at a rate he could not handle.

He realised his hands were trembling as he held the steering wheel. Chewing on the inside of his cheek, he tasted blood.

With chemical overload pulsing through his body and lack of sleep, he told himself to just drive. He clenched the wheel tighter.

He rapidly mouthed the same words . . . *drive, just drive.* He took several deep breaths. Eventually, his hands relaxed, and he sat further back in the seat.

"Yeah, that's all I have to do. Drive, and deliver Boudie's sister to The Belleview."

• • •

Florence, once she returned to her house, felt the cold settle its way through her clothes and into her skin and bones. She paced up and down the lounge, then moved to the bay window and glanced out at the empty street. Lulabelle trod the carpet in line with her. Florence impatiently pushed her bedraggled hair away from her face. She felt flushed from the chill outside. Annoyed at this waiting game, she checked the carriage clock on the mantelpiece.

"Where has Boudie's Wonder Boy got to?"

Should she leave a message on her sister's answering machine? She could make the excuse that the hour had passed, she felt too jiggered, or that the day was too cold to take the journey to Little Shore.

But Boudie had insisted for months that they enjoy a sisterly day together. She stood in the centre of the living room, still undecided.

Long-standing matters played on her troubled mind. Certain things needed saying.

Anxiety, and breathing through her mouth instead of her nose, gave her a dry throat. Only one thing for it, she decided—a hot cup of tea.

But she continued to pace up and down while considering her options. Still unsure, she questioned, *Am I being melodramatic and plain silly to cancel?*

She sighed. "The tea can wait. Sorry, Lulabelle, but I can't possibly let my sister down."

She headed for the stairs and plodded up the steep steps.

Florence paid no attention to fashion and dressed with simple practicality. In her opinion, Boudie made bold statements with her style and clothes and enjoyed drawing attention to herself. Without fear of the overuse of colour, Boudie dressed in passionate purples, or pretty pinks, her dainty feet always festooned with glittery shoes, her waist accessorised with belts, and buckles. Florence would never wish to compete with her sister and remained puzzled by the detail and time Boudie spent on creating such an image for the world to admire.

She, in contrast, sought refuge in plain taupe and beige. And her green Wellington boots were durable and comfortable friends.

She felt proud of her younger sister's business achievements, but she had never felt able to give her direct praise. The Belleview continued to blossom and reach great heights of success. Boudie always put this down to her organisation and vision, along with her and the young man's hard work.

Florence decided if the boy ever appeared, he could jolly well wait until she deemed herself properly dressed, ready to present herself to Boudie.

Florence opened the pepper-coloured doors of the cumbersome wardrobe, a piece of furniture of considerable age, inherited from her parents' home in India.

After the tragic partition of India, in 1947, her father, a former major in the Indian army, had returned to England. On Yorkshire soil, Major Scott Thomas readjusted to the life of a farmer, one he'd known well since childhood.

When Florence reached twelve years of age, her father sent for her to join him. There, in a dank and miserable village, she attended the local school. Her teachers sought control within the classroom, canes at the ready.

Parted from her mother, her baby sister, and wrenched from her one friend, Bryce, she missed the mornings she and Bryce had spent being home-schooled and later experiencing carefree hours of playing in the sunshine. Feeling abandoned, she became a detached young girl, retreating into the background since she was excluded from the school clique and bullied by the teachers. She became anxious.

When her teachers weren't present, her classmates took up the mantle and picked on her. Waiting in corridors, restrooms, or on the playground, they would pounce, mocking her accent and how she looked. Finally, they nicknamed her *Miss Sullen.*

Her only respite was time spent with her caring grandparents or the animals on the farm.

She felt she could not share with them or her father why she detested school. Each day dragged by.

She found some solace away from the sneers and jibes of the students when she walked through the open spaces of the countryside surrounding the farm. The family's flock of sheep grazed there, where two clever sheepdogs kept a protective eye over her and the sheep.

Desperate, she wanted to run away and board a ship that sailed back to her real home in India. She missed her loving mother.

One summer holiday, she shot up, seemingly growing the length of a vaulting pole. Her grandparents told her she would make an ideal model for *Country Life Magazine,* and her father joked by calling her his swivel stick.

With more confidence, she practised putting on a stern face in front of a mirror. When she returned to school in September, she towered over the gang of girls with their threatening tactics. She stood tall and gave them one of her rehearsed, *mess-with-me-at-your-peril* looks. It worked. The classmates backed off; even the authoritarian teachers seemed less aggressive.

A more self-assured Florence started to enjoy the power of her tallness, no longer dodging the bullies. Even the cliquey set included her. In the middle of class one morning the headmistress, a Mrs Bell, christened Beaky by the students, summoned Florence to her office.

"We are not sure what we can do with you, or indeed what you might do with your life, Florence Scott Thomas." Her tone came across crisp, devoid of emotion.

"It is clear you are no academic. Perhaps it's in your best interest, and that of your father's, for you to leave school. Have you thought about working on your grandparents' farm?"

Florence, lost for words, lowered her head. She hadn't given any consideration to what she might do after completing her education. Neither her father nor her grandparents had ever mentioned possibilities for what her future might hold.

Without referring to what had happened, and without discussion, the following week her father plunged her into learning the complete workings of the farm.

Often on her own, it made her question whether she would ever return to her beloved India.

Her father stalled when she asked, "Might Mother and Boudie join us here soon?"

She spent her nights in a cheerless bedroom tucked away at the top of the house. The room, lacked decorations, such as mirrors or pictures, with one single bed and a reddish-brown wardrobe that had no doors. Hemp curtains hid the few clothes she owned. Her grandfather's vintage reading lamp rested on an old metal and wooden school desk. Alone and with no close friends nearby, she felt removed from her previous life.

Determined to find contentment, vowing to find a way to communicate with the outside world, she decided to reach out to her mother, her friend Bryce, and her sister. If she didn't, she knew she would go mad from loneliness.

CHAPTER 10

FLORENCE STARTED TO WRITE LETTERS, THANKS to her grandparents, who gifted her a writing set that held the whitest of paper. Her father found a suitable ink pen from his study. She wrote furiously, sending weekly exchanges to her mother and sister. Whenever she conjured up pictures of them living a wonderful life in the heat and humidity, a jab of envy would strike.

She imagined herself reunited with her best friend, Bryce, envisioning the early morning lessons they'd shared with their English tutor, and how, after each lesson, she and Bryce would splash about and swim in the mosaic-tiled pool. Their shrieks of laughter had echoed throughout the house and across the sloping gardens.

She had a vision of her beautiful mother.

At a set hour each day, standing on their shaded

terrace, her mother entertained friends and served afternoon tea. Later, as the sun set over an orange-hued mountain, a servant would pour chilled champagne for her guests.

Florence clung to that little vision of heaven as she wrote.

She would run the entire length of the driveway to the red-and-white post-box that was nailed to a wooden post by the entrance gates to the farm. Once she unlocked the box and retrieved the envelopes, her heart would soar when sealed replies appeared. Later, in her bedroom, she would read the lengthy reports of family life in India.

> *Your sister continues to ignore both mine and Nanny's warnings and swings dangerously high on the ropes. Remember the ones your father made for you and Bryce?*

And her mother would sign off,

> *We miss you, dear Florence, and wait for the day we shall be reunited again. Your loving Mother*

Florence also wrote to Bryce, with tales of farming life from dreary Tamshire. She confessed to missing him. Months would pass without a reply. Then a brief letter arrived. Bryce wrote how he missed her, too.

She eagerly wrote again, but no further communication appeared. Utterly dismayed, she stopped writing to Bryce, for in her mind her friend had broken their solemn promise, a promise they fervently had made to each other before she left for England. She could not understand why, but in the depths of her heart she carried a small flame of hope that they would surely meet again.

Homesick, she yearned to return to vibrant India, for she loved her birthplace. Without a choice, she could do nothing, and she resigned herself to life on the farm.

As the sun rose each morning, she would set out into the fields, feed the animals, scatter seeds around the chicken hutches, and collect freshly laid eggs. Her father placed lofty expectations on her young shoulders, for she had to care both for him and her ageing grandparents as well as serve as both farmer and housekeeper.

Her grandparents often remarked on her natural gift for farming and told her how useful this would be when the time came for her to marry.

Florence, although grateful that the busyness gave order to her days, did not see a farming life in her future. She wanted to dream and be daring and have fun again, but she did not know how she might. Duty bound, she carried on.

Out in the fields, she embraced her freedom in the wildest of weather. The livestock, composed of flocks of sheep, two shire horses, and a few cattle, became her silent friends. She talked aloud and shared her worries with the farm's dogs, Blackie and Jessie. They gazed adoringly into her eyes, as if they understood her plight.

Sadly, her grandparents died within weeks of each other.

She remembered the stories they shared, their kindness, and the love they'd given her. Journalling helped her cope. By putting her thoughts and feelings down on paper, she could express sadness at their loss. And, re-reading her raw and emotive words, she continued to feel deeply connected to her grandparents.

After Florence celebrated her nineteenth birthday, her father broached the subject of another change.

"Now that your grandparents have passed, it's time you moved to a city and learned about the world, about work, and how to socialise."

Surprised at her father's willingness to let her go,

and still grieving for her much-loved grandparents, she bade farewell to the open, grassy fields, to the animals, to her father and, most of all, to the harsh life she had silently endured.

• • •

Florence travelled alone by train to London.

Near Brompton Road, she attended a secretarial course that a dear friend of her mother's had recommended. Florence rented a room from her too. A willing student, she did her best to type fast and learn shorthand . . . badly. She persevered for three months.

Following the course, and thanks to her father's fortuitous contacts, she started work as a trainee secretary at the War Office.

Soon, the farm became a distant memory.

Because of her father's rank and the high esteem he'd been placed in before Partition in India, and without her mother in residence, another expectation arose. Her boss, a friend of her father's, insisted she attend the occasional cocktail party. She found herself exposed to the higher echelons of public life and had to mix in an amiable fashion with wealthy lords and ladies, politicians, and civil servants. A far cry from her simple farming life in Tamshire, she felt unable to engage in this world of status and material trappings.

At her first party (she christened them Fickle Evenings), she literally bumped into the newly married and recently titled Colonel Bryce Beckwith.

Her heart almost stopped. She felt a flash of chemistry between them, and a burning ache flooded through her.

Why had fate conspired to keep them apart until now? It seemed the threads of their young lives had come undone. She wanted to disappear into the bland clothes she wore.

Her former friend tipped his head forward in acknowledgement. “Good to see you, Florence.” He smiled, and without any further engagement, moved past her to chat with another group of guests.

Upset by what seemed to be indifference towards her, she noted Bryce’s seamless confidence, a confidence she envied. He’d acquired an ease with people over the years. This was a far cry from the shy boy she’d known who had once been her closest friend.

She could not help but admire his impeccable style, but then feelings of rejection hit hard.

She searched desperately for a viable excuse to drop out of these gatherings, but her boss insisted she attend.

One evening, matters took a turn, and a woman sashayed towards her. Florence felt the differences between her and the woman who approached. She appeared as if she’d stepped off the ramp at a Christian Dior fashion show.

Unsure what to do, Florence wished the floral wallpaper would swallow her up.

The woman stopped and stood in front of Florence. “Good evening. I am Colonel Bryce Beckwith’s wife. My name is Diane. I hear you were once friends with my husband.” Her tone cast an air of superiority over Florence, who immediately found her irritating. Strained pleasantries followed about their families, and superficial discussions of how life continued to move forward since the Partition of India.

Florence tried to shake off a self-consciousness she felt standing face-to-face with the woman who’d married the man who’d betrayed their friendship.

Diane continued to attend these parties with Bryce. She wore off-the-shoulder ensembles in cream or white satin embellished with gold beading. Florence yearned for Bryce to speak to her alone, hoping for an explanation about why he had broken their connection.

On one occasion, with Diane present, he engaged in polite conversation.

"Good to see you again. How are you enjoying work at the war office and London life?" Before Florence could muster some courage to reply, she watched Diane press her hand into her husband's, willing him away. Diane's actions, Florence thought, revealed a lack of interest in having to employ small chat with a mere secretary.

"Come along, darling. My parents and friends await us."

Giving a nod of dismissal to Florence, Diane led Colonel Bryce Beckwith across the deep-piled red carpet to mix with her high-society crowd.

• • •

Florence stared at the open doors of the vintage mahogany wardrobe. When had she become this sentimental old soul with foolish thoughts of her old life? The full-length wardrobe mirror, although badly scratched, reflected her face, which was etched with a kind of wistfulness.

Her eyes studied her seasoned body. Without finesse or flair, what clothes could she possibly wear? Plain, muted skirts, trousers, and blouses all hung limply, many untouched since she'd moved to her present home.

"Not much in here to spruce me up," she told her disappointed self. Then her eyes fell on a warm, heathery tweed skirt and a silk lilac blouse with a bow. It had belonged to her dear mother and been passed down. Florence remembered having it altered to fit her.

An unworn knitted cardigan in a harmonious shade

of grey also caught her attention. The pockets, trimmed with a lacy frill, had been a gift from Boudie one Christmas.

She pulled the clothes off their wire hangers and threw them onto her bed. After changing, she turned to her vanity drawer and came upon a long-forgotten green satin box. Opening the lid, she scanned her mother's delicate pearl necklaces and treasured earrings. Before her mother died, she'd passed down some precious family heirlooms that reminded Florence of their once privileged life in India. She placed a transparent string of pearls over her head, and they rested on the silk blouse just above her waistline.

Florence reminisced again about her mother and the intoxicating perfume she wore. Her favourite had been Joy by Jean Patou. She thought, too, of the flimsy silk evening dresses her mother wore at cocktail parties, many in the palest of blue or shades of rose pink.

She remembered her father or mother reading her a bedtime story, kissing her goodnight, then departing for dinner at their club. She savoured these memories.

But time marched on.

Florence pinned up her tresses of grey hair into a chignon. She found one of her mother's silk flowers, now a faded lilac, and clipped it onto her pleated hair. Another drawer lay filled with makeup. She spotted an old tube of lipstick, once the colour of warm peach. She rubbed it onto her lips.

"I have no need for enhancement, but today I think I shall play the game of who is the prettiest of them all," she said, chuckling to herself.

Lost in recollections of times past, Florence gazed again at her image in the mirror. All six feet and a bit of her stood tall. Pleased and proud of her transformation, she said, "Mother, I hope you are looking down on me today."

She looked towards the old crystal chandelier above her head in the centre of the ceiling. "Remember the Lucy Clayton School of Grooming you once enrolled me at? Perhaps the course has finally worked a little magic." She had known it to be a preposterous idea, sending an awkward girl like her to attend a grooming and modelling course. After all, she had been a girl who never came out as a debutante, not even for one night.

Lulabelle appeared at the bedroom door and wagged her tail. Adoring eyes shone from her bushy grey eyebrows. She gazed at her mistress with a look of dignified approval.

"That's good enough for me." Florence strode over to give her prized dog a cuddle.

"Now, what to put on my feet?" She summoned her mind to concentrate. Turning back to the wardrobe, she kneeled down to search for appropriate shoes and found a pair hidden in a box covered in dust. She stood up, took the shoes out, and pushed her wide feet into them. They were accessorised with silver buckles and made of fine leather. She stared once again at her reflection, turning this way and that.

Tentatively stepping down the narrow-stepped staircase, she went into the kitchen, boiled a kettle of water, and made a pot of Earl Grey tea. She set out a tray and placed the teapot and a cup and saucer on it. She double-checked the calendar that hung by a single nail on the wall at the side of the fridge. No dates, appointments, or social activities marked the calendar, save for every Thursday's class of Karma and Calmer Yoga and the monthly Friday Frolics, Food and Fun. In bold red highlighter, today's date with her sister remained clearly marked.

Unsteady in shoes unlike her comfortable pair of

green Wellington boots, she picked up the tray and carried it through to the lounge. She placed the tray on an oak side table. Her feet already felt cramped, so she kicked off the black shoes. Flopping into a velvet wing chair by the window, she poured herself some tea, then sipped the refreshing brew while she viewed the front garden and the empty street beyond.

Keeping an eye out for the boy's arrival, she listened to the pitter-patter of rain on the windowpane. Lulabelle sat at her feet, the big dog's head resting on long, curled-up legs. The gold-plated carriage clock from her parents' house in India chimed eight forty-five. Wriggling impatiently in the chair, she set the cup down. With no sign of a car or a ring at the front door, her mood started to waver, her muscles tensed, and she felt her impatience grow.

CHAPTER 11

"WHERE ON GOD'S EARTH HAS THAT BOY got to?" Florence shook her head and peered out of the window. After a taking a few more sips of tea, she slipped back to when she first entered the world in India.

Filled with pride, her parents took delight in fussing and spoiling over their firstborn.

But when she reached five, her life changed.

One morning her father appeared in their sprawling living room. He lifted her into his arms and set her down on a chair. Then he knelt beside her.

The room opened out to manicured lawns filled with palm trees, and a swimming pool tiled in blue-hued mosaic glass.

Overhead fans blew out warm air. Little bubbles of perspiration appeared on the fine hairs of Florence's arms. The humidity made her fidgety, so she crossed her ankles, one on top of the other, and placed her hands in her lap. She waited for her father to address her.

"I bring good news, Florence. During the night, while you were sleeping, your mother gave birth. We are bestowed with another daughter and you, my dear, have a baby sister. What do you have to say about that?" Her father smiled.

She looked into his tired but twinkly eyes. She did not know what to say or how she felt, so she remained silent. After a few minutes, she smiled back at her daddy.

Her father took her hands in his. "It's quite a surprise for us, too," he reassured her. "I know it will take a bit of getting used to, but we'll all get the hang of this baby soon enough. Never forget you are loved, my dear, and will always be special to your mother and me." He stood up, patted Florence on the head, and left.

Later, she climbed the stairs with her nanny, and they entered her mother's bedroom. Half-drawn silk damask curtains allowed golden rays to pour through the gap, and she felt a mysterious glow to the room. The scent of her mother's perfume wafted around her. Her mother lay propped up in bed with plumped pillows for support. At her breast, she held the tiniest of gurgling creatures.

Curious, Florence moved closer to the bed. She stared at the baby's pink face and its fluffy blonde hair.

"Say hello to your new baby sister," her mother said.

Florence looked at her mother's pale face and the tiny beads of moisture that sat on her brow.

Her mother gave Florence a blissful smile and reached to take her hand.

"You must promise to take care of your sister. Always watch out for her wherever you are. Do you understand?"

Florence nodded.

"Your father and I thought the name Boudicea, after your great-grandmother, would be a most suitable name." Her mother looked at her as if she sought

Florence's approval.

"What a lucky girl you are to have a new sister. But we must not tire your mother out." Nanny moved closer to where Florence stood, took her by the hand, and bustled Florence back down the stairs and into the kitchen. Once there, Nanny instructed her to sit at the big round wooden table where she served Florence freshly baked biscuits and a glass of coconut milk.

Florence's thoughts lingered on her childhood as she sat sipping her tea in her wingback chair.

She had fond memories of her parents' colonial-style house and its perfectly trimmed lawns.

Sculptures of elephants had stood beyond the shade of the papaya and mango trees. Turquoise-striped chaise lounges and overhead fabric umbrellas with silk fringes accessorised the edge of the swimming pool.

She recalled Nanny calling her and Bryce (who she played with for hours every day) to sit underneath the leafy shade of the almond tree branches. They drank fresh lemonade poured from an Indian copper pitcher.

Florence often heard her parents describe her to their friends as a skinny bit of a girl, with wild, frizzy hair. In complete contrast, they called her friend Bryce a beautiful boy with floppy blond curls.

Small in stature, in comparison to her, Bryce followed Florence wherever she went. They played hide-and-seek in the coconut groves. The rolling lawns led to a swift and narrow stream at the bottom of their garden. The cool water meandered over rocks and stones and made babbling sounds.

They spent as much time as they could near the stream, intrigued by the teeny fish darting and gliding across the water. They played the game of "who can count the most fish" as they watched the fishes' backs glisten when the sun caught their gills.

Nanny constantly warned them not to follow the surge of water back to its source. "Too dangerous," she would say. "And what if you fell in? Who would save you?"

But she and Bryce ignored such warnings. When they thought nobody was watching over them, they sat by the clear flowing stream.

After removing their sandals, they'd gingerly dip their bare feet into the coolness and let the fish tickle their toes. The sensation always made them gasp. Sometimes she and Bryce would swing from handmade swings made of thick rope that her father had knotted and hung from resilient branches. They would push to go higher, amidst giggles and laughter. "Whee . . . whee . . . look at me," they would each squeal. "Look, look, we can fly all the way up to the sky," Florence remembered calling out. Her mother would sometimes appear and call to them from a shaded veranda. "Florence, Bryce, please refrain from swinging so high or you will fall off."

Florence remembered seeing her mother toss her glossy hair back as she laughed, amused by something one of her guests had said. More often than not, her mother held a chilled glass of champagne between her long, slim fingers.

• • •

Florence blinked, suddenly back in her living room. Shifting again in the chair, she checked the carriage clock. Lulabelle stirred, opened her eyes, and stretched full length into a dog pose.

Florence pushed herself out of the chair and looked out the window. A veil of rain steadily marked the panes of glass.

There would be no point in telephoning Boudie at this hour, she decided as she heaved an impatient sigh. Boudie would be running off those dainty feet of hers, cooking eggs Benedict or kedgeree. It seemed to Florence that whatever the hungry guests wished to eat at The Belleview, Boudie happily provided.

Florence did not use a mobile phone and had no interest in such fandangled contraptions. She simply could not get to grips with technology and wondered why anyone would want to use their fingers to type messages on such minuscule keyboards. It amazed her how people gripped the tiny devices and, even more of a mystery, how they read such small print on shiny screens.

She believed it a strange way to connect. *What had happened to old-fashioned traditional phones with robust handles and ringtones?* she often asked. What had happened to real conversations with people as they sat across a table?

Boudie would sometimes become impatient with her. "Oh, for heaven's sake, Florence, why can't you get with the programme and buy yourself a mobile phone?"

"Go digital. Become a silver surfer," Colonel Bryce Beckwith encouraged her. He already owned a mobile phone and knew his way around a computer. He patiently explained how it allowed him to contact friends and set up dates to meet ex-army folk when he visited London.

He offered to accompany Florence to buy a laptop and told her that with his help they could set up Skype with a camera. That way, he told her, she and Boudie could see each other while they talked and drank tea.

With as much grace as Florence could muster, she firmly declined his offer. "Maybe I am old-fashioned in my ways. I do not understand this technology lark that everyone else seems to think of as progress." She had made one exception in the 1990s. She purchased an answering machine and still found it reliable. The instructions had been easy to follow, and Bryce kindly recorded a personal greeting for her.

Florence turned away from the window and walked into the hall. The telephone and answering machine sat side by side on a round glass table. No lights flashed. Had Boudie remembered to give the young man her name and address?

• • •

Kit drove past signposted villages as they nestled in marbled grey clouds. Rain spat across the windscreen. The traffic crawled along due to road construction. An official-looking man, wearing a yellow high-viz jacket, stood and controlled the flow of cars holding a stop-go sign. Long silences had filled the car ever since he'd collected his passenger. He switched on the radio. A track from the Swedish group, Abba, belted out.

Does your mother know . . .

The song triggered memories of college life and writing a thesis about the music that had influenced him and expressed his young life. Hearing the song again brought him straight back to his mother. His chest tightened.

"How long before we're there, Cassie?"

The woman's wheezy voice startled him out of his reflections.

"Fasted since last night. I need food and water. I feel weak," she said. "Oh, oh, is that the news? Turn up the volume. Me and your father enjoy the radio. We like to stay ahead with what's going on in Kent." She turned towards Kit.

He peered at his passenger through the ridiculous mirrored shades he wore.

The woman twiddled her fingers and mumbled, but he had no idea what she'd said, apart from catching the name Cassie. The woman repeated the name.

Kit wondered, could Cassie be a connection to Boudie?

About to ask, he saw the woman had returned to the land of slumber. Her lips puffed out like Mick Jagger's and strange sounds popped out of her mouth. Her head rolled forward.

The noise hailing from the woman's mouth clashed with the words of the Abba song. Kit felt sympathetic about her frailty, but the cacophony played with his aching head. He switched the radio off and continued to drive.

A nauseous taste filled his mouth. He thought about the bottom of a parrot's cage. Ugh. He shook his head. He would have to stop soon and have a long drink of water or a can of Red Bull. He glimpsed a sign ahead that told him to turn left, and he steered the car towards the town of Battle.

CHAPTER 12

JAMIE STOOD IN THE DOORWAY OF HIS bedroom. Instinct told him to leave, but his heart said *stay*. He felt a spasm of wretchedness, but the time had come to leave the grind of city life and put the tugs of emotion behind him. The last weeks without his ex, Poppy, had been heart-wrenching. Maybe, he tried to convince himself, with a few weeks of respite he could clear his mind.

Picking up his backpack, he looked around the almost empty bedroom. It did not give him any pleasure to know that his mother would have to manage the move to Kent on her own. He felt another pang of guilt.

Resisting thoughts of how she might react when she found him gone, he held on to the banister, treading as lightly as a puppy down the taupe-coloured carpeted stairs. In the dimly lit kitchen, he stuck a note onto a packing box near the table where his ma's favourite crackled vase sat. A roughly made vase he had painted when he was young, covered with flowers in her favourite colours of pink and green. He had presented it to her one Mother's Day.

He carefully turned the key in the lock of the back door and walked out of the family home. He would post a few lines to his best friend, Matt, once he found his soft place to fall.

From the east end of London, he took a bus to Victoria Station. As he stood on the station concourse, a tangle of commuters rushed around him. He felt removed from the busyness and people's wish to reach their destination. He watched a queue form at the coffee and snack kiosks and breathed in the smell of freshly baked pastries. A whistle blew, train masters' warnings to passengers that a train was about to depart.

He scanned the departure board and listings of destinations. He felt a pull to take a train to the coast and visualised lapping waves reaching the seashore. The soothing beach would help him heal, he told himself.

Heading over to a ticket office, he stood in line behind a heavily built woman. Dressed from head to toe in black, she wore a statement velvet hat that sloped down on one side. Growling sounds came from a corner of the woman's large shoulder bag. A Chihuahua popped up and snarled at him.

Taken aback, Jamie talked in soothing tones to the dog, but the canine remained aggressive.

The woman turned to face Jamie. "Chico doesn't like strangers getting too close."

She waved her hand in a dismissive fashion, signalling for Jamie to step away. She turned back and, in a disapproving tone, spoke to the uniformed man behind the counter. "I shall make a full report about the service at this ticket booth. I am appalled that you deem it necessary to eat while serving your customers."

The man grunted, took the woman's cash, and passed her a one-way ticket. She huffed and puffed and pushed Jamie aside as she made her way to her train.

The booking clerk shook his head and lifted the half-eaten sausage roll from the greasy paper it had been wrapped in. He shoved the remains into his mouth. After a few moments of chewing and swallowing, he looked up and said, "Right, young man. Where you headed?"

Jamie hesitated, still a little unsure of his destination.

"Well, come along. I have customers waiting. Where do you wish to go?"

Jamie cleared his throat and requested a one-way ticket to Little Shore. As soon as he had the ticket in hand, he walked towards the correct platform and jumped on a train. With money in short supply, he would have to find a basic bed-and-breakfast as a place to stay.

• • •

Arriving in Little Shore, he passed a forlorn-looking pier that jutted out from the coastline. He stopped and read a notice that revealed the pier had been engulfed in a major fire some years before. Large, dark smudges of cast-iron pillars and burnt wood appeared to blend into the sea below. Together, they cast a mass of black ink across the foggy horizon.

He scanned the area from left to right. He stood for a moment longer and decided to take the paved public path. Seagulls cried out, squawking as they flew overhead. He inhaled the salty aroma of the sea. An unforgiving wind and high tide caused the waves to rise up, roll, and pound onto the shingled beach. Without gloves, Jamie's fingers felt numb, so he tucked them into the sleeves of his parka. He pushed through the merciless rain and wind and let his mind wander.

"Time is a great healer," he remembered his mother saying. Right now, he needed time and space.

He considered the intensity he'd felt as a student at the College of Performing Arts. The last year had taken its toll and hadn't helped with his broken love life. He felt such a fool for believing Poppy really loved him. He also had to acknowledge a fury that sometimes overwhelmed him because he hadn't seen his father in the last five years. In fairness, his father had tried time and again to reach out to him with letters and postcards. And, through communications with his ma, his dad had sent invitations for Jamie to visit him in France. Jamie had refused to have anything to do with him.

Now, thinking about the anger and frustration he felt towards the man he had once adored, he wondered why he had not been able to have a conversation and simply ask his father why he had left.

A fork of lightning ripped through the sky.

The power of the howling wind and rain persisted in pushing him off course. He looked around the empty walkway. To his left, on the opposite side of the promenade, he watched rivulets of water gathering and shining in the crevices of cobbled side streets. What madness had possessed him to come to a deserted beach town in the depths of winter?

The saltiness of the sea air sat on his tongue, and the smell of seaweed made him queasy. Waves connected with the bursts of incessant rain that fell on the rocks. He felt his shoulders slouch with the weight of the rucksack. Bending his body forward he walked uphill, leaving the smells and seagulls behind. Climbing the slope, the backpack seemed to grow heavier with every step. The wet air followed him, and an icy mesh swept across his face.

He stopped at an entrance with embellished gates

and two regal palm trees on either side. Beyond the gates, he saw an expansive lawn and an imposing period house. Above the gate, a sign painted in bright pink and black calligraphy hung from two robust chains. "Award Winning Belleview Boutique B&B" it boldly read.

The house stood three stories high and spouted decorative turrets. The entire image prophesied prices well beyond his budget, but for some reason he did not want to turn away. He opened the gates and stepped onto a crisscrossed mix of gravel and stone.

The rain had given the path a glossy shine, like marble. Twelve black-and-white tiled steps led him up to the front door. The arched porch was flanked by two plant pots, both filled with topiary bay trees. He glanced towards a stained-glass oval-shaped lantern that hung from a plaited rope above his head. Pressing the doorbell, the ding-dong sound vibrated through the doors of glass and rich wood. He waited. After some minutes without a reply, and turning to walk away, the door suddenly swung open.

An attractive woman, wearing pink corduroy trousers and a soft-knit off-the-shoulder sweater of the same colour, stood before him.

"Welcome to The Belleview. How can I help you?"

"Hi." Jamie hesitated. "My name is . . ." he stumbled over the words. "I'm . . . Kit. Kit O'Connor. I've travelled from London, and I need a room for a few days. Can you recommend somewhere for a poor student?"

"Hmm . . . there are not many B&Bs open at this time of year."

The lady opened the door a little wider.

Jamie, now Kit, felt a tingle of heat and comfort inviting him inside.

"You look chilled to the bone. There's fresh coffee brewing. What about a hot cup, and we can discuss rooms and my rates over the winter season?"

She ushered him into the foyer. Relieved, Kit dropped the backpack onto the floor. The woman took his parka, placed it over a satin hanger and hung it on a nearby coat stand. The warmth hit him like a thermal layer of reassurance. Guiding him into a conservatory, she promptly walked over to where an expresso machine sat on a counter near a back wall. After pouring steaming coffee into two china cups and arranging them with a jug of both cream and milk on a steel-coloured tray, she walked across the room and put them on a small table. Smiling, she seated herself in a tall-backed wicker chair and motioned to Kit to sit opposite her.

"Oh, dear. I forgot to introduce myself. My name is Boudicea. But family and close friends call me Boudie."

• • •

Boudie sat and assessed the young man who called himself Kit. Why would a lone student choose a seaside town at such a desolate time of year? He certainly wasn't here for the fishing or the outdoor life. But when she'd opened the front door to Kit, she'd heard one of her intuitional whispers, *Here is a decent young adult who is lost. You must help him.*

Observing Kit and always priding herself on being a good judge of character, over her years of living and loving, she had learned to listen to what her heart and gut told her. Sensing there could be a lot more to Kit but thought it better not to push him to explain himself.

They chatted about winter in Little Shore; a ghost town at this time of year, Boudie told him. She also spoke fondly of the loyal guests who continued to visit her B&B regardless of the weather.

Eventually, she leaned towards him. "Okay, Kit, here's

the deal. I have a tiny room at the top of the house. It holds a decent-sized daybed; it's my quiet place when I need to retreat from the daily grind. The views can be breath-taking once the clouds lift and the rays of sun streak through the windows."

Making a quick decision, she promised to charge him well below the minimum winter rate.

"As long as you give me your word that you are not a drug dealer and you haven't killed or maimed anyone recently. And I would not wish to harbour a bank robber who needs to lie low for a while." She gave him a stern look.

She decided that if this young man paid up front, she would embrace him wholeheartedly into The Belleview, just as she welcomed all her full-paying guests.

"I am happy to have you stay if you pay cash but, remember, this arrangement is only for a few days." She gave him another thorough looking-over before finally saying, "What about your family and friends? Have you informed them where you are?"

• • •

Kit sat on the edge of his chair and surveyed his surroundings while listening to Boudie's proposal. He already felt a bond with Boudie and had immediately spotted kindness in her hazel eyes. He continued to drink the restoring coffee in silence.

After a few minutes, and, encouraged by Boudie's arrangement for him to stay at The Belleview, he provided an edited version of why he'd bailed out of college, left London, and left his family home.

His voice change pitch, and a deluge of embittered words spilled out. Shocked at himself and the urgency to talk so frankly about his father, Kit realised he might have jeopardised his chance of getting a room. His skin prickled. Mentally pulling himself back, he swore not to talk about his broken love life with Poppy, who had almost destroyed him emotionally. The pain of leaving his mother earlier that morning, was not for discussion either. Such secrets, could not be revealed, not yet.

He collected his thoughts. "I promise I'm none of the things you mention. I just need a break from the stresses of life in London." He forced himself to grin at Boudie. "Many of my family live on the west coast of Ireland; as for the rest, there's always Skype or texting."

Swiftly, he reached across the table and firmly shook Boudie's hand.

CHAPTER 13

THREE YEARS PASSED. KIT AND BOUDIE HAD struck a more permanent deal, and he'd come to savour working in the cocooned world of The Belleview.

When he'd first offered to stay on and work, Boudie had replied, "My dear Kit, it would be a thrill to have you remain here. But are you sure this is truly what you want to do? If it is, then I believe we can work together. I will ensure you have many opportunities to learn new skills." Boudie confirmed she would pay him by the hour and that Kit could continue to sleep in the same room at the top of the house.

He did not bother to recharge his mobile, making it impossible for his mother or anyone else to contact him. Instead, he bought a pay-as-you-go phone. He stopped dwelling on the past and decided to reinvent himself by creating new memories.

He realised he had got quite a kick out of building the

character of Kit O'Connor. *A bit of an experiment*, he told himself. Whether or not he returned to the Performing Arts College to finish his degree didn't matter. Wearing this invisible mask, he congratulated himself on the ease with which he had been able to transition into this new role.

Boudie tested his commitment to work, giving him early morning shifts. First, he learned to set up, prepare, and serve breakfast. Later, Boudie showed him how to take bookings and follow up with daily administration. He became accustomed to Boudie's high expectations about service.

"It's showtime. Hope those eyes are open and your smile is ready," she encouraged him at the start of every morning, always upbeat, regardless of the hour.

Kit observed her greeting her guests with her warm smile and a cheery "good morning" as she guided them to their tables in the conservatory. Her greeting followed quickly with Kit and her serving The Belleview's renowned breakfast. Once a month, they both enjoyed reading flattering reviews on *Trip Advisor.*

Pleased with how quickly he had grasped the ins and outs of running the boutique guesthouse, after a few weeks, he took on some general maintenance. That became his most strenuous but rewarding task around the Victorian building. He took to cleaning, painting, and decorating, too. As a young boy, he'd spent his summer holidays in Ireland, where his beloved grandfather had patiently taught him such skills.

Kit paid special attention to Boudie's charm, which seemed to weave a spell on her guests. Some would travel from the other side of the world, year in and year out, returning to this, their favourite spot. He watched protectively when male guests flirted with Boudie. Some asked her out on dates, but she declined. "There are two loves in my life—The Belleview and my adopted grandson. I have little time for anything else," he'd overheard her tell one potential suitor.

One day Boudie surprised him by suggesting he register for a barista course. Eager, he signed up, and learned the precision and art of making great coffee. After he qualified, he heard Boudie regularly announce to her guests, "I have a most discerning palate when it comes to the quality and the taste of my coffee. Please, allow my chief wingman to make you a cup and I can promise you will never forget the taste." After which, she would introduce Kit with the grandest of gestures.

In pure theatre form, he would head to the expresso machine while his captivated audience watched and listened to the sounds of grinding, clanking, hissing, and the odd hum.

Within minutes, he served an espresso, americano, cappuccino, or a latte finished with a creative, foamy swirl of a heart.

Coffee sales soared, and Kit's popularity grew. The guests called him "an Irish charmer who creates art and passion in the best tasting cup of coffee."

Basking in Boudie's praise and her guests' appreciation of a job well done, Kit appreciated the generous tips, and his wings of confidence grew.

At the end of a day's work, he and Boudie would often sit together. In winter, they ate dinner in the warmth of the kitchen, thanks to the Aga. Over the summer evenings they lingered outside on a sunny terrace, eating al fresco and drinking a glass or two of wine.

During these evenings, Kit found himself captivated by Boudie's tales of a privileged world in London and in India, both places where she'd once lived.

He watched Boudie smile as she recalled her old life with her mother in a "sunny Asian culture", as she liked to call it. She spoke of the loneliness that engulfed her when the relationship with her older sister, Florence, became severed. Her father, long after Partition, had called Florence to join him at his parent's farm in Tamshire, England. Boudie regaled him with her other sadness. When she was eighteen, her father had insisted that she and her mother move from their vibrant and colourful life in India to live in what she considered a cold and dreary London.

He listened in disbelief when she revealed the unrealistic expectations of her parents, who nearly forced her to marry a man she did not love.

"You are lucky, Kit, to live freely and do whatever suits you. In my time, a woman held little or no status in the world unless, of course, she married." She reeled off what the role of a society wife entailed. "Obey and follow your husband's instructions. A society wife must entertain a husband's family, friends, and his business associates. She must engage in both her husband's and her own charity work. That's such an archaic and old-fashioned way of thinking," she said before continuing. "Damned if I'd be told how to live and who to marry. I refused to become locked into domesticity and the rules according to men.

"A friend of my mother's, who emigrated to America after India's Partition, regularly sent her women's magazines. Mother kept them under lock and key, but one day I managed to raid the cabinet. I pored over articles and read an advertisement promoting a book with the title *The Feminine Mystique*, by Betty Friedman. I sent off for a copy in my mother's name, and soon I had become a rebel. With waves of feminism blossoming, I felt I had no choice but to join The Women's Liberation Movement." She shook her fist in the air triumphantly.

"After much protesting, and wrangling with my

parents, they finally realised I would not alter my thinking. So, life changed. I remained single and began living on my terms." She beamed at Kit.

Another evening while they sat relaxing in the living room, Boudie shared with Kit about the years she spent with the sole desire to bear a child. She spoke of her vivid desire to bear just one healthy baby and admitted that, to her sorrow, her body had betrayed her.

Kit felt a greater empathy for Boudie after hearing this tale and bestowed on her the title of "adopted grandmother" just as Boudie had already given him the title of adopted grandson. He watched her eyes immediately radiate with a glow of delight.

Following these extracts from Boudie's former life, Kit felt a pull back to his mother. Thoughts of her appeared like fast-moving clouds, along with the memories of what she'd sacrificed for him to have a better life. In dreams, he'd sometimes see her face light up at the sight of him.

On another occasion, over dinner, Boudie looked directly at him. "Remember, I am here if you ever wish to talk."

He did not know what to say or how he ought to reply, so he averted his eyes from her gaze. In between Boudie sharing her life stories with him, he briefly spoke of his time at the College of Performing Arts. He talked of his passion, and his once-held dream to act in a big production on a stage in the West End.

One morning, following a busy breakfast service, he and Boudie were working side by side in the kitchen. Unexpectedly, she said, "Darling boy, don't you think it's time you lived a little? I do not expect you to hang around me or take part in everything going on at The Belleview every day and night. What about expanding your social life and interests? You might even join a local acting group. It's important for you to keep the flame of your talent burning. You could bounce a few ideas around, maybe allow a few creative projects to develop with other acting students. There are plenty of young men and women your age on the same path, and I feel certain they would welcome you into their circle."

When he agreed that would be fun, Boudie let him know a few days later that she had contacted The High Drift Theatre Company through some of her friends.

When he rang them up, the head of the group suggested Kit meet him, along with the other actors, to get a sense of what Kit enjoyed about acting.

At that first meeting, he'd felt barraged by questions about stuff he hadn't wanted to have to talk about. He thought it best to mention he'd taken time out to assist his adopted grandmother at her B&B. He remembered a long-held tradition used by his grandfather. His grandfather had told him, "Son, if anyone ever asks you a question that you don't wish to answer, simply reply with a question back to them. People love to talk about themselves. All you have to do is listen."

Kit adopted this technique, using a parry, repost, parry, repost—like the fencing lessons he once had pursued at college. By listening intently to his fellow actors' chatter and ramblings, he found he didn't have to answer questions directed at him. Before long, the theatre company embraced him into their tightly knit community.

A girl named Laylah showed an interest in him. She fished around enthusiastically with her enquiries.

Although flattered by this female attention, Kit also knew he would have to tread an evasive route.

One night in a local pub, as the group sat around discussing the evening's performance, Laylah sat close beside him.

As much as Kit fancied her and would have happily

held Laylah in his arms, he told himself, "No, it's not going to happen." Dangerous ground that could end up with pillow talk, he decided.

Over the course of his first summer, after joining the theatre group, he received invites to quirky pubs and blowout music festivals. The crowd often gathered amongst a tangle of lantern-lit woods and, later, they slept in various stages of undress in makeshift tents on mucky and soggy ground.

Or everyone partied till dawn.

They would watch a blazing ochre sunrise as they lay sprawled on the shingled beach, still maggoty with alcohol.

Much as he enjoyed his game of pretence, he knew at some point he would have to jump off his make-believe setup. He refused to dwell on the *when* or *how* he would reveal who he really was and why he had bailed out.

One drunken summer night, along with his mates, everyone ended up skinny-dipping in the freezing sea. Laylah appeared by his side and wrapped her naked body around his. He succumbed, kissed her passionately, and promptly regretted what had happened next.

CHAPTER 14

Following Molly's move to Kent and doing her best to adjust, she still occasionally lapsed into guilt. She knew words like *I should have, what if,* and *if only* wasted time and energy, but life and her future changed irrevocably the day Jamie walked away.

She did not want to worry her parents, so she relayed an edited version of Jamie's departure. They urgently suggested she employ a private investigator, for which, they said, they would foot the bill.

"Why would you not talk to the police?" they asked. "Surely there must be a team who specialises in this line of enquiry for missing persons. They must be able to do something that might lead you to finding our grandson."

She heard panic in their voices, but tapping into an inner strength, she sought her own path of investigation. Instinct told her that Jamie, whatever his reasons, did not feel ready to make contact or come home.

She did not tell her parents that she spent some weekends after moving to her new home camped out in a cheap Airbnb in London.

On these Saturdays, she would leave her apartment with an overnight bag on her arm. Like others preparing to attend the theatre, head to a friend's house for dinner, or eat out in a fancy restaurant, she also dressed up in her glad rags. Painting her lips and brushing her cheeks with a flash of colour felt the right thing to do to fit in with the crowd, but she had other pressing issues on her mind. Romantic notions were not one of them.

When heading to her car, she often bumped into Mrs Cornell from next door.

"Off somewhere nice, Molly?" Mrs Cornell would ask, squinting at her.

Molly always noted her neighbour's eyes would look down to check the holdall she carried.

"Haven't seen or spoken to a sinner all day apart from me husband. I like to take a walk to the gate at this hour. You never know who might walk past and have a chat like." Mrs Cornell would flash her false teeth. "I'll put money on there's a sweetheart waiting for you. Hope he takes care of you. Hard to find a decent man these days." Mrs Cornell would then wink at Molly. "My Cassie's days are caught up with her animals and her being a vegetarian. There's not a man in sight. And who would blame him, having to deal with all of that?"

"Thanks for the tips on men. I'll certainly bear them in mind," Molly replied kindly and gave Mrs Cornell one of her radiant smiles before getting behind the wheel and making the drive to London.

• • •

Arriving in London, she parked her car near the Airbnb

she had booked and would sleep at later.

She trawled the streets near Jamie's college and visited some of the crowded bars. Every spot seemed the same, with a sea of rowdy young men and women drinking, taking selfies, and planning their night ahead. She would order fizzy water with ice and slices of lemon, pretending it was vodka and tonic.

Younger guys sometimes hit on her, flirting by offering to buy her a drink, making comments about her shiny red curls, or speaking about the sexy sway of her hips. Embarrassed, and unacquainted with what someone younger might label as flattery, their behaviour told her they would happily boast to their friends of a night of passion with an older woman. Nothing could have been further from her mind.

Sometimes she would take a bus to the east end, a short distance from the family home and her old life.

Feeling every inch of being two decades older, surrounded by what appeared to be a cool crowd, she dipped into the madness of their Saturday nights. She wandered in and out of sweaty night clubs, the nightlife Jamie and his friends had once talked about and where they had once hung out.

On one such night, she spotted the opening of a glitzy nightclub. Pink and white-coloured balloons decorated the entrance door and a pink neon sign read *The Moody Attic*. Trendy and groomed young men and women waited their turn to head inside.

Weeks before, she had printed off hundreds of posters in her quest to find Jamie and kept a stack of them in her coat pocket and handbag. She pulled one from her bag. In her high heels, she awkwardly walked up and down the long queue. Projecting her voice, she asked if anyone knew or had seen the young man in the photo.

"Hey, lady, no hustling here or we'll have you

removed," she heard a man shout down the line at her. The tone of his voice sounded familiar. Molly turned and caught sight of a six-foot bouncer, dressed from head to toe in black and with an intimidating look about him. He had a walkie-talkie and earpiece in place, and he reminded her of some on-screen hulk of mammoth proportions. She realised that if he so chose, he could lift her up with one hand and simply dispose of her. Stumbling to where he stood by the entrance, she observed a gaudy square of candy-pink carpet on the ground. Sealed off with two poles linked with a piece of gold rope, she noted a sign clearly marked "VIPs Only."

"Are you on the guest list or do you have a pass?" the man asked gruffly. He didn't bother to look up as he checked his clipboard.

Then it registered with Molly. This was her friend, Brandon O'Neill. Usually dressed in work dungarees and a flat baker-boy hat, he and his team of men had helped her move to Kent after she'd discovered Jamie had left.

Molly knew Brandon to be a good guy. His son and Jamie had gone to the same school when they were young. A feeling of remorse stabbed at her about her lack of contact with Brandon since moving to Kent.

Brandon came from Irish ancestry and had been born in the Bronx, in New York City. He and his family had moved across the pond to the east end of London years before.

"Hey, Brandon. So, this is what you get up to on weekends?" She tried to sound upbeat and noticed his look of surprise as his gaze caught hers. That followed with a look of admiration flashing across his face. Feeling quite flushed, she took in his study of her. Finally, he focused on her eyes, and she watched him relax.

Brandon moved in closer and kissed her on each

cheek. "Wow, Molly. Where have you been hiding? You look sensational. Didn't recognise you all dressed up."

Molly grinned at him, holding on to her precious posters. "Well, I could say the same for you." She scrutinised his strong features, his smooth dark olive skin, and remembered the warm friendship they'd once shared.

"I did not know you were a man of the night. Look, I don't want to be a bother or cause any hassle." Molly went to move off.

"No need to leave. Really, it's okay. I just didn't expect to see you again and looking so gorgeous. You haven't changed one bit," he said, apologising for his gruffness. "Being a part-time bouncer pays well, but trust me, this is not my scene, nor am I looking for love."

"Well, neither am I," Molly said.

She felt obliged to tell Brandon that since Jamie had left, she'd put pressure on herself to check out his old haunts. She explained that some weekends she drove to London and stayed at an Airbnb.

"You can always stay at my place, no charge," Brandon suggested.

Molly laughed, ignoring this invitation. Instead, she showed Brandon the poster with Jamie's photograph. "Is there any chance you could hang a few of these notices around the reception area?" she asked.

"Yeah, sure, why not?" Brandon looked genuinely upset, and he placed his hand on her shoulder. "Honestly, there's not been a murmur of Jamie. If I hear anything or see him, don't worry, I'll be in touch. Look, next time you're up this way, maybe we could grab a drink, have a catch up?"

Molly did not respond, but thanked him, said goodbye, and walked towards another nightclub.

She continued visiting thronged bars and clubs during

weekends, hoping she could track down Jamie.

"Have you seen this young man?" Tears would well up in her eyes as she stood waiting at one of the crowded bars. She told the few who would listen the story of her son's departure and of her desperation to find him. Fuelled with alcohol, or off their heads on drugs, many revellers stared blankly at her, not bothering to check the photos or the words on the posters. They sometimes gave her a quick dismissal, saying, "Nah, sorry, Grandma, can't help. Never seen him."

She felt out of depth amongst this young, frenetic night scene and thought to herself what a far cry it was from her innocent courting days with Rory.

All those years she'd spent with just one man. The one she truly loved and gave herself to.

On these crazy Saturday nights she carried on, hoping to bump into one of Jamie's mates. If she did, she thought they might give her another track to head down or share ideas of where he could have gone.

From time to time, she rang Matt, his bestie. He'd had no further contact, he told her. She sometimes wondered if Matt could be hiding information. Had he and Jamie made a pact?

Often exhausted after coming up against one blank wall after another, she would later fall into bed at her pre-booked Airbnb.

The following day, reluctantly, she would always drive back to her home in Kent.

CHAPTER 15

Molly, having considered her career as a care worker and yoga practitioner, wished to further develop her passion for helping others. *Could she be the changemaker within her new community?*

Following her application and acceptance at an open university, she began working toward a degree in health and wellbeing. On her day off from yoga, she studied at a local library or at a nearby media and information centre. Occasionally, she also drove to a library in the East End of London, the halfway mark to Jamie's former college. In between using the online resources for the course, she sometimes checked the Facebook page she'd set up to find Jamie.

Today, she drove the short distance to the library close to home. After parking the car, she slung her bag over her shoulder and gathered files containing her coursework. Another folder held photos of Jamie and missing persons' posters. Placing them tightly under her arm, she walked up the steps to the steel and glass entrance door.

Once inside, the familiar smell of old perfume and leather swelled up and around her. She took a deep breath, then walked to the reception desk. The head librarian greeted her warmly.

"Hello, Molly. What can we help you with today?"

"Oh, the usual. Studies, reading, and research." Away from everyone, the library allowed her to work without interruption on her degree. Also, she could pursue the person she loved in these inner sanctums of calm. She often compared her dream of acquiring an honours degree to the anticipation of holding a new book in her hands—virgin pages waiting to be read, a rewarding story unfolding with a happy ending. In her mind, that also applied to finding and bringing Jamie home.

Moving across the pile of cherry-red carpet and heading towards a workstation and computer, she gazed around the almost empty room. She longed for a hit of coffee. That would have to wait, she told herself.

Performing what had become a ritual, she rolled her head from one side to the other, stretched her neck, and tucked her chin inward. That followed with an inhale of breath, and then a slow, long exhale.

To date, the results of her studies brought rewards, but investigations on finding her son had been unproductive. Aligning her focus on the gratitude for her yoga practice, her weekly classes, along with the support from her neighbours and her degree course, she looked upwards to the domed ceiling. Beyond the bubble of glass, a tumble of heavy grey clouds appeared.

She noticed the walls had recently been painted white, and new wooden shelves held rows upon rows of neatly lined-up books. A slim but robust ladder rested at one end of the aisle where she sat.

After a few minutes, she placed the files and folder on the polished mahogany table and laid out the contents. She stood to remove her coat and hung it on a nearby hook. She placed the strap of her bag over the padded chair. Once seated, she fired up the computer and clicked on the interactive activities she would take part in today. An hour passed.

She could not help herself. Like tiny magnets, her fingers sucked her in to click on Jamie's Facebook page.

His headshot appeared with a notice that read:

> ***URGENT***
> *Gone but never forgotten*
> *Jamie Mulligan*
> *Last seen February 2013*
>
> *If you have any information, please get in touch*
> *via DM and leave your mobile number.*
> *REWARD - £350.00*
>
> *With thanks,*
> *Molly Mulligan*

Meticulously, she checked and read the feed in the inbox. To her distress, no new posts popped up.

After Jamie left, and enduring that first year of grief, unexpected support came from the local East End Council. They gave her the go-ahead to put posters up on telegraph poles in and around the old family home.

Her brain a blur, she'd walked from door to door, showing neighbours a headshot of Jamie. Everyone had uttered words along the lines of, "Molly love, you must be heartbroken." The men and women from her surrounding community had shaken their heads in sympathy. Her elderly next-door neighbour took Molly's hand in hers. "Why would your Jamie leave? Surely things were not bad between you? You two always seemed close. I admired his passion for acting, and his ambition for a part that would whisk him onto the London stage."

Nobody reported any sighting of him. Instead, they offered her cups of tea, home-baked scones, and tried to comfort her with words of sympathy.

Always without answers, in a haze, she felt bereft.

The head of the College of Performing Arts contacted her when Jamie had not shown up for lectures. Concerned, he asked Molly to meet him. He remembered Jamie being close to his assistant, a Miss Poppy La Grange. "She became Jamie's mentor," he recalled. "I am sorry to say, but she left shortly before Jamie stopped attending his lectures." The professor flicked at some pages in a file and confirmed this information with Molly. He also mentioned that one of Poppy's reasons for leaving had been to take time out to travel across Europe. "I'm sorry, Mrs Mulligan, but Miss La Grange left no forwarding address." The professor closed the folder in front of him and stood up, signalling, Molly thought, that their meeting had come to an end.

She made to leave, but not before the head granted her permission to display posters on various noticeboards around the college. Finally, he promised he would see that a red alert be set up on the college website, along with a photo of Jamie. "I shall do my utmost to ensure everyone within the college shall remain vigilant. We shall continue to encourage our students to come forward with any information relating to Jamie." Molly and the professor shook hands, and she left.

As much as she appreciated the support of the College of Performing Arts, nothing cast any ray of light on Jamie's whereabouts.

Lying awake at night, she asked herself the same

question aloud. *Why did you decide to cut ties with college, your fellow students, and disappear from my life?*

She continued her health and wellbeing courses, delighting in learning new and practical skills. In between, she located online support groups, the official sites for those pursuing young men and women who had gone missing. Many of the members, like Molly, suffered day in and day out, and each person seemed keen to share their heart-breaking story. In time, members on these platforms became her allies. She found interacting with parents and friends of missing persons in live chat rooms enabled her to accept that she would never be alone. Some encouraged her to register a report with the police.

One day, calling on her courage, she stepped into the local police station close to her old home. The personnel team sympathised and logged Jamie's details into their system. Later, the officer in charge explained to her, "Madam, we have levels of priority regarding children and adults who go missing. If an adult decides he or she wants to start a new life, that's their prerogative.

"We understand this must be impossibly hard on you to accept, but there is nothing else we can do. If more information appears to show this was anything more than a choice, please contact us." The police officer then handed Molly information pamphlets, along with lists of telephone numbers for more helplines.

Disheartened, she'd exited the station.

Trying hard to accept Jamie's departure, she carried on with her yoga classes and fun Fridays. Proud of her success, keeping a smile on her face, she continued into year two of her degree. Taking her mind off her reality and the secrets she kept, she never lost sight of the belief that Jamie would return when he felt ready.

During one of her visits to the library, she had a

moment of inspiration. She searched for Poppy La Grange and checked the name on several social media platforms. All she found was a cockapoo who appeared to be quite the princess and a bit of a celebrity—one whose videos were shared with a fan base of almost one million followers on Facebook and Instagram. She wanted to scream in frustration. Instead, she howled with laughter.

Molly thought back to Brandon O'Neill. On the day he assisted with her to move to Kent, he had found Jamie's passport behind the empty wardrobe in Jamie's bedroom.

It at least comforted her that Jamie could not travel abroad or he would find it challenging to organise a new passport. Once at her new home, she had placed the passport in a drawer by her bedside table.

Against that same wall in Jamie's old room, wrapped in one of Rory's old shirts, she and Brandon had also uncovered an oil portrait of Molly, painted by her ex.

CHAPTER 16

MOLLY CONTINUED TO SIT AT HER DESK in the almost empty library. Her fingers curled as she tapped on the keyboard. Distracted from working with her study group, a photograph loomed large on the screen and tempted her in. Clicking on London's Google Maps and zooming onto the street of her old home, the front door flashed up and time fell away, pitching her back to the morning Jamie disappeared.

She remembered that last evening spent with her son, and when he'd kissed her goodnight. The night followed with a restless sleep and a strong sense of foreboding. The next morning, she'd had to face the anguish of Jamie being gone, having left her only a scribbled note.

She reflected on her struggle that day, having to say goodbye to the home she had shared with her ex-husband—Rory—and Jamie. If not for her friend Brandon's support, she would have crumpled and refused to move to Kent.

She backtracked and recaptured herself as a teenager. Walking home from college, Rory and his friends would sit on a wall and wolf-whistle as she passed.

"Hey, beauty, what about being my sweetheart?" one boy called out to her.

Blushing, with her eyes to the ground, having already spotted Rory, she'd noted his sparkling eyes and high spirits. He displayed a light-heartedness she admired. Soon after that, they'd become smitten with each other.

"Carefree, wild days of love," Rory had said, describing the start of their blazing romance. He'd told her what good fortune he had found when she chose him.

"Hey, you got it all wrong. You chased me, remember?" she had laughed.

Within two years, they married. Her parents, Sean and Alana, blessed the marriage and helped them buy their first terraced home.

She would never forget the feeling of pure excitement of owning their own home, a red-bricked, two-up, two-down house, joined to her neighbours on either side by a wall. She relished living in a piece of history, for it had been built before Victorian times.

In a daze, Molly continued to envision herself walking through that same front door again. She stepped into the hallway, which led to a cosy extended kitchen. The windows threw a bright light onto the garden, filled with flowering plants in colours of white, purple, and cream. Observing the overgrown fig tree that spread its wide green leaves for shade over the summer months, she recalled harvesting the soft, purple fruit in August.

Rory, a creative artist, had worked long hours for an advertising company. Molly had trained as a care worker and committed herself to what she viewed as a privileged vocation. Within a few years, their son Jamie had arrived. Their irrepressible emotions spread like a web of pure and unconditional love for their baby boy.

Once she and Rory had settled into parental bliss, Molly's parents retired to their beloved home along the west coast of Ireland.

The years tumbled by.

Rory came home one lunchtime, his facial features haggard against a pale complexion. "Made redundant with a small payoff from the agency," he'd told her.

She'd done her best to soothe him. "Another job will appear. You'll see. You have a great reputation and a most presentable portfolio. The powers that be will headhunt you. You'll soon return to leading a team, just like your colleagues." She'd reassured him with kisses and held him in her arms.

Weeks passed. She'd watched Rory's once incurable energy and passion buckle. He'd ceased to care about his appearance. He would often slouch in a chair in the kitchen, staring for what seemed like hours through the window at the lushly planted garden.

To Molly's disappointment, Rory refused to contact any of the creative agencies. A few friends telephoned him, saying, "Don't worry, bud. We've got this. We have contacts." They promised to make introductions and set up some job referrals for Rory. Empty words.

She remembered Rory's increased drinking. His moods would waver between fury and a helplessness she'd never witnessed before.

"I drink to forget," he'd admitted. He would pick fights with her and Jamie without reason. "Oh, for heaven's sake, don't buy into it. I'm letting off steam," he would say later by way of an apology.

Molly had found their new situation unsettling when Rory became more uptight. Wishing to calm his agitation, she tried appealing to his emotions. "What about us? Jamie and I love and need you. What about our son's future? You can't give up on your family."

Rory had hung his head in defeat. He appeared at a loss to explain his behaviour. After that, Molly saw a sense of despondency settle in.

A vivid memory returned to her. One night, following dinner, Jamie was upstairs in his bedroom, working at his desk to complete his homework. Rory sat in his usual chair at the kitchen table. She sat opposite him and reached across to take his hand and kiss it.

Oblivious to her show of affection, his eyes glazed. He kept them fixed on his half-drunk glass of wine. Without warning, he banged his fist down hard on the table. The glass toppled and shattered. The red liquid splashed across the surface and dripped onto the terracotta-tiled floor. Tiny specs of glass scattered like fireflies in the candle-lit room.

"What happened to us, Molly? What happened to those heady, lustful days? What brought us to this place?" He looked up accusingly. "You always take our son's side. I say left, he says right, and you go along with him." He almost spat the words out, his tone fuelled with bitterness. He pulled his hand away from hers.

A realisation had hit her. Nothing would pacify him. Rory had become a victim of his circumstances and blamed her for everything.

Without a word, she pushed her chair away. Shaken, she walked out of the kitchen to the hallway, where she caught sight of the shadowy figure of her son standing at the top of the stairs. He darted into his bedroom and slammed the door. She put her hand to her mouth. Had he heard yet another of his father's outbursts?

After that night, Molly had become the main breadwinner. She increased her workload. She showed the best care and empathy to her clients, and sometimes she was even asked to sleep over at her patients' private residences. In some ways, it was a relief to be away from the turmoil and stormy atmosphere that had crept into her beloved home.

Rory, a stubborn and proud man, would not accept their new circumstances and sank further into depression. He resisted her suggestion of seeking professional help.

One year turned into two. Finally, Rory walked out and left Jamie and her behind.

Although grateful for a newfound peace, she missed the man she loved. It felt as if the lifeblood had been sucked out of her.

After that, Jamie no longer listened to her words of encouragement. She'd watched him struggle without his father. He became rebellious towards her.

"I don't get it," he'd shout. "Why would a father up and leave his wife and only son? He didn't even try to make stuff better between us."

Two more years went by. She carried on, working tirelessly.

With no sign of her husband returning, his friends appeared like busy bees who could not resist the honey pot.

"Hey Molly, I happened to be passing," said Archie, Rory's closest friend, often knocking at the door unannounced. "Any chance of a cuppa? Or something stronger if you've got it."

Every time Archie returned after having spent time with Rory, he would insist on relaying news about him.

"Whoa, Archie," she finally said. "Can we be honest? You and I both know this is no casual drop in to give me updates on Rory. Where were you when my ex-husband needed you most?"

"I had no idea that talking about Rory is a sensitive subject." He continued to tell her Rory had picked up the pieces of his tattered life, gained some fervour, and had turned his life around.

According to Archie, in the south of France in the town of Menton, famous for its lemons and music festivals, Rory had found a property—a tired-looking bistro/bar on a calm backstreet.

He reported that Rory had injected colour into the old building and opened the subdued space. Mirrors of an art déco design illuminated the walls and reflected brighter energy, he'd told her. He also confirmed to Molly that Rory's melancholy had dissipated. He spoke of a few suspicious locals who questioned Rory, him being the foreigner, on what he hoped to accomplish by coming to take up residence in their town.

"After Rory opened for business, miraculously, this community let go of their scepticism and arrived in droves at the bistro. I speak a little French and understand from his customers that they now like and trust your ex."

Molly became irritated by Archie's embellished tales of her ex-husband, how he sat amongst the locals who gathered every morning to read their newspapers, sipping coffee noirs, or gossiping amongst each other.

"After Rory learned Churchill painted landscapes in the area, he felt eager to renew his hobby of painting. Your Rory has without doubt reinvented himself. It appears his finances are back on track, too." Archie smiled at Molly, showing pride for what his friend had accomplished.

As if to convince her further, Archie continued. "I am sure it will please you to know Rory has cut right back on his drinking. These days, he is seldom seen hitting the bottle hard." Archie looked to Molly for her approval, following what she considered long and winding stories of her ex-husband's success.

Unimpressed by Archie's exaggerated bulletins from France, one day she said, "Enough. Archie, you are happy to 'pop in' as you call it, and relay news about Rory. But, the truth of the matter is, did your supposed best chum have to disappear off to France and leave his family? As glad as I am that Rory is doing well, I don't need the details of how wonderful he has become." Molly put her hand up. "Please leave. You are no longer welcome here." Even with her protests, Archie, flushing bright red, looked determined to continue.

"He has mentioned on more than one occasion how sorry he is for wallowing in self-pity, causing you and Jamie such heartache. Moll, he'd have you back in a flash. His words, not mine." Archie tried to hold her eyes. "Anyway, if his new career path continues to take off, you could join him. Start over or not, eh?" Archie moved closer and brushed his hand across Molly's.

She flinched at his touch. "I am asking again. Please leave. I am not interested in having your company or your lengthy updates. You have not been a friend to Rory or me. Now go."

"Hey, come on, that's the way it flows. It's called life, and it keeps changing. Maybe you are ready to move on." Archie's smile did not falter. He said, "You must realise I've always thought of you as special. Tell you what, why don't we plan a date for lunch or dinner soon?"

Leaning in, he kissed her on each cheek. Molly looked away.

"Don't be a stranger." He walked down the path and blew her a kiss.

Cringing, she wiped at her cheek and waved him and his invitation away. "Don't come back," she shouted and banged the front door shut.

Months passed, then an unexpected postcard arrived from Archie.

Hey Molly,

Rory has opened a small art gallery next door to the bistro/bar, exhibiting his work of seascapes and landscapes.

Buyers have shown a particular interest in the portraits of a beautiful, pale skinned, red-haired woman.

Thought you'd want to know.

Let's make a trip to Menton soon?

"Be on your guard," her father had warned during their weekly telephone calls. "Remember, Archie, a supposed best friend of Rory's, did not come to his rescue when he needed him most. He's not interested in what Rory is up to. He wants to freeload, and trust me, it's you he is hoping to snare."

"It's okay, Dad," she told him. "I've wised up to Archie and his little games."

• • •

Molly averted her eyes from the screen where her old life and family overshadowed her. She mourned the years when Rory's and her love blossomed and what she had believed would be their forever love.

She reprimanded herself about how her heart could still feel a tenderness towards him.

Lost in times past, she looked up and checked the vintage black and white clock on the other side of the library wall. Familiar faces had congregated without her noticing. Silently, they had taken their places at various desks across from her. She nodded at each person.

Once again, she allowed herself to be whisked back in time and her eyes bore into the Google Map on the screen.

CHAPTER 17

FLORENCE SAT IN HER LILAC ENSEMBLE, TAPPING her foot impatiently. Lulabelle's sympathetic whimpering did not help. She checked the old carriage clock that no longer chimed on the hour. The hands showed nine thirty. "Half my day already wasted," she tutted.

Moving to the window and pulling back the cream-coloured lace curtains, she spied Colonel Bryce Beckwith on the other side of the street. He appeared lost in some daydream. To further her irritation, she watched him whistle as he walked down the path and pushed his red wheelbarrow. After attending to the DIY at the church, Colonel Bryce Beckwith always grinned broadly on his return. His animated face bothered her this morning. Whenever this happened, Florence would have to swallow hard when he enthusiastically spoke of taking tea and homemade cake with the vicars' wife. He often described her as "exotic Gabriella."

Until today, she'd held back on discussing personal matters, emotions, and questions that had tormented her for years, and suppressed a longing to share them with Bryce. In the last weeks, these questions had incessantly played on her mind and in her dreams.

One such question referred to her frustration about not knowing the truth about Colonel Bryce Beckwith's relationship with his late wife, who had died over ten years ago.

And what kind of affection does he hold for me? she wondered. Florence decided leaving this earth without knowing the answer would be unthinkable. Surely at this stage of their lives Bryce could be more forthcoming and reveal how he truly felt. Time had become startlingly precious. She would have to confront him and ask if they could rekindle a more endearing relationship.

In her stockinged feet, unable to endure stepping back into the uncomfortable shoes she'd kicked off earlier, she hot-footed it to the front door and down the path, waving furiously to catch Colonel Bryce Beckwith's attention.

"Bryce, Bryce? I need a word. Come, come," she beckoned impatiently.

Bryce returned Florence's wave and gave her a thumbs-up. After which, he marched down the lane and into his garage. He ditched the wheelbarrow, zapped the automatic door shut, and hurried back to the street.

"Well, I never, Florence Scott Thomas! What a sight for sore eyes. Pretty as a picture you are today. I hardly recognised you." His eyes twinkled. "And what a fetching flower in your hair, reminding me of your dear mother, God rest her soul. A beautiful and kind lady. Do tell, where are you off to, and in such finery?"

Florence felt a flush of red spread across her face, but she did not want to waste a moment. "Come, follow me," she ordered Bryce. He obligingly walked into the house and through to the living room.

Once there, almost pushing him into her winged chair, she poured the remains of the Earl Grey tea into a second china cup and saucer that she'd placed on the tray earlier. Handing over the cup, she remained standing.

"Bryce, there are things on my mind I wish to share. They cannot wait a moment longer." After taking a nervous breath, she asked herself, *What could Bryce see in me? A seventy-five-year-old woman, firmly set in her ways, with a wrinkled face and unfashionably long grey hair.* Touching her lips, stained with the old coral lipstick, she put her hand to the chignon festooned with her mother's silk flower. He'd paid her a compliment a few moments before. That must count for something. Perhaps it was a sign, a chance to enable her to make a final stab at uncovering the truth of his feelings. Her mind searched for answers. With a fluttering heart, she paced the room back and forth. Lulabelle's ears perked up and her eyes peered towards her mistress.

Florence blurted out, "Something has bothered me for many a year." Moving closer to Bryce and stretching out her hand to touch the side of his face, a giddiness crept into her body. One not felt for a long time. *Steady,* she told herself. *Steady.*

Florence hesitated, then took a step away from him. "Why did you forget about me when my father summoned me back to England? Because I never forgot you. We were bound together forever, or so I thought. But without a word to me, you went and married that Diane woman. You allowed her to take a place in your heart. I felt utterly betrayed, if you must know. As we are at this ripe stage of our lives, and with time of the essence, I must ask why you behaved so?"

Her heart pulsed. Feeling faint, she went to sit on the rich brown velvet sofa opposite him. The pain of lost days and nights of grief caught her off guard.

She would not allow the overpowering misery of rejection to torment her. Unblinking, she continued to stare at him.

Following her outburst of emotion, Bryce cleared his throat, as if covering up his sense of awkwardness.

Moving to the edge of the sofa, she said, "Are you thinking that our friendship is the same as that of an innocent boy and girl like when we lived a cocooned life in India?" With tension building and a panic in her voice, she kept talking. "When you moved next door, did you assume I would believe you had given me a sign you still cared for me?" She stood up and paced the room. Lulabelle followed closely by her side.

"I have to ask. Did you ever love me? And if that is so, what feelings do you still carry? It's probably ridiculous to expect an answer, but I pined and cried for you more than I care to remember. Maybe it's all been in vain, and I have wasted the years." She stopped in the middle of the floor. Lulabelle went back to her bed in the corner of the room and curled up, but she kept one open eye on Bryce.

Colonel Bryce Beckwith raised his hand. "My dear, I never in my wildest dreams expected you to share such sensitive feelings. I hoped and prayed over the years that you might feel we had more than a friendship."

A long silence descended on the room.

• • •

When Florence did not respond to Bryce's comment, feeling embarrassed, he decided it was best to take his leave. He stood up and his bowler hat toppled from his head and rolled across the polished wooden floor. The dog growled and followed the hat into a corner, taking it into her mouth. Bryce tried to retrieve his now spit-ridden bowler from Lulabelle, but she kept his headwear firmly between her teeth.

As he tried to wrestle his hat from the dog, his mind pushed for answers to Florence's questions and declarations. *What about the countless invitations I made over Sunday mornings, suggesting she join me for coffee at my breakfast table? Did that not show how much I valued her company?* In a flap, he recalled the times he asked Florence to walk with him to church and attend Reverend Horatio's service and how she'd flatly turned him down with one excuse after another. What was he to think? Holding his body still, he allowed his eyes to dart around the room. Once he felt more composed, he said, "My dearest. Through mutual friends, I sought you out. After Diane died, my friends supported me in buying the house next door. In my opinion, this displayed, perhaps incorrectly, the high regard you are held in. My sole desire was to be close to you, and that is still my wish."

Having secured his hat, and unsure what to say next, Bryce went to the side table, picked up the bitter tasting cup of tea, and handed it back to Florence.

Her brow frowned with what he believed to be anger.

Finally, she broke the silence. "Lulabelle come here. There's a good girl."

Lulabelle left her bed and padded across to sit at her mistress's feet.

"I have not finished." Pointing her finger and gesturing for Bryce to sit back in the winged chair, she said, "In the last hour, I have come to a decision, which includes you."

Bryce sat down, loosened his tie, and wondered what else Florence had to say.

"Today I was due to visit my sister, Boudie. The plans have been scuppered with a no-show from the boy my sister calls her adopted grandson." She waved a hand in irritation and continued. "The evidence of this morning has shown me he is a most unreliable chap. I intend to report this to Boudie when I next see her. No more sitting around. It's time to act. My decision is made. I propose you and I take my esteemed father's car for a long drive. We, my good man, shall drive to The Belleview in Millie Morgan."

He wanted to protest, but Florence interjected.

"No buts, no fuss, no argument. The Morgan is in prime condition, ready to face this winter day and the journey ahead. We can too, with due courage. I intend on driving to Boudie's. It's your choice. Will you join me, or do I drive alone?"

"My dear, this is sheer madness. It's the middle of a harsh winter. We would have to take certain measures for such a drive. And what about your creaky bones?"

He watched Florence roll her eyes.

"I will not be put off and can assure you my bones are already unsettled this morning. Another two hours could not possibly add to my current pain. Anyway, it will be a wonderful surprise for Boudie. She has plenty of room at The Belleview. We shall have to pack an overnight bag and if you decide to join me, you have half an hour to get ready."

Flummoxed by Florence and her unexpected decision to drive to the coast, he did not relish the sharp ultimatum. After Lulabelle and Florence escorted him out of the house, he hastened down the path. He turned and looked back quizzically at his headstrong neighbour.

"Think of it as an adventure," she called out.

My day has been turned upside down. What shall I do? He considered his options and firmly closed his front door.

CHAPTER 18

MOLLY BEAT HARD ON THE KEYBOARD WITH a clenched fist. Angry tears flowed.

She heard a whisper in her ear. "Are you okay, Molly?"

A hand touched her arm. Molly looked up, and several sets of eyes stared in her direction. Other library patrons shook their heads at the intrusion. She had broken the code of silence and the promise she had made to herself to remain cheerful today. She struggled to contain her sobs. Her breathing felt laboured, and a pain spread across her body.

"Molly, let me take you outside and get you a glass of water." The head librarian picked up Molly's shoulder bag and firmly guided her away, taking her through a door and into a corridor.

"I'll be fine, really. I'm sorry, but today is a bit of a day. Old and sad memories."

"I am concerned, that's all," the librarian replied. She

handed Molly her bag, disappeared, and returned with a glass of water.

Molly put the glass to her lips and tasted salty tears as they mingled with the chlorine tap water. Hearing a kettle boil in a nearby open kitchen, she watched a member of the staff vigorously stir granules of coffee and hot water in a mug. A queasiness from the aroma of instant coffee overcame her.

Excusing herself, she slipped into the nearby ladies' room. Catching a reflection in the mirror of the woman peering back at her, she thought, *what a sorrowful-looking figure.* Her face displayed pale and blotched skin.

Until today, she'd only ever released her emotions from her old life when lying in bed at night. Occasionally amplified, they felt as if some other force powered them. Like a pendulum swinging two ways, one side took her in the direction of the future. The other could drag her back to her old life, one where she continued to search for news of Jamie. Today, a sad tale of her private life pressed against the cracks. Summoning up when Rory had left, and later when her son slipped quietly out of her life, she felt shame for allowing emotion to trickle out in a public library. For three years, she had covered over the fractures and tried hard to blend in and become part of a community again.

Ripping the rough paper from the towel dispenser and wiping away the remains of her lipstick, she splashed her face with cold water and dabbed at her eyes. After pulling out her makeup bag, with a shaky hand she traced the outline of her lips with a lip pencil.

With the colour refreshed, she whispered, "That's grand." Listening to her heartbeat finally tuning in to the rhythm of slower breaths, she looked herself over again in the mirror. Running her fingers through her hair, she said, "I have survived these past years. I'll not allow myself to become buried in grief."

She called out the word *courage* and felt white, light-feathered wings encircle her.

Throughout her life, she'd been aware of angels, for her grandmother would often comment after someone had passed. "You must never worry when heavenly spirits appear in times of angst or grief, for they are a sign life will go on and all will be well. You simply must trust the process." A beautiful blue-eyed child stood close to her right side. He resembled Jamie as a young boy and engaged her with a smile and blew her a kiss. "No need to worry, it's okay, I will return," the child said. A rainbow-coloured light radiated towards her. In that moment, a rush of anticipation pulsed into her heart.

Rolling her shoulders back and forth a few times and placing a smile on her face, she checked her reflection again. She willed the smile to reach her eyes, then stepped into the corridor. The head librarian stood patiently waiting, holding Molly's coat, file, and blue folder. She gave Molly a look of empathy.

From a nearby shelf, Molly reached for the glass of water and slowly sipped the liquid.

"Thank you for your kindness," Molly said. "Please pass on my apologies to the other patrons." Allowing the librarian to help her with her coat, she placed the file and folder under her arm. Stumbling through the exit door, she headed towards her car.

A voice called out, "Mrs Mulligan, hey, Mrs Mulligan."

Molly turned to see a young man wave a striped scarf in her direction.

"Hey, where have you been?" the young man asked once he caught up with her.

Startled by the greeting, she recognised Matt—

Jamie's best friend—a short and muscular young man, in complete contrast to her tall, lean son. Matt's curly waves of black hair stuck out from underneath a wool hat.

"Good to see you, Matt. It's been a while. How have you been?"

"I'm good. My girlfriend lives nearby with her father. We're supposed to be swatting for our final exams, but you know what it's like." Matt shrugged. "But hey, whoop, whoop, in a few months we'll be free."

"It's probably never the right time, Matt, but I have to ask. Have you had any contact with Jamie?"

"Not a thing. Sorry, Mrs Mulligan."

"It's been three years since he bailed out on us. A bitter pill that I have swallowed each day," Molly said. The sight of this young man before her brought back more memories of the day Jamie left.

Every possibility, it seemed, had withered the day her son made a choice and her responsibilities as a devoted mother had been whisked away.

"Jamie and I were due to have a fresh start with a move to Kent. Not an hour goes by . . ." her voice trailed off. She felt tears escape and roll down her cheek.

"Terrible situation for you . . . I mean . . . the not knowing. Me and the friends talk about him. We do our best to keep his memory alive. I miss him." Matt bowed his head. "I'm sorry I haven't been in contact, and I know I've let life stuff get in the way. Look, I've got a bit of work to do here." Matt pointed to the library. "If I hear any new info, I promise I'll be on the phone to you immediately. And you can call me anytime, really. I hope, I really do, you can deal with Jamie's decision to opt out." He paused, appearing lost in his thoughts.

"In his note, the one he posted to me, he stated he'd be in contact soon. He just needed time and space. I guess things changed, huh?" Matt fidgeted with his scarf, wrapping it in and out of his fingers. "Like brothers, close we were, both being only children, and over the years we leaned on each other." He sighed and looked at Molly. He kissed her on each cheek and headed for the library entrance.

He turned to walk back to where Molly still stood and tapped his head. "I've just remembered and there's probably no connection, but me and the girlfriend went grape picking last year in the south of France. Over a weekend, we explored the area. We sat and drank coffee in a square in some small town and watched the world go by." Matt tugged at his scarf, then continued. "I saw a woman who looked vaguely familiar. She passed us by, pushing a baby in a buggy. A few days later, it dawned on me who she could have been." He hesitated, then said, "She worked as an assistant tutor at our college. I remember at the beginning of our course she'd specifically taken Jamie under her wing and helped him get over his lack of confidence. We teased him all the time about her. But, one day Poppy La Grange just upped and left. Sorry, Mrs Mulligan, I didn't think to let you know. Anyway, there's probably no connection." Matt reached out and took hold of Molly's hand. He told her again how sorry he was and abruptly rushed off.

Molly, left speechless upon hearing Matt's update, could not find her voice, fighting the strongest urge to run after him and scream, "How could you have forgotten?" She chose to remain calm after the scene she'd caused earlier.

She clearly remembered the professor relaying to her some years before that Poppy La Grange taught at the college. He confirmed she had taken an interest in Jamie, but then he gave her the bad news; she'd left with no forwarding address. Nobody had heard from her since.

Surely, she is not hiding Jamie, because his passport is in a drawer at home. What can I do? How can I get hold of this mystery woman? She kicked at the front wheel of her car in exasperation. Molly considered Matt and his life ahead of him, filled with promise. Her eyes fixed on him. She watched him holding hands with his girlfriend, the two of them already in the library on a pretext of working.

Putting her weary body into the driver's seat, she placed the key in the ignition. The relentless cycle of her brain never stopped. On high alert, tension gripped her. Why was she putting herself through this torture? There was always a possibility of a knock at the door or her mobile ringing in the middle of the night. Sometimes feeling half crazed, right now, she needed something to sustain the hope of a happy ending.

Mumbling, she said, "My son is still out there somewhere. I have got to keep believing he will return." She sought her mobile, stalled, and asked out loud, "Is it too late after all this time to check in with Rory, ask if he can throw some light on a Poppy La Grange?"

CHAPTER 19

FLORENCE REMEMBERED HER FATHER'S WORDS when, in 1976, he gifted her his classic sports car, a Morgan, in shiny black and trimmed with chrome.

"My dear, this machine is a cracking car, originally bought by my father in 1946. A model with a reputation for speed back then. I recently read that Morgan's are still hip. Why, only last week, *The Times* reported a young Mick Jagger bought one in buttercup yellow. Not the colour for a Morgan, in my opinion, but times are changing." Her father kissed Florence on the forehead. "I trust you will drive her with due caution and great care."

She'd christened the car "Millie."

For years, Florence spent weekends, her hands stained with oil and dirt, working on her beloved car. After Colonel Bryce Beckwith came to live next door, he offered to assist, and she accepted his help.

On balmy summer afternoons, Florence's vintage Morgan would take them to the heart of the countryside. On these occasions, she filled a hamper with fresh food and added one of her vintage bottles of pink rhubarb gin. She and Bryce would sit side by side in chairs or on an old wool blanket by the edge of a field or near a babbling brook. Delphiniums and lavender swayed in the light breeze, facing the warm sun. A nearby church clock chimed on the hour. They listened to the buzz of bees, lightly dancing, gathering pollen as they flitted from flower to flower. Birdsong added to her happiness in the glow of the day.

• • •

Back in the present, Florence, still in stockinged feet, picked up her formal court shoes and went upstairs to the bedroom. She caught sight of her body in the wardrobe mirror and did not approve of what she viewed. A quiet dismay lingered. Colonel Bryce Beckwith had not declared his love for her. Disenchanted, she may have been, but she refused to allow words like *rejected again* to inflict themselves on her mood. After unclipping the lilac flower from her hair and throwing it into an overnight bag, she thought,

Where have I hidden my favourite silk scarf? It has swallows in green and red, so it should not be hard to miss.

Spotting the bright colours on a nearby shelf, she pulled the scarf towards her and wrapped the comforting fabric around her shoulders. Tossing the uncomfortable shoes to the back of the wardrobe and summoning up reserves of energy for the drive ahead, she told herself, *I'll not be beaten.*

Back downstairs, after placing her overnight bag by the back door, she pulled on her green Wellington boots.

Patting Lulabelle, she peered into her loyal companion's eyes. "I must apologise, dear one, for you shall be left alone for twenty-four hours."

After slipping into her wool-lined waterproof raincoat and picking up her bag, she walked out the kitchen door with renewed purpose and headed for the garden gate. On reaching the garage and undoing the catch, the door swung up. Stepping across to Millie Morgan, she caressed the shiny bonnet.

Florence almost jumped when a voice of command boomed from the garage entrance. "My dear Florence, I must stress again, this impulsive plan of yours makes no sense."

Disregarding his words and letting out a massive sigh of relief, she watched Colonel Bryce Beckwith walk towards her. Delighted, she saw he carried a small overnight case. "Ah, the Colonel has decided to accompany his neighbour after all. Your navigating skills will be appreciated." Florence smiled at him.

"I cannot see you drive alone to your sister's in such weather. Have you checked the oil and water? Of course, the air in the tyres must also be checked. Have you telephoned your sister to inform her of your intention?"

"Enough of this interrogation, Bryce. I have not contacted my sister. As I mentioned earlier, it will be a wonderful surprise for her."

"Okay. I accept your wishes. Regardless, I have made us a flask of tea." Bryce held up the metal flask. "We can stop halfway, take a break, and stretch our legs."

Florence observed the etched creases on Colonel Bryce Beckwith's forehead that seemed to have grown deeper in the last hours. Knowing him as she did, he probably felt this to be another of his military operations that would require his utmost concentration. Pleased to have him on board, Florence resolved they would have a successful drive to Boudie's.

Two hours of driving alone with the car's particularly narrow design would have been a challenge for anyone, but especially for someone of her years and bones, as Bryce had reminded her earlier. She secretly admired the perfect knot of his silk tie at his throat and found herself quite taken by his shock of thick, white hair and his neatly clipped moustache. "Allow me to take your overnight bag," she told him.

Florence strapped both her bag and Bryce's firmly to the rack at the back of the car. After which, she ensured the bonnet was securely attached. Thankfully, with the waterproof fabric roof firmly up, and the side screens in place, they would be protected against wind and rain. "Right, Bryce, let's get going. There is no time to waste."

She studied him as he walked towards her and pulled back the driver's door. Aware of her height, which always posed a tricky task, she valued Bryce's assistance helping her into the driver's seat. Awkwardly sliding one leg into the footwell, leaning across to the passenger's side, and dragging the other leg in, she wriggled this way and that.

Once comfortable behind the wheel, she signalled at Bryce to close the door. Grateful for his patience, she placed the key in the ignition and Millie Morgan's engine took a minute or so before it came alive, her purring sound music to Florence's ears.

She beckoned for Bryce to close the garage door and to follow the car down the lane. They had both learned over the years that the doors of a vintage Morgan could be a most destructive force to the uninitiated. Once she'd reached the end of the lane, Bryce got in, carefully lowering himself into the black leather passenger seat. She accelerated to turn into the street.

"Stop. Who will feed Lulabelle?" Bryce called out.

Florence jammed her foot hard on the brakes and

became aware Bryce had been thrown forward. “For heaven’s sake, man, you frightened the living daylights out of me. Let’s not panic. I know what to do.” She ordered Bryce to check the inside pocket of his trench coat to confirm his mobile was in place.

“You can text Molly. Update her of our circumstances and relay our plans. No doubt she will be happy to pop over to my house, feed Lulabelle, and take her for walks until we return tomorrow afternoon.”

Following her earlier distress about talking openly about her emotions and feelings, and the lack of response from Bryce, she’d hastily decided to undertake this trip. In the rush to get away, she had quite forgotten to ring Molly and update her. In agitation, her shoulders hunched, and her hands gripped the small wheel. After a bit, and with a nod to Bryce, she put her foot back on the accelerator and allowed Millie Morgan to take off like a ribbon of black metal down the street.

Glancing back at her house, she caught sight of Lulabelle staring wistfully out of the living room window. Remembering she’d not given the dog a special treat before leaving, guilt overcame her. Not wishing to share her thoughts with Bryce, she pushed her remorse away and continued driving into the mid-morning.

CHAPTER 20

Excited by Florence's pending visit, that morning Boudie's internal clock woke her long before the buzzer rang on her mobile phone. Her eyelids flicked open. She jumped out of bed and swished back the pink silk curtains. Thick blankets of grey cloud greeted her, blocking out views to the sea.

On grim winter days, Boudie knew she'd have to cajole the few guests who visited at this time of year. She'd tell them, "It's a soft day. Wrap up and enjoy a walk in the healing sea air. Don't worry, the skies are sure to brighten up later." With a warm smile, she seemed able to convince them weather miracles would happen.

This morning, in between preparing and serving breakfast, she dialled Kit's mobile number. After several rings, he finally picked up. Reminding him of the importance of the day, she asked if he had the piece of paper on which she'd written Florence's address. On hearing him hesitate, she realised he'd forgotten, and calmly relayed the information again.

An hour had since passed. Checking the clock on the kitchen wall, she muttered, “He’s late.” She knew she would not relax until Kit arrived safely with his passenger. Concerned by his lack of attention to time, she reminded herself of the spark of energy Kit had brought to The Belleview.

Thanks to her suggestion, Kit had learned the art of barista coffee-making, and, with her encouragement, he’d continued to develop his talent for performing.

After executing another applauded breakfast, she and her part-time help cleared away the crockery and leftovers. Next up, they would refresh the guest bedrooms.

Before heading upstairs, she stopped by the reception desk and gazed at her treasured photographs. Framed in gold, they hung on the walls behind the desk, exhibiting accolades of a job well done. Viewing the handsome man in one photograph, she felt a glow of pride. Kit smiled out from the frame with his certificate as a full-fledged barista.

Moving closer to the photographs, she touched one set in the centre of the wall. Every now and again, she’d asked herself, *Why would a young man leave his family and the College of Performing Arts to live by a coastal retreat like Little Shore?*

Following Florence’s visit, she decided she would propose a grandmother-to-grandson kind of chat. Could she encourage Kit to talk honestly? What had really brought him to her three years ago?

Heading up the marble staircase, she walked into each bedroom and plumped up the cushions on the newly made beds and chairs. She heard her part-time help hoovering at the far end of the corridor.

Her thoughts rambled to her sibling. *How might I*

persuade Florence to stay for a few days?

In her opinion, Florence never seemed to need people in the same way she relished good company. She assumed time had touched her sister, following the imposed separation from her and her mother after their father brought her to Tamshire. Boudie considered her father's frequent comparisons between her and Florence.

"Why can't you be like your sensible sister?" he would ask.

"Because I'm not my older sister," she would tell him, trying to remain chirpy as she responded. "I'm your second daughter. Why can't you accept each of us as we are?" She wondered what her father would think now. It seemed she had become the sensible one and Florence had turned into the animated one.

She'd been struck by Florence showing signs of being more spirited, following a recent conversation.

"A miracle has happened," Florence exclaimed. "We have a new neighbour and since her arrival even grumpy old me feels upbeat. The community and I have joined her 'Karma and Calmer Yoga for the Young at Heart' on Thursdays up at the church hall."

Boudie could not remember when her sister had shown such fervour.

"Until we took these classes, we had no idea what it meant to become *bendy*. Our yoga teacher plays us mystical music in between instructions and that helps us stretch our bodies. Since we started yoga, we stand up straight, breathe into our stomachs, and tip our toes as if our lives depended on it. I know you and Molly Mulligan would hit it off. You have similar attributes. You're both outgoing and happy."

Boudie enjoyed hearing the eagerness in Florence's voice.

"Of course, you are not as young as Molly, but like

you, she is filled with contagious energy, and everyone loves her."

Boudie had looked up to her sister, but she had been torn away from her. She wondered if they could rebuild the closeness they once shared.

A cloak of anticipation enveloped her as she stepped into her bedroom suite. She knelt by her bed, reached underneath, and plucked out a pile of faded parchment letters—untouched for years—out of a pink box. Emotions stirred within her.

Systematically, Florence had written from Tamshire to her and their mother. Like a wave of recordings in ink, memories of her sister's old life appeared. She settled on her bed and gathered one thick package of envelopes wrapped in a satin bow. She untied the knot, and the letters scattered onto the duvet.

While she had remained in India with her mother, her father insisted Florence travel to England to join him. The wrench of her sister's departure had left a gaping hole and marked the end of their sunshine days together. She remembered weeping through sleepless nights, imagining Florence's new life in the hills of the Pennines.

In order of the date written, Boudie re-read details of when Florence attended the village school. In later years, her sister revealed that she'd frequently been bullied by some of the pupils.

Sparked by Florence's writing, Boudie held a vision of her sister describing the workings of her grandparents' farm. Under the supervision of her father, Florence explained she'd taken to farming and told Boudie about her new friends—mountain sheep and cows—and waxed on about her love of tractors and her enjoyment of working on anything to do with mechanics. Boudie presumed that the bullying had forced Florence to reserve her attention for animals and inanimate objects.

In one of her letters, Florence said their grandfather had boasted to his farming friends, "Give that girl a broken-down tractor and she can make it sing again."

Sitting upright against the headboard, Boudie couldn't resist reading more.

Florence's words gave her a chance to reflect on the monumental changes her sister had undergone. She accepted their separation had brought more than a physical distance between them.

While she continued to read, she could not help but admire her sister's use of pen and ink. Florence's writing, in her opinion, appeared like flowing art on the page and held a surprising neatness for one who'd gained the reputation of being clumsy.

She skimmed through Florence's plan to grow rhubarb.

This might sound like a crazy idea, but having mulled it over, perhaps I can grow rhubarb. I have no idea why it intrigues me, but I guess one reason is the flavour. After building two sheds at the back of the farmhouse, I've filled them with nitrogen-rich soil. We have no electricity, but I fancy giving this project my best shot. Will write and let you know of progress made. Father thinks it better that I take up a "woman's hobby" as he likes to call it. "Join the local WI, a knitting club, or take some dancing lessons," he suggests.

As you both know, I am not that kind of woman.

With fond affection,
Florence

Boudie continued to read the letters detailing Florence's rhubarb exploits.

Florence reported success with the wide-leafed vegetable. She spoke of winning prizes and became known for selling her produce at the local county fairs.

She also relayed that her curious community wanted to know her secrets. She said one of them had asked, "What magic have you conjured with those green thumbs of yours? I tell them it's a credit to our Siberian weather. I suppose the soil being nitrogen-rich helps, too."

Boudie noted Florence was a reluctant star in her rhubarb achievements, often asking her mother and herself, "Why is everyone taking such a keen interest in my rhubarb?"

Florence did not appear to understand why people also came from miles around to coo over her homemade sweet-and-sour rhubarb pickles. She described presenting the pickles in clear glass jars with frilly red cloth labels, and she said queues formed outside her shed to buy the fresh rhubarb as well as the pickles.

Boudie scanned Florence's rhubarb ideas and noted her sister's wish to develop a recipe for Pink Rhubarb Gin.

Boudie never found enjoyment in the flavour of rhubarb, nor did she take to the idea of a lethal concoction with gin. She remained a firm champagne girl. For her, the bubbles conjured up feelings of a romantic nature. In her opinion, champagne resembled tiny pearls interlaced with exotic fruit.

But she championed Florence's efforts even if she would not be imbibing. She recalled her father's words about Florence's gin recipe, thoughts shared while sipping the tangy alcoholic mix at their home in Belgravia. "Good grief. This gin mix would knock the head off a demon."

Boudie smiled at the vision of her father so many years ago.

She continued to read Florence's recanting of her and their father's routine each evening at the farmhouse.

We sit by a roaring wood fire in the kitchen and listen to the hourly chime from the gold carriage clock. We live in a rambling house built of ancient stone with sections worn away. In between the fine cracks in the walls, I am convinced there are ghostly whispers from a long ancestry of hard-working farmers.

Water gathers on the ceiling, drip, drip, then plops onto the surface of the rough floors. Father and I run around, setting down old pots and pans to collect the water.

She tried to imagine Florence surviving howling winds and rain pounding against the building, the cold air forcing its way through the gaps.

Clutching a bunch of the handwritten letters, she decided if she found a bottle of the alcoholic pink stuff stashed under the main staircase of The Belleview, and should Florence agree to sleepover, she would serve the rhubarb gin to mark their renewed bond. If the alcohol wasn't worth drinking, she always had a bottle or two of chilled champagne waiting to be opened.

Being a quiet time of year, she would savour precious hours in her sister's company. Her spirits lifted as she thought about her sister's arrival and the celebration of them being together at last.

CHAPTER 21

Closing her eyes, Boudie continued to reflect. Memories of life in India with her mother after the war filled her mind. She remembered a particular letter arriving for her mother, following her father's return to England after Partition in India and the end of World War II. In that letter, he explained he spent time researching England's programme of redevelopment. Having trained in the ways of army life, he confessed he did not relish the offer to become a civil servant based in London. A desk job held no appeal, for he also had accomplished farming skills.

My dear Elisabeth Rose,

After much scrutiny, I believe the best way forward is for me to remain in Tamshire, working my parents' farm.

It seemed her father had decided to take heed of Florence's original idea with rhubarb, too.

I am convinced growing rhubarb could become a commercial and lucrative enterprise.

Letters appeared every few weeks. He wrote to her mother about his trials in developing such a business. Finally, correspondence arrived with good news.

I have managed to organise the rhubarb to be sent by train to London's produce markets. With distribution in place, the company is starting to blossom. We are now known as Scott Thomas & Co.

One day Boudie spied her mother sitting on the veranda, crying softly, a letter spilled out upon her lap. Later, when Boudie's mother read aloud some of the letter, Boudie discovered her father had broached a sensitive subject.

My dear, I believe the time has come for you, along with our youngest, to join me in England.

Perhaps noticing Boudie's discomfort, her mother told her, "I am most unsure about your father's proposal." A few days later, her mother read to Boudie the letter of reply to her father.

If you insist, we will come to live back in the homeland, but Boudie and I must be assured of a promising life. Country living is not for us.

As London reawakened to an era of change, her mother suggested they could take up residence in her parents' empty house in Belgravia. Eventually, Boudie's parents made a bargain. Monday to Friday, Major Scott Thomas would deal with his affairs in the north of England, and on weekends he'd travel to London to be with his family.

Boudie did her best to comfort her mother on the day they left their home in India. They both shed tears in the taxi that took them to the ship sailing for England. "I have completed my time here," her mother said. "All I have left are beautiful memories, but I pray one day either you or Florence will return to our home. I've left a secret message under one of the floorboards in our bedroom," her mother half-whispered to Boudie as she pulled out the last letter from Boudie's father.

My dear Elisabeth,

I know you and Boudie reluctantly leave the heat and the warmth of the people behind you. We must never forget the open canvas of the colourful life we shared in our beloved India.

You must take heart and believe life in London can and will flourish once you both settle into this great country.

Your esteemed and ever-loving husband.

Boudie reminisced about her struggles following her arrival in London. Overcast days of misty grey slapped at her, however, she stubbornly adjusted to the atmosphere of a city.

Without delay, her mother took to rearranging her parents' home. Eventually, Florence came to live there while still working as a junior secretary at the War Office. Major Scott Thomas joined them on weekends.

She thought back to those Friday evenings. At exactly six thirty, her mother would call out, "Girls, girls! Your father is here."

Standing on the front porch, in a sombre tweed suit, the lapel of his jacket adorned by a small rosebud, her father would hand her mother a bouquet of red roses. He would then take her mother in his arms and kiss her.

Boudie wrinkled her nose at the memory of her father reaching out to hug her. His clothes reeked of tobacco and cigar smoke. His grey moustache scratched at her skin when he kissed her forehead.

After dinner, the family would adjourn to the salon, where Major Scott Thomas sat in a velvet, high-backed chair. He always poured himself a large shot of brandy.

"My dear Boudie," he said one evening, "I shall never understand you and your love of the *froufrou* way of living. It appears you take far too much heart in wearing shimmery evening dresses accessorised by your mother's jewellery, then you disappear into the night. A flimsy lifestyle."

She protested loudly, saying, "Father, I am part of a hip new London scene. Whether or not you approve, I feel perfectly comfortable within this group of people." Secretly, she admitted, his words were indeed true. Following her arrival in London, she'd chased a social life and liked nothing better than to dress up and party until dawn. But she could not understand why her father continuously compared her to *sensible* Florence. On these nights, her father often became tipsy on brandy. She appreciated her mother stepping in and admonishing him for his comments.

Boudie realised that she and her sister walked different paths. Florence—intense, serious natured, and now in her mid-twenties—remained aloof. In Boudie's opinion, she concentrated only on her work.

Florence claimed to have no interest in joining her sister at cocktail parties. Nor would she dream of dressing up with the sole intent of meeting a future husband.

Around noon each day, her mother tapped loudly on

her bedroom door. She wouldn't reply, but after a few minutes her mother would step into the room and draw back the floor-to-ceiling curtains.

Boudie recalled the feeling of a blazing light beaming down on her near-lifeless body while she lay on her king-sized bed like an embalmed princess. She would cover her half-open eyes. Frequently, unmerciful headaches hit her after too much alcohol from the night before. She always said, "Can't a girl get her beauty sleep?"

"You say that every day, dearest." Her mother always came in with a tray of food, placing it on one of the side tables near the vast bay window. Boudie knew she did this because if she wished to eat or drink some freshly squeezed orange juice, she would have to get out of bed.

"Couldn't eat a thing," Boudie would say, ignoring the temptation. Mid-afternoon, she'd pour herself a Bloody Mary or two. She told herself it was medicinal and helped get her through the void of facing another boring day.

On weekday evenings and weekends, while her mother and Florence sat in the salon to take tea and read, Boudie would disappear upstairs and dress in one of her fancy ensembles. She'd then head out into the night and immerse herself in the ritualistic cycle of alcohol-fuelled parties in the private bars and clubs in Mayfair.

In the end, visiting one hot spot after the other until dawn left her weary of hangovers followed by cures that didn't work.

One morning, nursing a mind-blowing headache, she decided the time had come to seek a proper career.

She asked Florence for advice. To her disappointment, her sister showed a lack of interest in Boudie's wish to change.

"How could I possibly advise you? I have lived a solitary life without you, our mother, or my best friend."

To Boudie, her voice sounded intolerant and unhelpful.

"I am employed in a job I did not choose, and father will not allow me to engage in the dealings of what he calls 'his flourishing rhubarb business.' May I point out, *my* idea gave him his success?" A disgruntled Florence turned away from Boudie, refusing to be drawn in on the matter of her sister's future.

Her mother's acquaintances gathered for afternoon tea in the salon and suggested that Boudie should "settle down." Boudie would listen while they chatted of their challenges with marrying off daughters and sons. In between, they nibbled on tiny mouthfuls of Victoria sponge or Battenberg baked from a recipe from an up-and-coming cook, Mary Berry.

"What you need is a rich young gentleman to settle down with and have a family. Two children would be quite enough to give you a sense of worth and accomplishment," said one of her mother's acquaintances. Another of her mother's friends emphasised to Boudie, "A wife must excel at house design and produce the finest cuisine, too. Husbands of today expect their wives to attend to the affairs of the home, his social commitments, and to organise dinner parties for his close friends and work colleagues."

"Change is afoot," said her mother, breaking into the conversation. "We are stepping into more modern times, and this is your chance to make a respectable name for yourself."

Boudie looked around the table at the women, who were all nodding in agreement. Like most fledgling debutantes, she had once dreamt of being swept away by a handsome white knight who would protect her. In reality, she recognised her enthusiasm waned easily, but she truly desired purpose in her life. She resolved she would definitely not go down the route her mother and friends spoke of.

The end of the glorious sixties became a time of protest for equal rights, free love, and women gaining more independence. Embracing these changes, she decided to step out, to strive and to achieve.

• • •

Boudie heard a loud knock at the door.

"Mrs Scott Thomas," one of the women who helped her called out, "I've seen to the rooms and the corridor. Time for me to leave. I'll see you tomorrow."

"Oh, dear, is it that time? I must have dozed," Boudie replied. Flustered, she put aside the pile of letters with their recaptured memories.

She pushed herself off the bed, shook out the duvet, and re-settled the cushions. Walking into her marbled bathroom, she stared in the mirror. After fiddling with her blonde-highlighted hair and refreshing her lips with glossy lipstick, her heart tingled at the thought of Kit's arrival with her sister.

She'd dressed from top to toe in shades of calming blue, along with a jumper trimmed at the neck in similar-coloured feathers.

The doorbell rang. Elated, she skipped down the stairs, taking two steps at a time. With an exaggerated sweep of her hand, and a welcome speech ready, she opened the door.

Kit, wearing oversized sunglasses, stood before her. Beside him, a feeble-looking lady had her arm linked in his. The woman tilted her head, almost resting it against Kit's waist.

"Hey, better late than never," said Kit. "May I present your long-awaited dear sister?" He bowed his head majestically.

CHAPTER 22

BOUDIE NARROWED HER EYES. STARING HARD at the two people on her doorstep, she said, "Kit, what the hell are you playing at? Why are you still dressed like a pirate? Peeking around his shoulder in case he was up to something and had Florence in the car, she noted he had parked her car by the main entrance, and no one remained inside. Turning back to Kit, she said, "This is not my sister. Where is Florence? What have you done with her? I did not have you down as incompetent." With one hand on her hip, she tapped one of her suede kitten-heeled shoes on the parquet floor. She softened her tone and spoke to the woman. "Who might you be, dear?"

The woman gaped back at her, understandably upset. Her glasses had fogged up and were perched on the tip of her nose. The woman spoke in a barely audible voice. "This is not the hospital I normally come to." She turned and cast her eyes up at Kit. "You are not Cassie. Where is my daughter? Have you kidnapped me? My name is Rita," she said, looking back at Boudie. "That's right, I am Rita or Mrs Cornell, and . . . I've been fasting. Not a morsel of food has passed my lips since eight o'clock last night." Raising her voice a bit, she said, "Who are you people? I need to sit down. Anyways, my Cassie will worry, as will my Stanley."

Boudie thought the woman might faint after the exertion of speaking. "My dear woman, be assured that you have not been kidnapped. There's been a mix-up, that much is clear." Boudie glanced over to see a red-faced and embarrassed-looking Kit.

"You see, Mrs Cornell, I expected my sister to visit today. My adopted grandson was due to collect her." She gave Kit a look, one she knew had once frightened the horses she rode as a young girl in India. "I am Boudie Scott Thomas, owner of The Belleview Boutique B&B, and this is my assistant, Kit O'Connor." The poor woman's face looked geisha-girl white. "Might I make you a pot of restoring tea and prepare some food for you, Mrs Cornell? There's no need to worry. After you have eaten, we shall deal with my adopted grandson's faux pas. I'll let your family know of your whereabouts and that you are safe."

She patted the lady's arm and noticed her gnarled fingers, tinged blue. She left to find a warm cardigan to replace the well-worn tracksuit top that hung from the woman's bony shoulders. Known to take the incidentals of running her business in stride, and being a dab hand at calming troubled waters, this moment had her struggling. Disappointment and anger coiled itself through her body at Kit's stupid blunder. Returning to place the cardigan across the woman's shoulders, she willed herself to remain cheerful and asked Kit to escort the woman into the conservatory to a comfortable armchair overlooking the garden.

"Please serve Mrs Cornell some water and do not leave her side until I return. We will talk later."

Without giving him a chance to reply, she briskly turned on her heels and walked through the swinging doors and into the kitchen. Pulling open the fridge door, she grabbed two eggs, butter, and marmalade, then moved to the marble-topped preparation area near the stove.

Fresh croissants sat at the bottom of the bread bin. She quickly fried the eggs, heated the croissants, and made a pot of tea. She set a tray with crockery and cutlery and added two pieces of fresh fruit on the side. Back in the conservatory, she laid everything on a table which she moved to place in front of Mrs Cornell. She watched the woman's eyes blink and open wide at the sight of food.

"Ah, me breakfast at last. Thank you. Where did you say I am?"

Surprised she had not noticed earlier, Boudie noticed one of the woman's arms was encased in pink plaster, supported by a sling.

"Would you like me to look at your arm once you've eaten?" She moved to sit opposite Mrs Cornell. Her unexpected visitor nodded vigorously, and Boudie thought of a small child with scratched knees after having had a fall.

"If you want coffee," she said to Kit, "you know what to do." She did not look at him. "After that, perhaps take a shower and change into fresh clothes." Pretending to busy herself, she encouraged Mrs Cornell to eat. She heard Kit leave the room, his footsteps heavy on the sweeping staircase.

"What a treat," Mrs Cornell said, smacking her lips and taking another slurp of tea. She wiped at her mouth.

"I quite like it here. What kind of place is this?" she asked, looking towards Boudie.

Boudie confirmed again to Mrs Cornell that her adopted grandson had got things mixed up and collected her by mistake. "Would you happen to know of my sister, a Florence Scott Thomas, Mrs Cornell?"

"Of course, I know Florence. Lives right across the road from me and my Stanley. A tall, sharp looking woman. Has a giant dog named Lulabelle. Been our neighbour for years. Keeps herself to herself, she does. Apart from Thursday's. That's our 'Yoga and Stretch' class with our teacher, Molly Mulligan. Joins in then, towers over us all with her long arms and gangly legs."

Boudie, relieved upon hearing this relevant piece of news, again assured Florence's neighbour she was completely safe at the Belleview.

"Don't worry luv, as long as this is not some care home. I haven't lost me marbles yet." She took another bite and said, "If my Cassie's been up to her tricks with some scheme to take me away from Stanley, she'd better watch out."

Boudie watched Mrs Cornell try to push herself out of the chair with her stick. She looked like an old rag doll. Boudie smiled in sympathy as the woman flopped back down. Her scrawny legs and plimsoled feet went up in the air.

Boudie went to the bar and opened a drawer where the first-aid box lay tucked away. She took out a tab of painkillers and broke one tablet in two. She walked over to Mrs Cornell and handed her the pieces to swallow. Her eyes were drawn to her guest's little feet, bare and veined, angry looking bruises marked black and blue. Her heart leapt with pity.

"Can I trust you? May I call you by your first name?" Mrs Cornell asked. "Promise you will not put me wrong today? You're sure I haven't been kidnapped?"

"You've not been captured. I assure you it's been a case of mistaken identity."

"So, you're saying I'll remain here until my Cassie or me neighbour, Molly Mulligan, might collect me?"

Boudie wanted to hug Mrs Cornell. She saw her reach into the pocket of her thin track-suit top and pull out an ancient mobile. She handed the phone to Boudie. "I'll be happier when you call Stanley and let him know where I am. Cassie will be in a rage. 'My precious time wasted,' she'll say." Mrs Cornell's eyes twitched. "The way it is these days, young boys and girls of this generation, well, they all look the same to me. Their fancy cars and long, unnatural-looking hair. Every one of them is covered in jewellery and tattoos. In truth, I can't tell one from another," Mrs Cornell half muttered. "Honestly, I could have sworn your boy was my Cassie." Mrs Cornell grinned a big, toothy grin. "Like your grandson, she has black matted hair that hangs down her back and she wears big, hooped earrings like his."

Mrs Cornell's yellowing false teeth began to move loosely in her mouth.

"Mrs Cornell, before we make plans, why not sit for a while and enjoy the view of the garden? I know it is stark at this time of year, but soon spring will arrive in a colourful hail of splendour."

A sudden sense of desperation overcame Boudie. She wanted to telephone her sister and explain this confounded mix-up. She excused herself.

"Where am I?" Mrs Cornell called out.

Boudie turned back to patiently explain. "You are in Little Shore, safe and well."

"Little Shore by the sea, eh? That's where I spent me honeymoon with Stanley, me husband."

Boudie watched Mrs Cornell strain her eyes beyond

the double doors of the conservatory. *I believe the poor creature is lost in time*, she thought. Backing out of the conservatory, she left Mrs Cornell to reminisce.

In the kitchen, she picked up the handset. She could hardly bring herself to think about how discontented Florence must be, at home and alone, waiting to be collected. "Stupid boy. One simple request: bring my Florence to stay, is all I asked." She dialled the number, heard only the sound of ringing, and tried again. Finally, she listened to a recorded message.

"Hello, Colonel Bryce Beckwith here on behalf of Florence Scott Thomas, who is unable to talk right now. If you would like to leave a message and your contact number, she will respond when available. Don't forget to wait for the beeps." There was a cough and a click at the end of the message, and Boudie's heart sank. She remembered Bryce, that blond-haired young boy who seemed happiest in the company of the equally young, lanky Florence and who later became known as Colonel Bryce Beckwith.

She held the phone and tried to smile one of her wide smiles so her tone wouldn't come across as irritated as she felt.

"Hello, darling sister. I do hope you are sitting down. We have a situation. My silly adopted grandson has collected another woman near to you. Her name is Mrs Rita Cornell, and she's a most frail woman. She has confirmed she is your neighbour. Sit tight, dearest one. Wait for my next update. No need to worry. All is in hand."

Why didn't Florence pick up? That stumped her. Walking into the reception area, she found a pair of socks and warm slippers in a nearby cupboard and returned to the conservatory.

"How are you feeling now, Mrs Cornell?" she asked,

noticing the woman's cheeks were flushed bright pink. Her eyes looked hazy with cataracts. Her visitor nodded, as if that was answer enough.

Boudie knelt and removed the thin-soled footwear from Mrs Cornell's feet and dressed them in silk and cotton socks and a pair of fur-lined pink slippers. "There, that's better. Your feet will soon feel like warm toast." Boudie stood up and placed a hand on Mrs Cornell's thin shoulders. She sighed heavily, knowing she would not rest until she put the pieces of this distressing puzzle back together.

CHAPTER 23

"TIME TO STOP FOR TEA." FLORENCE PATTED Colonel Bryce Beckwith on the arm. Placing her foot on the brake, she parked the Morgan by the village green and insisted they get out to stretch their bones.

She appreciated Bryce helping her out of the driver's seat. After slowly uncurling herself to a standing position and cursing the horrid weather, she rubbed her cramped legs. Once she'd shaken out her sinewy arms and raised them above her head towards the sky, she walked around the car a few times. As she mulled over her mad idea to make this journey, she spotted a deserted wooden hut in the distance, covered on one side with a striped awning for shelter. The pavilion faced a cricket pitch.

Observing Bryce as he marched up and down on the other side of the vintage Morgan, she went to the back of the car, pulled out the flask of tea and the two china cups he'd remembered to pack.

"Bravo, Florence. Well done, for driving in such conditions," said Bryce.

Feeling self-conscious, she handed him the flask and cups, and reached for her overnight bag to unzip one of the pockets. Two packets fell to the ground. She bent down, gathered them up, and with a smile said, "Just for you, Bryce. See, I never forgot. As a boy, these biscuits were your favourite. Of course, had time allowed, I would have made you sweet Jalebi. You will have to make do with these British stalwarts." She held the packets in front of him. He flushed bright crimson.

She sighed. Memories of innocent days spent with Bryce flooded her thoughts.

She recalled their childhood days in India when they would sit side by side in her parents' garden, she with her cropped wild hair, and Bryce in contrast, with hair as lightly coloured as the moon and blond curls framing his sweet face. The Indian cook would serve them lemonade, digestives, and custard-cream biscuits on fine bone china plates. She remembered when friends of their parents brought them packets of sweet treats from the old country and their excitement when they opened the boxes. They could not wait to taste the biscuits.

Bringing her thoughts back to the present, she nodded her head towards the building, nudging Bryce toward it. They discovered the hut had a narrow bench and an overhang that would give them a resting spot away from the mesh of rain.

Florence's silk scarf clung to her disarrayed chignon. She settled her body on the seat, untied the scarf, and the limp grey of her hair collapsed about her shoulders.

Bryce sat by her side while she poured the hot tea from the flask. She watched the steam rise from the china teacups, and she opened the foiled packets of biscuits. She nodded at him to dip in.

Bryce took one of each. Oohing and ahhing, he bit into them. “This takes me back. I’ve not eaten these since our childhood.”

She chose a digestive, dunked it into the hot liquid, then closed her eyes and savoured the taste. A reflective stillness, apart from the sound of water droplets trickling down from the awning, enveloped them.

“I hope Molly received news of our plan,” she said, turning to face Bryce. Fretting about Lulabelle being all alone, she berated herself for such fool hardiness and her insistence on driving to Boudie’s. She knew how headstrong she could be, but she believed a firm stance had been required today.

She refused to wait for some young man to turn up when he felt like it. Screwing up her face in irritation, she said, “Selfish youth, only thinking of themselves without consideration for those considerably older and wiser.” Bryce did not respond. *He’s lost in his own world*, she decided.

Swiftly the rain withdrew, the clouds lifted, and a rainbow spread its arc.

She pointed to the sky. “Bryce, look. Maybe this rainbow is a lucky omen.” They continued to sit, and she puzzled as to whether this could be her last opportunity. Could she finally explain to Bryce that he’d always been the one for her and always would be? She realised neither of them had ever learned the knack of expressing feelings of love.

Her mind drifted back.

After Bryce moved next door to her, to her immense surprise, she’d already acquired a beau from a chance meeting. A fellow named Cyril Clarke. But the romance only lasted during the ten-week course she’d taken under his direction. He’d been a professor of American culture and engineering at the University of Kent. She believed he sought her out and seemed interested in more than their equal passion for machines and engineering. After class, they would head out to eat at a local café. The memory of him had faded, but she remembered one of his features, a scar above his left eye. According to Cyril, a suitcase fell from his wardrobe one night as he lay sleeping . . . the same suitcase he packed his belongings into and left to return to America.

By way of an apology, Cyril left her a puppy in a basket at the front door, along with a brief note: *I must leave post-haste to be with my godmother who is dying.* So went his story, without a goodbye. She accepted that Cyril Clarke did not see her romantically, nor did he wish to take matters further. Weak and without backbone, is what she thought of him.

After Cyril left, Boudie suggested, "Why not take a trip back to India, or visit Africa? Now that you're sixty-five, perhaps you could commit to missionary work," her sister urged. "The puppy can be sold or gifted to a decent family."

Florence repeatedly told Boudie and anyone who'd listen, "I took a certain vow as a young girl. I shall never be of the mind to take another vow to become a missionary." She acknowledged she was ungainly and sometimes grumpy, but she wanted to be accepted for who she was. "Call me cynical, but I've come to distrust people." She told Boudie.

Instead, she showered unconditional love on her one loyal and faithful companion, her Lulabelle, now old and ageing like herself.

Sitting on the bench with Bryce, she considered the defunct Cyril encounter. She could never compare Cyril to her stable and clear-headed Bryce.

The skies cleared and a sparkling winter sunshine tried to poke through. She allowed herself to snatch a look at Bryce's profile. The greatest and most painful love of her life, he sat looking into his teacup, apparently lost in his thoughts.

She loved the way he always kept his shock of thick white hair trimmed neatly like his hedges, and she liked the look of his slim moustache that twisted at the edges. She yearned to stroke that moustache. His eyes, pools of Omar Sharif brown, never ceased to draw her in. In her opinion, Bryce still looked dashing—an attractive man to a single woman of her age, or younger. She shrugged off feelings of being elderly. These days, according to the experts, age was simply a number and a mindset.

Could she fool herself into some dreamy notion of pink candy-floss hearts, cherubs with arrows, and a promise of a happy ending? She looked at Bryce again as he poured more tea for them and reached for another biscuit.

"Penny for your thoughts," she said.

Bryce placed his cup on the bench. From the inside pocket of his trench coat, he pulled out a yellowing AA map. Puzzled, she watched him spread the chart across his lap.

"If we head off in fifteen minutes, we will arrive at The Belleview within an hour." He refolded the old map and slipped it back inside his coat.

She'd never allowed Bryce access to her true feelings. She'd borne a potent love, an eternal flame that shone deep in her heart for more years than she cared to remember. Following her father's summons back from India to a cold and merciless England, she never lost her belief and hope that Bryce would follow her. He remained her night and day. To her disappointment, he had stayed away.

Now, sitting next to Bryce, she recalled an evening at the farmhouse before her move to work and live in

London.

Her father and she sat in the kitchen, eating dinner. He mentioned he'd received a letter from his friend, Bryce Beckwith's father. "Such good news, my dear Florence. Your mother and I are formally invited to a wedding. Young Bryce Beckwith is due to marry a lady by the name of Diane Wilson-Brown. You may remember that family from when we lived in India. They were renowned for generations as importers of tea." Her father told her a mutual arrangement had been made on both sides that guaranteed their extended legacy.

She held a vision of that evening and her reaction upon hearing this news. Normally a placid girl, she had shrieked and wailed, "Oh no, this cannot be!" Placing a hand over her mouth, her tears had come fast and furious. Uncontrollably, they'd rolled down her cheeks. She'd pushed her chair away from the dinner table and fled from the kitchen, climbing the stairs to her bedroom. She slammed the door shut and threw herself onto her bed. Punching the pillows, feeling embittered, she sobbed until exhaustion overtook her.

How could her Bryce agree to this union? Surely, he did not love this Diane woman. Had he been blinded by wealth and forgotten the pledge they'd once made? "Best chums, always watching out for each other."

"I'll never forget you, Florence. I will come and find you," Bryce had said.

Following her departure, it felt like he had deserted her. With eyes red from crying and a pillow soaked from tears of grief, that same night she vowed, "I'll never marry or trust a man again."

Florence sat in the chill of the wet day under the awning. Bryce had only been fifteen when he uttered his words of commitment. A big promise for a youth, she lamented.

Already weary from the drive, she decided it was best she didn't share how tired she was. Bryce would only fuss and insist they drive back home. "I'll not allow further delays on what was supposed to be a day with my sister," she mumbled to herself. Taking a deep breath, she said, "I apologise for my impatience earlier at the house, but I have questions and I have waited to ask them for far too long. It's time, Bryce. I must know what you feel for me." She hesitated, then added, "Well, about us." After wiping a crumb from the side of Bryce's mouth, she moved closer to him.

CHAPTER 24

Embarrassed, Colonel Bryce Beckwith sat upright. He wanted to reach out and take Florence's hand. He silently wondered, if he made this gesture, would she react in her usual brusque manner? What would he do if she pushed him away?

Years before, he'd accepted that he'd been unable to learn the ways of expressing affection—which hadn't been helped by his marriage to Diane. She expected him to keep his emotions firmly locked in.

After Diane died, he searched for Florence, congratulating himself when he discovered where she lived. By chance, the house next door to hers had been for sale. Following his move, and her refusals to join him for coffee or to attend church on Sundays with him, he concluded that he'd best not pursue anything that spoke of romance. He had told himself time after time that he must accept Florence's wishes that their relationship be purely one of companionship.

He had carried an overwhelming ache in his heart after her attention seemed drawn for a time to a man by the name of Cyril Clarke. The fellow's interest in Florence proved short-lived, and his guilty flashes of jealousy dissipated.

Shaking off those memories, he dwelled on his already upturned day. He'd been ill-prepared for her directness earlier. What did she expect after years of living on the other side of the hedge?

Unable to articulate words that could show his love for her, he turned away. Placing the old flask under his arm, he put the remains of the biscuits in one of his pockets. Turning back around, he watched her from the corner of his eye. She threw her eyes towards the sky, then stood up and confounded him by walking quickly towards where the Morgan was parked on the green. He swiftly stuffed the creased silk scarf Florence left behind into his trench coat pocket and tried to catch up with her. The soles of his polished brogues would not grip the squishy wet grass, and he slid this way and that.

"Wait, Florence! Wait! Please don't rush off. I know I've not been clear about how I feel, and I agree we have important things to discuss. But you took me off-guard. You've got it wrong, my dear." His words dispersed into the damp air. A breeze started to gather. "Come back," he cried out. "Let us sit again under the awning. Allow me to tell my story about the lonely years I spent without you in India and, indeed, London. You must believe me, I'm at my happiest when we spend time together." He pleaded and continued to follow her, but she continued to stride across the cricket field.

He had to conclude she'd either not heard him, or she'd decided to ignore his words. Frustrated by his cherished friend, he slowed his pace. He heard a ping from his mobile. Taking the phone out of his trench coat, he glanced at the screen and read a text from Molly.

He felt the wet lawn suck at his shoes. Without warning, he slipped and fell face down, landing in a waterlogged strip.

His mobile flew out of his hands onto the sodden ground. The biscuits escaped from his pocket, and the metal flask dropped from under his arm, rolling along the soft surface.

CHAPTER 25

FLORENCE, UPON REACHING HER CAR, PACKED the teacups carefully into her overnight bag and laboriously put herself into the driver's seat. She tapped on the steering wheel impatiently, waiting for her co-driver to appear. Minutes passed. She couldn't see through the fogged-up windscreen. Frustrated, she rummaged around the side pocket nearest her and whipped out a chamois cloth to wipe the screen. After a few more minutes, she started the engine, beeped the horn, and switched on the wipers. She tut-tutted at their inefficiency. Speaking to herself, she said, "They will have to be replaced, and I know of only one person for that job."

Peering through the misty windows, she caught sight of Bryce's figure lying on the wet ground. She flinched at the thought of him being injured. Immediately she switched off the engine, and with an almighty heave extracted herself from the Morgan. Clambering across the marshy surface, she reached Bryce. Awkwardly, she knelt to whisper into his ear, "Oh, Bryce, are you okay? Can you lift yourself up and onto your knees?"

Bryce eventually raised his mud-streaked face to stutter some indiscernible reply. Slowly, she encouraged him to lift his body from the ground and turn over.

"Apologies, my dear. In my quest to catch up, I slipped on this confounded surface. No harm done. Simply took my breath and pride away."

"Best if you sit with your legs spread out in front of you for a few moments," she said. But seeing him in this sorry state, she could not stifle her laughter. Doing her best to contain herself, she scrutinised his face. Reaching into her pocket, she pulled out a cotton hanky, spat on it, and tried to wipe the mud from his face.

"You almost gave me a heart attack. One minute you were speed walking across the cricket lawn, then I spotted you lying on the ground. We'll get you properly cleaned up once we get to Boudie's." She couldn't help but continue to chuckle at the sight of the undignified Colonel Bryce Beckwith.

"What's so funny?" Bryce cried out.

She spotted a solitary tear rolling down Bryce's muddied cheek. Unsure whether to tell him to man up and pull himself together or to place her hand on his shoulder in assurance, she merely stood watching him.

Overhead, brighter skies continued to expand and shoo the voluminous grey away. Florence's heart skipped a few beats. Perhaps some hope remained for her and Bryce.

Finally, he began to talk.

"Please, may we continue the conversation you started this morning, and again, over there on the bench? My dear, I felt thrown by your need to show me what is in your heart. I realise my ungainly flop onto the cricket field has not helped matters. If you could, help me up."

Florence mustered every ounce of her strength and hauled him to a standing position. His look told her he was worn out, like some floppy scarecrow following a rainstorm. She paid no heed to his grubby trench coat, his neat silk tie streaked with wet soil, his sodden trousers, or his stained leather shoes. It seemed to her that a dishevelled Bryce paid no heed to his bedraggled state, either.

"Bryce, I believe we have been unlucky in love. But we can change that right now. Can't we?"

"I agree. This can no longer wait." Bryce's voice quivered. "First, I must ask for absolution for the many wasted years. I know I am inappropriately dressed for the declaration I wish to make, but I have come to realise, like you, that time is of the essence."

He fixed his eyes pleadingly onto hers and raked his normally pristinely manicured fingers through his damp grey hair. She watched him twist his sullied moustache. To her surprise, he removed his soiled trench coat, allowing it to drop onto the wet grass. He inhaled deeply and rubbed his hands furiously together.

"Florence, here we are, just you and me. Even the sun has appeared in our favour. Whatever time I have left to make some final footprints on this earth, I would like to make them with you. Please allow me to take your hand in mine, for that is where it belongs."

She became impatient with his ramblings. "Oh, just get on with the speech, Bryce. What are you trying to say, man?"

"Very well." He spoke in a stronger voice and took her hand in his. "I, Colonel Bryce Beckwith, believe we have been courting for the best part of our lives. Will you make me the happiest man alive? Will you marry me? The sooner the better, I say. I love you totally and will not take no for an answer."

Had she heard him correctly? Had Bryce just asked for her hand in marriage? She checked his imploring eyes. There seemed to be no obvious sign of injury. She took his other hand and looked straight into his handsome face.

Biding her time, she pondered his question and felt him squeeze her hand tightly before she at last replied. "I have waited the best part of sixty or more years to hear such words. If that is what you have truly carried in your heart for all this time, you, my man, can wait a little longer to hear my answer."

Despite still being streaked with mud stains, she saw Bryce's face redden. He pulled away and picked up the trench coat, the mobile, and what remained of the soggy biscuits. Checking the screen on his phone, he looked up at her in horror. "My phone is blank and obviously dead. Without a source of communication, we must hasten to Boudie's, telephone Molly, and confirm that Lulabelle will be taken care of." His shoulders sank as he walked to where the ancient flask had rolled. He picked it up and nearly slid back to where Florence stood waiting for him.

"Whatever happens," she said, "We shall remain the best of friends and neighbours." She stroked his cheek and noted he appeared lost to her. Perhaps his thoughts were on the drive ahead. Or had she shocked him with her terse reply?

To her amazement, he took her hand and kissed it. "Make it a good answer, for this is our last chance." Limping back to the Morgan, his arm linked in hers, he looked up and pointed.

She raised her head to see another rainbow sweeping across the sky.

CHAPTER 26

IN HIS ROOM, KIT UPTURNED HIS RUCKSACK and allowed the contents to spill onto his pristinely made bed. He longed to slip under the fresh white sheets, wrap up in the comfort of the goose-feather duvet, and lose himself to sleep.

Instead, he undressed, stepped into the bathroom, and turned on the shower. Throwing his head back, he allowed the pressure from the hot water to splash onto his tangled mass of hair. He welcomed the heat, massaging the knots in his shoulders. A bottle of dissolving fluid sat on a nearby shelf. After unscrewing the cap, he poured some of the gloppy liquid into his palm and rubbed the solution around his hairline. Helped by the condensation, the wig he'd worn for thirty-six hours began to release from his scalp.

The weighty mass of hair slid down his back, landing in a heap on the shower floor. His brain still buzzed as he turned the tap off. He grabbed a bath towel and slipped back into the bedroom. Glancing in the mirror, he pulled his short blond hair this way and that. From the wardrobe, he chose a pair of skinny blue jeans and a white T-shirt, along with his favourite jumper, one that once belonged to his father. It was a well-worn blue fisherman's knit, frayed around the collar, with overstretched sleeves and almost threadbare elbows. He could never wash or part with it, even though the loose cable stitching had piled, and the entire garment had become moth holed.

He rubbed the knitted fabric across his face and caught the faintest smell of his father's aftershave—sandalwood and leather. Gathering the tatty clothes and the smudged boxes of theatre make-up from the bed, he stuffed everything into his travelling bag and flung it onto the bottom of the wardrobe. After rolling the pirate's jacket into a ball and pushing the fabric into a bag with the boldly typed words, Dry Cleaning, his gaze turned back to the bed. He was so tempted to climb in. Frazzled from fatigue and guilt, emotions twisting in his mind, he unhooked his parka from the back of the door. He snuck down the marble staircase and heard Boudie talking on the phone in the kitchen.

"There's been a bit of a mix-up. No need to be upset, Florence. This situation will get sorted. Call me." Her voice seemed agitated, much like he felt.

He retrieved his walking boots, along with a beany hat from a cupboard in the reception area. Exiting by the front door, he walked around to the back of the house to the shed, where bicycles were stored over the winter months. Unlocking the door, he steered one bike out, giving little heed to the fact that the bicycle helmet he'd grabbed was decorated in wacky shades of bright pink and silver stripes. Pushing the bike towards the main gate, shafts of grey clouds bore down on him. He believed they might be a descending frown of ill-fortune.

In the distance, he spied the swell of the sea rolling in with its lacy edges. A scattering of birds, mostly seagulls, followed a red and blue fishing trawler. The boat sped through the curling waves, heading towards the mist-laden harbour. The moisture-ridden air gave off a stench of fish and decomposed seaweed. He gagged as the scent filled his nostrils and he began cycling away from The Belleview, down the path and beyond the pier towards a neighbouring coastal town.

• • •

Molly parked her car and walked across the street to check on her neighbours. She knocked on Colonel Bryce Beckwith's front door. Not getting a reply, she went to Florence's house. She spotted a wide-eyed Lulabelle. A smile flickered across Molly's face as the dog pushed her head through the beige net curtains and peered at her from the living room window. The sound of a telephone rang out in Florence's hallway and shattered the silence. Molly lifted the rectangular flap of the letterbox on the outside of the door and listened to a woman's voice as she left a message on Florence's answering service.

Molly turned and observed Stanley sitting by his front window. He tapped frantically on the glass pane, signalling her to come to his house. She sped across the road. By the time she reached the gate, he was already waiting in his wheelchair by the open front door.

"Come in, come in. I'm glad you're back." She pushed his chair into the living room to keep him out of the breeze. Settling Stanley in a corner beside his table, she noted a glass half full of apple juice with a chewed-up straw dangling to one side. A bowl containing sullied liquid held bits of vegetables floating on top.

"Can't drink Cassie's soup." Stanley's pallid, round face wrinkled in distaste. "Will you make yourself a cup of tea? I could do with a decent one meself." His bushy eyebrows squeezed together.

She headed to the kitchen to put a kettle on to boil. After a few minutes, she brought two mugs of freshly made Builder's Tea and set one in front of him. Stanley sipped the scalding liquid.

Molly held the clear box containing Mrs Cornell's cheese and pickle sandwiches under her arm. She handed it to him. "Sorry, they're crushed. They've been stuck in the boot of my car since this morning."

Stanley clicked open the lid and devoured the contents. "Ah, that's more like it."

Once the colour returned to his cheeks, she sat down.

"Let me update you on the events of my day," he said.

She listened as he plunged straight to the details of Cassie surprising him by dropping by mid-morning. "I asked her, what are you doing back so soon? Where's your mother? Has something happened at the hospital?" He slurped at his tea, then said, "I told her the last I'd seen of her ma was her taking off at top speed in what I thought was her bat machine. You were supposed to be headed to the hospital," I told her. "Molly, I got quite a scare when I noticed you hanging on to the door handle. You could have been dragged along and badly injured."

Molly appreciated him shaking his head in concern for her.

He carried on, relaying that Cassie had given him one of her ill-tempered sighs, and glared at him. "She told me her ma did not have an appointment at the hospital. Can you believe that?" Rheumy eyes looked at her, awaiting acknowledgement.

She gave an empathetic nod, and he continued.

"Cassie would never win awards for her patience

unless animals are featured. As for Rita, what a waste of time with her fasting for nothing, convincing us, she did, she had been due for blood tests." He gave her a despondent look. "What do you have to say about that?"

Before she could voice her thoughts, Stanley continued to report on the saga of his daughter. "Once Cassie calmed herself, she promised me she would make a few calls. Where in God's earth could my Rita have got herself to?" His chin trembled. After a few more slurps of the hot tea, he continued the story.

"Cassie left soon after, claiming her pregnant sheep needed her attention. Don't understand why she refuses extra farming help," he muttered. "She warned me not to telephone the police for missing persons. I suppose it was her way of assuring me her mother would waltz back in later with some tale or another."

In Molly's opinion, his voice had hit an anxious staccato level.

"Children and wives, eh? More of a responsibility as they get older. You're the lucky one, being on your own and all that."

Molly dropped her head, feeling a dull throb in her chest. She willed herself to take long, slow breaths.

"Rita obviously pencilled in an incorrect date on the calendar. Her appointment is for next week." He shook his head in disbelief. "She's become worse, I'm telling you. She gets so easily confused these days. What do we do?"

Molly's mobile pinged twice. She reached into her bag and saw a text from Cassie.

Hey Molly. Cassie here, Rita's and Stanley's daughter. There is no need to upset my father any further, but can you shed any light on my mother's whereabouts? I am out in the fields until dusk, but call me with any updates after that.

Molly made a sign to Stanley, holding up her mobile, and went to the kitchen to listen to a recorded message. The voice she realised she'd heard earlier on Florence's answering service said, "Hello, Molly. Boudie here. Florence, my sister, was due to visit today. My adopted grandson promised to collect and drive her to Little Shore. Silly boy, he's picked up the wrong person, a Mrs Rita Cornell, who's confirmed that you are her neighbour. I've given her food, and she's drunk lots of tea and water. She is concerned her husband will worry. Can you please let him know she is perfectly safe here?

"Of course, now I'm gravely concerned about the whereabouts of my sister. I've telephoned, left messages, and requested she contact me post-haste, with no response. Call me anytime, either on my mobile or the landline."

The message cut off. Molly heard the desperation in Boudie's tone.

Walking back into the cluttered living room, she moved close to Stanley. "I have good news. Your Rita is safe and currently with Florence Scott Thomas's sister. Her name is Boudie. She runs a B&B in Little Shore. There's been a bit of mix-up, and Boudie's grandson collected your Rita instead of Florence."

"Well, hallelujah that she's safe." Stanley put one hand to his forehead.

"But the question remains, Stanley, who will attend my Karma and Calmer Yoga class tomorrow? There's you, Reverend Horatio Jones, and his wife, Gabriella. Of course, we must not forget Lulabelle." She tried to sound upbeat, but behind her cheeriness, Molly wondered where indeed Florence had taken herself off to, apparently along with Colonel Bryce Beckwith since he appeared to be missing, too. She looked at Stanley.

Head tilted to one side, eyes closed, Stanley's snoring shook the room.

Amused by the sounds, her thoughts wandered back to a nature programme she'd watched on TV some months before. A stampede of water hogs came to mind. How did Stanley sleep while making such a racket? And poor Mrs Cornell, she thought. It's just as well the woman suffered from a lack of hearing.

She slipped out of Stanley's house, heading back to her cosy apartment.

CHAPTER 27

KIT PULLED HIS BEANY HAT OVER HIS EARS. The biting wind stung his face. He continued to peddle hard. Black and white frames shot across his vision like a film, images of him walking away from his ma and friends three years before. He thought about the pain he'd probably caused. The wheels of his bike wobbled, and he almost fell off. Why had he left everyone he held dear, and the course he'd once had a passion for? Soul searching did not help him find an answer. Harking back to that winter's morning when he arrived at Little Shore after he climbed the hill, he'd stood on The Belleview's doorstep, and in a flash of a second, gave himself the name Kit O'Connor. He'd welcomed the possibility of a new life.

Following his decision to remain and work with Boudie at The Belleview, he'd cocooned himself with his only outlet—the theatre group. He'd never allowed anyone in the group, or Boudie, to get too close. Part of that might be because of beautiful Laylah, he thought. He cringed, recalling his drunken night of passion.

A line of boats lay moored by the shoreline, some crumbling and in need of a repaint. Kit paid little attention to them, or the shingled slope where white foamy waves crashed on the beach. Cyclists overtook him, their bodies covered from head to toe in Lycra and waterproof attire. Union Jack flags flapped from the back of their saddles. Through the wind and rain, they shouted, "Keep pushing those pedals, bud." Too wrapped up in emotions that tangled in the rain, he ignored their friendly greetings. Breathless after reaching the brow of a hill, he began to formulate a plan.

Time to fess up to Boudie, he thought. And, he decided, *I shall also contact Ma and ask for her understanding.* But would they understand? How could he explain that he'd only meant to hide behind the mask of Kit for a short while? He couldn't justify why he'd remained behind that mask and realised his imaginary life had escalated. He'd nearly convinced himself that he really was Kit O'Connor . . . and Boudie only knew him as Kit.

Seeing his mother earlier on the street, chatting to the stranger he now knew as Mrs Cornell, caused a fever of guilt to wash through him. *I freaked out.* Salty tears rolled down his face, the moisture warm against his chilled skin. He slowed his peddling and wiped his eyes. Had his father and mother perhaps reunited as a result of his disappearance? Until this morning, that question hadn't occurred to him. Lost in time as Kit O'Connor, not seeing himself as missing, he'd made a promise to return one day. That day had arrived. He cycled on.

Flashes of the portrait of his mother, the one his father had painted years before, came to him. He'd hidden the painting behind his wardrobe at the old family home, wrapped in an old shirt belonging to his father. Had his ma taken the portrait to Kent? His father's brushstrokes captured her in oil, giving his ma an ethereal loveliness. Eyes closed, he imagined his mother's fiery red hair flowing like a curling brook, her contoured features and her perfectly animated smile.

After battling another steep hill, he pulled on the brakes, stopped, and swung his leg off the bike.

Shame overtook him as he thought of the note he'd left and how he'd deserted her and her wish to start over.

Raindrops trickled down the back of his neck and seeped into the collar of his father's loose-knit jumper. The dampness permeated his body and the saturated wool beany weighed heavily on his head. After getting back on the bike, he held on fast to the handlebars and peddled hard. Through the misty shadows of the rain, he spied a conservatory built of glass and white bricks. On the wall by the entrance gate, he was greeted by the café sign.

• • •

Boudie watched Mrs Cornell nod off, a broad smile spread across her face. She decided once Mrs Cornell awoke, she would suggest they take a jaunt to the seafront. Getting her outside might calm her and relieve her ongoing fears of having been kidnapped.

She still had not heard from Florence. A sense of unease grew within her. Leaving Mrs Cornell to sleep in the conservatory, she went upstairs to the room that had once been her retreat, a calm space she'd handed over to Kit three years ago. She knocked on his door. Without an answer, she knocked again, this time louder. She waited, then gingerly turned the handle, calling Kit's name. On the carpeted floor lay a clear plastic bag. Inside the bag, she saw Kit's pirate jacket and thought of how she'd patiently sewn black and gold braiding onto Kit's costume for his tour with *The Pirates of the Caribbean*. At the bottom of the open door of his wardrobe sat his overnight bag, stuffed with clothes and theatre paraphernalia. His bed remained empty. She tapped on the bathroom door. "Kit, are you in there?"

Again failing to get an answer, she walked into the shower room and glimpsed a pile of black hair spread out on the tiled floor. Gathering the long wig, she threw it into the washbasin and smiled at the happy memories she'd shared with him these last years. Walking back into his bedroom, she spotted a curled-up photograph near his bed. She picked up the glossy print, immediately recognising the smiling child. Sliding the photograph into the fold of her trouser pocket, she left the room and walked onto the landing. Something has happened, she thought. Instinct told her he'd become unsettled. They would talk—and the sooner the better. She would get to the bottom of this behaviour. So much for enjoying a quiet season of planning The Belleview's months ahead. She shrugged her shoulders in resignation. Mrs Cornell could sleep in the bedroom originally prepared for Florence's visit, she decided. Later, she would telephone Molly Mulligan. Between them, they could hatch a plan to return the frail woman to her home.

After months of persuading Florence to come and visit, anticipating that they could spend proper time together, her plans had been aborted by Kit. Once she succeeded in talking to Florence, she would encourage her to make another date to visit. Perhaps she'd drive to Kent to collect Florence herself.

Downstairs, she found a pair of sturdy boots and a warm fleece jacket that she hoped would be a snug fit for Mrs Cornell's emaciated body. Tiptoeing into the conservatory, she saw Mrs Cornell sitting in a chair, her hands resting in her lap. She seemed motionless, staring out the window at the stark garden, watching two blackbirds feasting on some dried fruit Boudie had placed on the bird table the day before. To her relief, Boudie saw the flurry of rain had all but evaporated. An angelic light of winter sun peeked through. Trees and plants bereft of flowers and foliage still produced a stark beauty for her.

"Here we are, Mrs Cornell. I've found you a warmer top. What do you say we go fill our lungs with sea air?"

Assisting her guest to stand, she linked her arm through Mrs Cornell's, guiding the woman to the front door. They walked down the path to where Boudie's car was parked outside the main gate.

"Where am I, and where is my Cassie?" Mrs Cornell gave Boudie a vacant stare.

CHAPTER 28

KIT PARKED HIS BICYCLE IN THE CAR PARK near the café. He cursed as he pinched each of his fingers to get the feeling back. They had grown stiff from the cold and holding the handlebars too tightly. After removing the bike chain from around his neck, he locked the wheel. Ahead of him lay a decked platform. Metal tables and chairs sat empty. He pulled off his drenched beany hat, squeezed the moisture-ridden wool, and smoothed his spiked hair. Shivering as he stumbled across the stony path, he poked his head inside the entrance door and called out, "I'll be sitting outside."

The server appeared with a menu, wiped the drops of rainwater from a table and the accompanying chairs, and welcomed Kit, who sat down and ordered a hot chocolate and the first thing he saw on the menu.

Surrounded by damp air, he became aware of a tightness building in his shoulders and an ache in his calf muscles.

The sky changed colour, the rain slowly retreating into low-lying clouds. Spots of blue pushed through. He closed his eyes and bathed his face in the glimmer of weak sun. A renewed purpose filled his thoughts, and he resolved to tell Boudie the truth, whatever the cost.

Slicing through the calm, car tyres crunched on gravel. He heard the vehicles stop, but he kept his eyes tightly shut. He heard children chatter and the sound of people pushing buggies on the uneven path to the café. The harshness of the sounds tore at his nerves.

He heard the voice of a woman cajoling a child. A familiar waft of perfume triggered memories.

"Come along, Melina. Let's sit outside and read your favourite story, or we could colour in your doodle book."

That voice couldn't be mistaken. And the perfume: Weekend by Burberry.

"As I live and breathe. I thought handsome Jamie Mulligan would be gracing the stages of the West End. Or his name would be on grand-scale billboards promoting his latest film."

The hairs on the back of his neck prickled. The sound of metal chairs scraping against the decking and a child being encouraged to settle into one, made him open his eyes. He swallowed hard. "Poppy, what the hell are you doing here?" Stumped to find words that could express his feelings, he carried on staring, and the name Melina rolled around in his brain. The little girl sitting opposite him looked at him, all sweet innocence. Soft, strawberry-coloured curls spilled onto her shoulders. His heart softened. The child spoke to Poppy. "Mummy can we feed the ducks?" She looked away from him and nuzzled under her mother's arm. After a few seconds, she turned her head shyly again towards Kit, stretching out her chubby arms and hands towards him. He noticed her chocolate brown eyes and thick curved eyelashes as she pulled away.

"Looks to me like a certain Mr Mulligan has been burning a candle or three, and he's not looking his best today," said Poppy.

Melina pushed her illustrated cloth storybook towards him and pointed to the title, *The Bear and the Cat*. "Meow, meow." She laughed, and he clasped the child's book and outstretched hand. This time she hung onto his fingers. He looked uncomfortably in Poppy's direction.

"Are you just visiting, or do you live around here?"

"You've forgotten. This is my part of the world. My family has lived along this coastline for many years. I returned to my roots, following the responsibility of having Melina. Poppy stroked the top of Melina's head. "I also happen to co-own this creative cafe." Poppy swept her hand towards a large black-and-white sign hanging over the entrance door. *Melina's Arty Café*. "My ears about things creative in Little Shore never mentioned we had a rising star amongst us. One Jamie Mulligan, actor and dancer, with a half-decent singing voice. A young man who showed great promise when I knew him."

He peeked at Melina as she mimicked Poppy's sing-song voice. He turned and checked the wall behind him, seeing a blackboard that listed events, live music, children's arts and crafts, acting workshops, even comedy open-mike evenings.

The server appeared and served his hot chocolate and a cheese and chorizo panini. "Are you going to join me for something to eat or drink?"

Poppy waved her hand to decline.

He thanked the server. After a few sips of the creamy hot liquid, he bit into the panini.

"Okay, okay. I changed my name to Kit O'Connor. And you are the first to know, Poppy La Grange, if that is still your name."

"I promise my lips are sealed and ears closed." Poppy made a sign, moving her two fingers across her mouth as if fastening a zipper.

He blushed in embarrassment. "Funny, when I heard you call my name, it felt at odds to the person I have become." *Stupid to change to Kit,* he thought to himself. "After you ditched me, I needed a break from everything and everyone." Desperately wishing to dismiss the hurt Poppy had caused him, and the game of pretence he had played, he told himself it was time to own up and call himself Jamie again.

"If I remember correctly," he said, "you ducked out, telling me you were on your way to France or Italy to escape the pressure and hustle and bustle of London life. I believed you when you listed the reasons you needed to travel. Even believed you when you told me you would not hold me back from the brilliant career I was destined for." Like the angry waves and wind that whipped around him earlier, he could no longer contain his irritation. Three years of pent-up frustration and unanswered questions spewed out. Jamie stared at Poppy. "You abandoned me, for God's sake. After you left, I couldn't cope. I needed to hide and pretend to be someone else. You must have known leaving without warning did not help my situation, reminding me of when my father left my ma and me?"

Poppy remained quiet, her eyes fixed on him, cold and without emotion.

"My ma wanted us to start over in Kent, but I couldn't face the move. On the morning I ought to have been helping her, I boarded a train and ended up here. I promised myself a few weeks away would sort my head out. I have to confess, as I stood on the steps of The Belleview, a bonkers idea came to me, and I changed my name to Kit O'Connor."

He reminded himself of the morning he left his ma, just as his father had left her, leaving for France. And in his first year at college, Poppy had done the same to him. How bizarre that by running away, he should end up in Little Shore, where Poppy had been living all this time.

Jamie looked across at the child. Lost in her bubble, she carried on, drawing bold squiggles up and down the pages of her doodle book.

"So, I guess I am guilty of living a life of deception. Like you, it appears we both carry secrets."

He placed his hands on the table to steady his nerves. A heavy silence pursued. Before he could stop himself, he blurted, "Who is Melina's father?"

Poppy didn't say anything for a bit. Finally, she said, "I can explain."

He cut her off. "You know something? I can't do this today. It's too much to take in. I have the mother of all hangovers and there's an urgent situation I must deal with back at The Belleview."

"I agree. It might be better to do this when it's just you and me. Let's plan to have a conversation. I wouldn't want you to return one day and find I'm not around." Poppy grinned at him as she called out her mobile number.

He tapped the number into this phone without commenting.

The winter sun had waned, a sign the chill of dusk would soon appear. He looked at Melina's soft pink hands and her cherub-like face. She smiled, and he blew her a kiss, but she cast her eyes down, pretending to concentrate on her doodle book.

A new sadness overcame him. "Bye." He nodded at Poppy and waved to the little one before plodding across the stones to unlock his bicycle. The temperature slumped, as did his heart. Standing by the bike, he waited until Poppy, with Melina in her stroller, walked into the hub of the café and settled by an open log fire.

He felt his face burn bright in annoyance. *How dare she suddenly appear back in my life . . . and with a child in tow?*

Walking away from the café, he pushed the bike along a shingled pathway, then freewheeled down the hill. Yellow and orange-coloured streetlights reflected their shadows onto the sea, twinkling towards the harbour.

He cycled back to The Belleview.

CHAPTER 29

MOLLY KICKED OFF HER BOOTS AND HUNG her coat on a hook in the hallway. In the living room, she gazed towards the skylight windows. Regardless of time or season, an enchanting light always shone into the room. Placing her bag on the carpeted floor, she flopped onto the cream sofa to rest her head against the silk peacock-coloured cushions. Her eyes drifted across the room, and she fixed on the framed photos that rested on a glass table. They reminded her of happier days spent with Rory and Jamie. Their smiles, bright and loving, still warmed her heart.

Wiping her eyes, she curled up on the sofa and tried to relax. Feeling distracted, she thought about Rita. Who would chaperone her home? Molly decided she would contact Colonel Bryce Beckwith. Where had those two adventurers taken themselves off to? Knowing how bloody-minded Florence could be, nothing would surprise Molly about her neighbour. Stretching her body and rising from the couch, she padded to the bathroom. Splashing her face with cold water made her feel refreshed. She moved back to the living room, took her mobile from her bag, and read a text.

> *Molly dear, Florence got it into her head this morning, to drive to Little Shore to visit her sister, Boudie. The young driver due to collect her did not show up. We have taken Millie Morgan. I could not let her drive alone. We are sorry to ask, but could you see to Lulabelle? Otherwise, Florence will worry. We plan to return tomorrow and will contact you before our departure. With sincere gratitude,*
> *Col BB and Florence*

Molly studied her watch. The message eased her concern, and she noted the text had been sent before lunch. But why would her dear neighbours drive in such risky conditions—and in Florence's vintage car? Perhaps, she thought, they were caught up in the days' excitement and Colonel Bryce Beckwith, who she knew to be fastidious, forgot to text her about their safe arrival and plans to drive home the following day.

She walked into the hall, unhooked her coat, and grabbed her scarf, making her way out of the apartment. Florence's spare set of house keys jangled in one pocket, and a flashlight rested in the other. Slipping across the road to Florence's house, she opened the front door. An eager, waggy-tailed Lulabelle greeted her. Molly attached the dog's leather lead to her collar, and they headed out.

The day's weather had been a constant drizzle, but the ground underfoot felt icy in patches. The building fog bit into her skin. She pulled her scarf and coat tighter around her body and walked Lulabelle around the block twice. Following her arrival back at Florence's, Molly fed the dog chicken livers from the fridge and served the meat in a bowl already half full of dog biscuits. She gave Lulabelle cuddles, then uttered words of reassurance, saying, "Don't worry, I'll be back later for your night-time stroll." Molly could not remain sad, having Lulabelle to take care of, and she remembered part of a quote, *Happiness is a walk with your dog.* To cheer Lulabelle, Molly suggested, "How about I bring you a bone to chew on later?" Lulabelle appeared uninterested in what Molly had to say and padded without grace over to her bed in a corner of Florence's living room. After double-locking the front door, Molly stepped across the road again, entering the mellow warmth of her apartment.

Pondering her long day, she accepted the fact that her core students would miss their Thursday yoga. Lying back on the sofa, and closing her eyes, a thought came to mind. She would suggest to Stanley that he call and update Cassie on her mother's whereabouts. Perhaps Cassie would surprise everyone, leave her sheep and animals for a day, and drive to Little Shore.

CHAPTER 30

JAMIE WALKED INTO THE BELLEVIEW RECEPTION area. He removed his walking boots and caught the smell of dampness from his parka. The wet collar of his father's jumper stuck to his neck. He padded through the kitchen door in his socks and inhaled the aroma of a casserole and studied the simmering pot on top of the Aga. Probably one of Boudie's delicious recipes of meat, herbs, and vegetables encased in red wine, he reasoned.

He stared at her as she sat at the kitchen breakfast bar, lost in her thoughts. Filled with love and appreciation for all she had given him without any expectation, he settled his broad frame onto a bar stool opposite her.

"Hey, Boudie." Guilt gurgled in the pit of his stomach.

She filled a glass with water from a carafe on the granite tabletop and crossed her hands one over the other before raising her head to look at him.

"Ah, my adopted grandson, I wondered when you'd

return. By the way, you left your black pirate's wig in the bathroom. I assume nobody needed you to rescue them today." She paused for a second, then said, "What's going on Kit? I've never seen you in such a state."

"I have been a total idiot. I allowed myself to get swept up in the theatre performances. A lack of kip following the show's success, along with too much celebrating, has made my head scramble all over the place. I'm still in a muddle."

Boudie waved his apology away. "As you have often said, 'stuff happens.'"

"The thing is, I'm not sure I know where to begin." His eyes hurt like hell. He looked down, forcing himself to concentrate. "If I don't let this out, I feel like my body will implode. You deserve to hear the truth." He bit his lip and put his elbows on the table.

"Don't look so worried. You're safe here."

Boudie's tender voice tore at his heart. He raised his eyes to hers. "Please make allowances for what I am about to say." He puffed out his cheeks and let out a big sigh. "My name is not Kit O'Connor. It's . . ." He paused out of habit, then surged ahead. "Jamie Mulligan. The only son of Molly, who is Mrs Cornell's neighbour. You must believe the core of me, the one you have come to know, is still the same." He struggled for words. "You remember when I first arrived on your doorstep and told you I'd opted out of London life? On that same day I broke a promise to set up a new home with my ma in Kent." He paused. "Left her a note, telling her I couldn't join her, but would be in touch. After loading up my kitbag and leaving the house, I jumped on a train, without a plan, ending up in Little Shore. I wanted to be anyone but Jamie Mulligan and had the notion it would be fun to become someone else, get into some other character's head. The name Kit O'Connor only came to me after ringing your doorbell on that winter's day. That may sound bloody weird, but I swear it's the truth."

He briefly shared with Boudie how he got lost in reinventing himself, then continued. "After what happened today, I've concluded that I've caused nothing but upset, both for my ma and for you."

Colour drained from Boudie's face. Unsure what would happen next, his eyes followed her as she slid off her stool and went to the fridge. She took out two flutes and a bottle from the wine fridge and finally spoke. "I think we might have to open the bar early tonight." She set the flutes on the table and popped the champagne cork.

He watched the effervescent fizz hit the bottom of Boudie's glass. The bubbles ascended to the top, filled with vitality, none of which he felt.

"Will you join me?" She held up one of the flutes.

He shook his head and waited for Boudie to sit again, glass in hand. Nausea overcame him as the fruity aroma of the alcohol reached his nose. He sat poker straight, every muscle in his body on fire.

He could see she was fighting the urge to cry.

Silence hung between them. Finally, he said, "You've shown me only kindness, and I think of you as my family."

Boudie lifted the glass of chilled bubbles to her lips and, after a few sips, placed the frosted glass back on the polished surface. "On the day you stood on the porch, I could have sent you away, but I chose to welcome you into my home. After we came to a long-term agreement, I was cheered to have the company of a young adult. I admired your keenness to fit in and you adapted well to a working life.

"I admit I knew there had to be more than you revealed when I invited you into The Belleview. I suppose I hoped that in time you would come to trust me and share your family story and why you really left London." She took another sip from her glass. "I trusted you. You lied."

Jamie put his hand to his face and felt his skin prickle.

"What else are you hiding?"

He watched her unfurl a photograph and place it in front of him.

"Are these your parents?" Boudie asked.

Jamie nodded at her, picked up the photo, stared at the family shot, and confessed his shame. "My mother worked tirelessly to support me in my effort to gain a place at a Performing Arts College in London. I realise I have been selfish, leaving my ma while she carried on alone. I simply disappeared from her life." Jamie clicked his fingers into the air. "As for my father, well, I've not been properly in contact with him for years. I ignored his efforts to keep in touch when Ma and I still lived at the family home. He pushed the photo back to the centre of the table.

"When I showed up at your door, you must believe me, I felt grateful for a place of refuge. Honestly, it became my soft place of comfort, a real home." He continued to hang his head. "What have I done?" After glugging some water, he slammed the empty glass on the tabletop. "My father left me and my ma when I was young. As an angry teen, I refused to acknowledge him after that. I wanted him to feel the pain of rejection. As for my ma, she didn't need her son to opt out without any explanation. I made excuses to myself that I had been thrown into the business of college life and felt out of my depth. The other students came from diverse and wealthy backgrounds. I was only there thanks to a scholarship. I struggled with relationships. At one point, I thought I might drown in the despair of trying to fit in."

"Darling boy, you don't need me to confirm you've messed up," Boudie whispered. "I always knew there had to be a backstory. From the first time we met, you had a fragility. I often wondered about your family and thought perhaps a girl had given you the heave ho." Boudie tapped her fingers on the crumpled family photograph. "I have been equally selfish by pretending you were the grandson I could never have. If I feel betrayed, what about the torment that has surely plagued your mother? I should have insisted you come clean at the start."

Jamie observed her mouth twist in a hard line. Gone was her usual exuberance, replaced with a sadness that clouded her features.

"Now that you know the complete story, where do we go from here?" He waited for her to decide.

"I can play this one of two ways," she finally said. "I could kick you out right now, never to see or speak to you again. You either go back to whatever life you choose—and it won't include staying here if you're not honest—or you agree to contact your mother. Tell her the truth and bear the consequences. And finally, you must decide; who do you want to be, Kit or Jamie?"

CHAPTER 31

WALKING INTO THE BATHROOM, MOLLY gazed at the bathroom mirror, noting the dark circles under her eyes had become more prominent. Her skin remained blotchy from earlier weeping. She turned away from the mirror. "I will not let myself get gloomy."

Moving to the bedroom, she threw on a pair of yoga bottoms, a matching vest, and a sweat top, and headed to the kitchen. After boiling a kettle of water and preparing some restoring Earl Grey tea, she sipped the liquid from her favourite china mug. Wandering into the living room, she sat on the sofa.

She tried calling Colonel Bryce Beckwith, but he was unreachable. Deciding to text him to confirm she would take care of Lulabelle, she typed in:

If I can be of more help, please let me know.

Best Wishes, Molly

The text failed to send.

Disheartened, she set about preparing and cooking dinner for herself and Stanley. Once ready, she laid Stanley's hot food on a tray. She wanted to eat later in the comfort of her home.

After putting on her coat and scarf again and picking up the covered tray, she stepped out into the subdued light and frosty air, making her way next door. Once inside Stanley's house, she set Stanley's tray on a table, serving him his dinner.

Stanley pulled at the tea cloth and foil wrapped around the casserole. "Aw, Molly, you've saved the day." She watched him grab the spoon, scoop up the chunks of meat, and shove them into his mouth.

Molly removed some newspapers from a nearby chair to sit and keep Stanley company while he ate. The only sound came from his slurping as he sucked up the gravy from the bowl.

She took his slurping as a compliment and could not help but grin, pleased he enjoyed her cooking.

Once Stanley finished the last morsel, he incessantly scraped the bowl with his spoon. Finally, having practically licked the bowl clean, he looked at Molly and smirked.

"There's more." She stood and, retrieving the warm dish of apple pie and custard she'd brought, she placed it on his table.

"Ah, yer the best. Now that's what I call a real tasty meal." She caught the twinkle in his eyes as he gobbled the contents and licked his spoon again.

"Have you updated Cassie yet?" Molly asked.

He shook his head. "After her visit this morning, I didn't want to get another earful of her wrath. Would you do the necessary and call her on my behalf?"

Once she had cleared away the dishes, she went to the

kitchen, boiled a kettle of water, and made a hot drink, which she poured into a flask for Stanley to drink later. Back in the living room, she put his flask on the table.

"Okay. I'll text Cassie after I've finished my meal. Let's see if she will bring your Rita home tomorrow."

She watched him pat his stomach and looked contentedly in her direction. Then, picking up the handset, he flicked across his favourite TV channels. She knew he'd ease himself into his single bed in the living room around ten o'clock and bunk down to sleep. She waved good night.

Checking her phone as she walked into her apartment, she saw there was still no word from the two elderly rascals.

Replying to Cassie and confirming Cassie's mother had been driven by a neighbour's grandson to Little Shore by mistake, she added that Mrs Cornell, by all accounts, had been fed and well taken care of.

> *Your mother needs collecting. Call me once you have planned her return home tomorrow. No need to worry about your father. I cooked dinner for him this evening and he's settled in for the night.*

A sense of weariness hung over her. Not feeling up to setting a table for one, she treated herself to dinner from a tray on her lap. Retrieving her meal, still warm from the oven, she sat on the sofa, wrapped in the comfort of a wool throw.

While doing her best to concentrate on her food, she pushed the meat and vegetables around the bowl with her fork, never quite lifting the food to her mouth. A different hunger grew within her.

The ping of a text message caught her off guard. She set the tray down and felt cheered upon seeing Brandon O'Neill's name flash up.

> *Hey, beautiful lady, why have you been hiding? When are we going to have that date? Come on, what are you afraid of? Thinking of you. Call me soon. Brandon.*

Had the time come to let go of the past? Was she ready to make a full-hearted connection with Brandon? She shrugged at the idea of encouraging romantic thoughts. Even so, his message bolstered her mood as she faced the hours ahead.

CHAPTER 32

BOUDIE WALKED AROUND THE KITCHEN countertop to where Jamie sat on the other side of the bar. She took him in her arms just as the Zen-like bell of The Belleview rang, startling them both.

She pulled away from Jamie. No matter the hour, an enthusiastic welcome must be extended. She hurried towards the front door.

She swung the door open. Between planters of bay trees on each side of the entryway stood two dishevelled travellers, their overnight bags resting at their feet.

"Any chance of a room or two for the night?" the woman asked.

Boudie threw herself at her sister.

"Oh, my darling girl, what a surprise! You left me frantic with worry when you did not return my calls. How on earth did you manage to get here?" Boudie looked from Florence to the stranger and took heed of the mud stains on his coat.

"I drove the Morgan. After much deliberation, I decided I would not allow your rascal of a grandson to take away my chance of visiting you today. And here we are," said Florence, "me and my navigator."

Boudie delighted in seeing the sparkle of triumph in her sister's eyes, but after appraising the man beside her, she thought, *What a tremendously scruffy individual.*

"Surely you remember young Bryce from our days in good old India?" Florence shot Boudie a smile.

"My dear lady," said Colonel Bryce Beckwith, "Pardon my shoddiness." He put his hand out to shake Boudie's and said, "Please don't let my appearance put you off. Unfortunately, I fell when we stopped for a break earlier. I slipped on a waterlogged cricket lawn and landed face down in a puddle. I am happy to remake your acquaintance. Colonel Bryce Beckwith at your service." He bowed towards Boudie and then stood at attention. "My parents and yours were friends for many years. And as you may already be aware, Florence and I became next-door neighbours some ten years ago."

Relieved, Boudie nodded at her sister's friend.

"Yes, indeed, I remember you as a young boy." She took his grubby hand, squeezed it firmly, and stretched to give him a kiss on his stained cheek.

"It is evident you both have been in the wars today. Such driving courage. I want to hear about your escapade."

She ushered them into the reception area, took their soiled coats, and placed each one in a dry-cleaning bag from the nearby closet. She fetched two large-sized pairs of slippers from the same closet. Once they had removed their footwear onto newspaper laid out on the parquet flooring, she guided them to sit on chairs near reception. After putting the slippers on, they stood again.

"Jamie, darling, we have visitors. Do please come and help," she called out. He appeared through the kitchen doors, acting sheepish as he approached them. Boudie's heart softened upon seeing his pained face. She introduced him to her sister and friend.

"So, you are the young scoundrel who failed to collect me this morning," Florence boomed, standing to her full height. She eyeballed Jamie. "Pray, what's your excuse?"

Seeing Jamie's face redden, Boudie stepped between them. She explained a mistake had occurred and relayed that she'd left messages on her sister's main phone line without any response. Boudie's worry eased after Florence's look of disapproval melted away.

"As it happens, you, Jamie, have been a catalyst to making a love story almost come true today," Florence said.

Boudie considered the rosy glow on Florence's cheeks and turned to face Colonel Bryce Beckwith.

Before she could say anything, Florence said, "I hear you're a star barista coffee maker, the best this side of Little Shore. You are forgiven if you'll create one of your masterpieces for me right now."

Jamie nodded, apparently taken aback by Florence's formidable presence, and inched backwards towards the bar in the conservatory.

"Indeed, it was a most fortuitous drive," Colonel Bryce Beckwith declared to Boudie.

Florence placed her hand in his.

"I hope you do not mind, but I took the liberty of packing a bag and insisted Bryce do the same. We wish to take advantage of your hospitality and rest our tired bodies. May we stay over?"

Boudie nodded. In sheer delight, she again threw her arms tightly around Florence's waist.

"As it happens, dear one, The Belleview occupancy is down to two single gentlemen who are checking out in the morning. After tomorrow, I have no guests booked until next week. It will be just us, *en famille*." Boudie shooed her beloved sister and her friend towards the grand staircase.

"Jamie, darling, can you fetch clean towels? I shall escort Colonel Bryce Beckwith to the honeymoon suite. Florence, I insist you have my room."

She led the way up the sweeping stairs while Jamie went to grab some guest towels.

After a few moments, he followed behind Bryce a nd Florence, carrying their overnight bags, one in each hand, the fresh towels under his arms. Once they reached the top of the landing, Boudie made an announcement.

"Food will be served in the conservatory at eight o'clock sharp. Simple fare, I'm afraid. You will be pleased to know, Florence, I found a lone bottle of your famous Rhubarb Pink Gin. We shall toast to old and future times by cracking it open before we eat.

"And please say you will stay for a few days. What's the rush to go home?" Boudie validated the invitation to Colonel Bryce Beckwith with an approving gesture, bowing her head, assuring him he was welcome, too.

She turned and whispered to Jamie, "You look quite haggard. Go and put your head on your pillow. I shall make your excuses. I am perfectly capable of pulling dinner together."

Squeezing Jamie's arm, she swished past him and showed Florence and Colonel Bryce Beckwith to their respective suites. After which, she considered her unexpected guest, Mrs Cornell, who would need her care and attention until the following morning.

CHAPTER 33

PUNCH-DRUNK WITH TIREDNESS, JAMIE ALMOST fell through the door of his bedroom.

"Jamie Mulligan, what have you done?" He kicked the leg of a chair tucked away in the room's corner. He rolled back the covers of the bed, peeled off his clothes, and slipped under the duvet. Placing his head on the crisp cotton pillowslip, he closed his eyes. A million monsters hissed around in his overloaded brain.

An image of his mother and himself in a yoga-tree pose flashed before him. "Pay attention to your breath," she would often say, helping him find calm before he took exams.

Disappearing into rippled waves of sleep, dreams of Poppy La Grange and visions of college life floated past. He scanned the people whose lives he'd passed in and out of before he left them behind. Poppy La Grange stepped forward. "What happened Jamie? Why did you disappear from London? You walked away from a bright future in acting and music to bury yourself in a small fishing town. What were you hoping for—that you'd survive by becoming someone else? Did you think nobody would ever wonder about the stranger who came to live amongst them?"

"I could ask you the same question. What happened to you, Ms La Grange?"

"I ask the questions today." In his dream, he felt the coldness of her gaze tap into his thumping heart.

"No, no, it can't be," he cried out. "You gave birth to my child and chose not to tell me?" he heard himself shout into a murky darkness. His eyes shot open. He threw back the bedcover, swung his legs around, and sat on the edge of the mattress. "It's just a nightmare," he reassured himself.

Droplets of sweat rose on his brow. Filled with anxiety, his hands clammy with perspiration, he placed them across his forehead. "That bloody woman set me up so she could have a child. Living in Little Shore."

The bedroom door opened. Wiping his eyes, he looked up to see Boudie pop her head around the edge of the door. He grabbed the duvet and wrapped it around his body.

"My darling boy, have you seen your face? You look as if you've seen a ghost."

Battling with harboured emotions like a dam no longer contained, words flooded out, and the story unveiled about his love for Poppy La Grange.

Boudie came all the way into the room and sat on the bed, taking his hand in hers.

"During the first months of life at college, I realise Poppy, who was an assistant tutor, purposely sought me out." He talked of the compliments Poppy gave him in her appraisals.

She told me, "You have a gift to act and sing and I can help develop your star quality if you let me." He told Boudie he'd been shy and unable to respond to such praise. "She would frequently suggest we meet for a glass of wine, set goals, and plan a strategy for my first year. And she claimed she could introduce me to the right people to fulfil my dreams of becoming an actor. Although flattered, I hadn't a clue how to react to her advances and flirtatious manner."

Boudie nodded for him to carry on.

"Observing me at lectures, she spoke of me being detached from everyone, but once I stepped into a character, I could immerse myself fully in a role. I felt uneasy when she spoke of my capacity to weave spells on the stage. Poppy constantly repeated success and fame could be mine if I desired it enough." Rising from his bed, he wrapped the duvet tightly around his body and paced back and forth across the room. "I finally surrendered to offers to meet for a drink. That followed with a first date, then another. Our relationship developed. When we sat together in a pub or restaurant, Poppy would move in close, our knees and feet touching. One evening, she turned and whispered in my ear, her lips close to my cheek, and said she wanted me. I admit I blushed." He returned to sit alongside Boudie, who squeezed his hand.

"Saying she felt our chemistry, she asked why I did not throw caution out the window. She said we should enjoy more of each other. Boudie, I swear, her eyes flashed when she placed her fingertips on either side of my cheekbones. Before I knew what was happening, she pressed her mouth on mine and kissed me on the lips."

He stared down at the bedroom floor.

"I cannot believe I am sharing these intimate details, but you asked for honesty. That first kiss felt pretty intense and filled me with dizzy promises."

"I have experienced life. Believe me, I am unshockable. Do continue," Boudie reassured him.

He regaled her with stories of his life with Poppy, admitting he disappeared into a surreal world of blatant sex, lust, and an obsession for her. He told her how their fiery conversations were intense, like their lovemaking. Changed by her, he said his assertiveness and confidence grew as Poppy guided him at every step.

"I became hooked by the thrill of being with her. We would sit on her four-poster bed, shrouded in black silk voile, with Baroque music playing as we drank champagne. We spent most days and nights together. I craved her body tightly bound by mine and counted the hours and minutes whenever we were apart."

He shared the question he'd asked her.

"If this is what love feels like, how can we remain lost in unadulterated bliss?"

Jamie watched Boudie patiently listen while he recalled the day Poppy became his reason to walk away.

"One afternoon, away from prying college ears and whispers, Poppy and I sipped coffee in a café. She leaned across the table, kissed me on the lips, sat back, and took my hands tightly in hers. As ever, I sat transfixed by her. Poppy casually mentioned she'd handed in her resignation to the head of the college to relinquish her post and would leave before the end of term. Following this statement, she said the time had come for change. She wanted another kind of life and that meant getting away from the crowded city and relentless noise."

He visualised Poppy gazing out through the windowpane of the café to the bus lanes, then onto the street filled with people.

"'But what about us?' I asked her, but she simply shook her head and reiterated that I had a wonderful career ahead of me. 'Why would I stand in the way?' she said. Then, like a knife straight through my heart, she summed up our time together, saying she'd been terribly fond of me, but we'd agreed it would never be a big love thing. 'How can you just ditch me?' I yelled back at her. 'Why do the people I care about most, leave? What gave you the right to trample over my heart when you already know I've never fallen for anyone before? You are the love of my life. I thought we had a future.'"

Jamie's thoughts lingered on Poppy. He stared out at the starry skyline. Feeling his jaw twitch, he turned to face Boudie.

"After hearing this bombshell, I became frantic, willing her to retract her decision. But Poppy let go of my hands and tried to dismiss our conversation by laughing.

"Poppy made to leave, but I jumped up and stood over her. The table rocked. A hush filled the café, and even the sound of the coffee machines ebbed away. I grabbed her shoulders and lightly nudged her back into her chair. I sat down and said, 'Look me straight in the eye and tell me you don't love me. Tell me it was only a fling.' She would not meet my eyes."

"I asked her, 'Are you planning to simply walk away, leave without any sense of responsibility about how I might be feeling?' Boudie, I pushed my chair away and cocoa froth and coffee overflowed onto the saucers and brown liquid trickled onto the shiny table surface. I blindly stormed out of the café and heard her call after me, 'I hope one day, you will find it in your heart to accept my decision.'

"I did not look back. Nor did I listen to her calling after me. After that, I disengaged from life and eventually opted out of college. And as you now know, I left my ma on her lonesome." He squirmed in embarrassment and noticed Boudie's eyes were spotted with tears.

"I did not realise your backstory had such a hold

on you. You are not the first, and certainly not the last college student to have become enraptured by their tutor."

She pulled him to her in a hug. After a few seconds, she rose from the bed, walked to the bedroom door, hesitated, and turned around.

"I am sorry this Poppy woman dumped you. A real slap in the face—one I can empathise with. You must reconcile with your mother and perhaps in time you'll consider rebuilding a relationship with your father, too."

He remained silent, still seated on the edge of the bed. He saw her check her watch.

"Time is pressing. I need to prepare dinner. There's no need to play Mr Charmer tonight or answer a bundle of questions. Best if you eat in the kitchen away from us oldies. I can explain you have an overpowering migraine. By the way, in view of your blunder, you should drive Mrs Cornell home. I've since decided it best if she stays over. The poor woman is confused. Once she's had a good night's rest, she will be set for the drive."

He exhaled a long, slow breath, and blew her a kiss as she slipped out of the bedroom to leave him with his thoughts.

CHAPTER 34

Before heading downstairs, Boudie crept in and checked on Mrs Cornell. The woman sat upright, her eyes tightly shut, her head resting against propped-up pillows. Mrs Cornell's florid complexion and her gaunt, childlike body in the oversized bed reminded Boudie of an old china doll she had owned as a child.

"Mrs Cornell, time to wake up and get ready for dinner." Boudie placed her hand on the woman's shoulder.

Opening her eyes and scrunching up her nose, Mrs Cornell said, "Where am I? Is this the honeymoon room? Where is my Stanley?"

Boudie reassured Mrs Cornell of her whereabouts and encouraged her to get out of bed. Guiding her to the en-suite bathroom to refresh herself, Boudie told her through the door, "I have just the outfit for you for this evening."

Boudie waited patiently until Mrs Cornell finished and, with faltering steps, came back into the bedroom.

With ample cajoling, she helped Mrs Cornell change into a pair of French-blue velvet tracksuit bottoms teamed with a shimmering T-shirt in the same colour. After which, Boudie led the woman to the dressing table. Sitting her down in front of a mirror, she combed Rita's fine hair and painted her lips in pale pink gloss. Mrs Cornell grinned as she stared at her reflection.

"Are we going to dance in the ballroom? Stanley and I love dancing, and it's our honeymoon." Mrs Cornell chuckled, but then Boudie saw sadness spread across the woman's face. "Where's my new husband gone off to?"

"Rita dear, you are staying at The Belleview. Tomorrow, you will be reunited with Stanley. Stay here and rest. I shall escort you downstairs once dinner is ready." Boudie waited until she felt Mrs Cornell had collected her thoughts and understood her suggestion, then headed downstairs to the conservatory.

She set the grand table, pulling out her best linen from a nearby cupboard. Placing cream ceramic pots filled with purple cyclamen down the centre, she decorated the spaces in between with candles resting on crystal candelabra. After striking a match to the pillar candles, both the crystal and candles flickered. She looked around the room and absorbed the burnt orange and ochre light casting a certain magic across the walls. Appreciating the warmth of the dinner setting, she then went to her iPad and selected some Adagio classical music.

She considered Jamie's troubles. *What can I do to help ease his pain? And there's poor Mrs Cornell, lost in her world of times past.* "Cheer up, old thing," she said to herself. "Focus on the evening ahead. Tonight is about bringing happiness to everyone sitting at my dinner table."

About to leave for the kitchen, she heard a tapping

sound on the parquet flooring and caught sight of a perky-looking Mrs Cornell as she entered the conservatory. "Oh, Mrs Cornell, what a fright you've given me. Why didn't you wait for me to walk you down?"

Oblivious, the woman did not reply. Boudie paid close attention to how Mrs Cornell concentrated on each step, moving towards the table.

"I shall sit right here in the centre," Mrs Cornell said, letting out a snort.

"Today, I've won the lottery, just like my wedding day when I married my handsome husband." Mrs Cornell looked at Boudie. "Wait till I tell Stanley I've laid down on a king-sized bed and rested my head on pillows made of goose feathers. Can I stay and visit the sea again tomorrow?" she pleaded.

"But Mrs Cornell, what about your husband and daughter? Surely they've been worried and want you home as soon as possible," Boudie said in soft tones.

"Well, Cassie won't be concerned. She'll be out in the fields or in the barn with her pregnant sheep. We could ring Molly and ask her to keep an eye on Stanley until I return."

Mrs Cornell seemed quite determined to stay, Boudie concluded. Once dinner had been eaten, she would share with Mrs Cornell that she would be driven home the following day.

CHAPTER 35

With time to spare before dinner, and feeling more courageous, Colonel Bryce Beckwith wandered down the corridor. Noting a group of photographs on a wall to his right, he moved closer. Boudie posed with famous actresses that he recognised. They wore splendid kaftans, and he was determined to ask questions about the glamourous stars who were featured with her.

At the end of the corridor, an arrangement of red roses and white hydrangeas caught his attention. They sat in a vintage vase on a pale wood table. On further inspection, he noted they were made of silk. Gingerly plucking one out, he proceeded to knock on Florence's bedroom door.

He wondered if she would be patient in allowing him to speak of his life story. Gathering himself, the door opened. Reassured by her look of affection, he pressed the single red rose into her hand and believed the response in her eyes said, *I am pleased to see you.* They stood facing each other in the doorway.

Disheartened earlier, not helped by falling on the waterlogged cricket ground, he spoke with renewed determination. “My dearest one, I confess, following your insistence that I wait for your reply to my marriage proposal, I felt mightily disappointed. Can you find it in your heart to give me a favourable answer?”

Without warning, her hands wrapped themselves around his.

“Sorry for being my usual stubborn self. Without question, my answer is yes, and yes again. I shall happily spend the rest of my days with you. You are my one and only true love. Why do you think I have remained single all this time? Silly man. Nobody could ever match you.”

His happiness at her declaration was short-lived when she pulled away and pointed a finger at him.

“There is one condition before any announcements or wedding bells ring out. I need some long-awaited answers. The truth of why you took so long.”

“You have my word that I’ll provide a complete and honest explanation,” he replied. He pulled her close and kissed her chastely. Feeling a tingle like cascading feathers skimming across his lips, he’d quite forgotten when he’d last been kissed. They moved into the bedroom, and both sat on the edge of the bed, tightly clasping each other’s hands. He monitored her face, anticipating her reaction, and began to share his story.

• • •

At reception, the clock struck eight o’clock. Arm in arm, both Florence and Bryce made a regal entrance into the conservatory.

Both freshly showered, Bryce inhaled his beloved's perfume—Lily of the Valley. He noted her mother's lilac flower in her hair, which enhanced her reset chignon. He wore a grey suit, a white shirt, and complimented his outfit with a coloured silk bow tie.

Catching sight of their neighbour, Mrs Cornell, sitting in prime position at Boudie's dinner table, he saw Florence's disapproval spread across her face and her posture stiffen. Mrs Cornell stared at them, grinning like a Cheshire cat.

"Hello, neighbours. Fancy, we're in the same house, eh?" Mrs Cornell cackled in delight. From her tracksuit pocket, she pulled out a giant stick of pink rock with the words "Little Shore" inscribed in black ink across the wrapping. "Was going to wait until I got back home. Wanted to say sorry for the mix-up, Florence. You see, I became befuddled this morning, between me cataracts and fasting all night. I believed it was me daughter, Cassie, who was driving me to the hospital for tests."

Bryce moved to escort Florence to sit opposite Mrs Cornell.

"Didn't realise I'd been collected by your sister's grandson. He looks the spit of my Cassie," Mrs Cornell continued, looking to Boudie and then to Florence. "Anyway, it's ended well. You managed to get here in one piece with yer reliable Colonel Bryce Beckwith." Mrs Cornell sat back, breathless. Then she threw the bit of rock at Florence through a gap in Boudie's accessorised dinner table.

Bryce squeezed Florence's hand on seeing her facial expression change. He watched her take hold of the rock.

"Thanks for the thought, but I'll not be eating this sticky piece of sugar. My ancient molars have left me without any bite. But the rock shall be a reminder of the drive to Boudie's ending on a positive note," she finished curtly.

Bryce placed his arm across Florence's shoulder.

"I've enjoyed one of the best days," Mrs Cornell said, animatedly carrying on, telling her audience in detail the hours she and Boudie spent on the promenade. "We ate fish and chips with mushy peas. Puffed up swooping seagulls tried to pinch our chips." Mrs Cornell laughed and spoke of how they took refuge on a seat, facing the wrong way around. "It faced the road instead of the seafront." She chuckled. Then she grew quiet and closed her eyes.

To his relief, Boudie appeared in the room and offered them both a glass of restoring sherry.

"No alcohol for you, Mrs Cornell," Boudie called out.

Stirred from her catnapping, Mrs Cornell said, "That's right, Boudie, a Cherry Coke will do me fine if you have one," she mumbled.

They all raised their glasses to each other. "To a happy reunion and the surprises of today," said Boudie, making the toast.

Seeing his beloved move awkwardly in her chair, looking first to Boudie and then at him, he stood up. "We bring good tidings. I seek your blessing. It's all been rather sudden, in the end." He cleared his throat and picked up his glass of sherry.

"How can you call waiting a lifetime to receive a proposal, rather sudden?" Florence uttered impatiently.

"My dear, let's not spoil our good news." He patted Florence's hand. Turning to face Boudie, who sat at the end of the table, he raised his glass in salutation. "After a break from our driving through inclement conditions, I went down on one knee on a waterlogged cricket green and proposed marriage to your sister. She's had her way and kept me nervously waiting for the last hours." Bryce placed one hand on his heart. "You see, Florence needed to understand why I did not follow her back to England years ago. To my shame, I never found the courage to explain until we sat together this evening. I am delighted your sister has accepted my hand in marriage. I am the luckiest man alive, but we must have your approval."

He shared his story and the pressure he'd received from his parents to marry Diane. As quickly as he married their choice of his bride, he told them, he'd joined the army. "I felt nothing but discontentment throughout my married life. Diane was a kind lady in her own way, but she could never take the place of my Florence."

He spoke of remaining a companion to Diane until she passed. "I looked for Florence and heard she'd moved to Kent. I constantly checked the property pages. One day, a little miracle came to pass. An army friend contacted me and spoke of a property for sale next door to my dear one." He looked at Florence for her reassurance.

"I thank your sister for her patience, waiting for me, although I had let her down. The past is firmly behind us, and we look to our future together." Bryce sat and wiped his brow with a cotton handkerchief from his top pocket.

"Hurrah, hurrah," Boudie cried out. "Darlings, it's never too late for romance. In the end, love conquers all. Quite marvellous news and a positive conclusion to a tumultuous day." She clapped her hands and rose from her chair to skip around the table to kiss Florence on both cheeks and to give Bryce a hug.

"I feel honoured to give my blessing. Have you set a date? Where might the wedding take place? Who will give you away? What will you wear?"

Bryce watched Boudie make a dive towards the bar, unlock the chiller cabinet, and grab a bottle. She presented him with Florence's Pink Rhubarb Gin.

Curious, he watched her retrieve three shot glasses, pour the alcohol, and swiftly move back to the dinner table.

"My sister has come to visit. If that is not enough jubilation, the man of her long-held dreams accompanies her. I officially announce Florence's engagement to Colonel Bryce Beckwith. May your days and years ahead be filled with joy. Hip, hip, hurrah! My congratulations to you both."

A tear splashed down Boudie's face. She thrust her glass into the air and the dark liquid spilled onto the table. She called out, "Cheers! Sante!"

Bryce looked around the table, clinked his glass with the others, and smiled at his future bride. Sipping the odd coloured alcohol, he did his best not to grimace at the taste.

Florence boomed out, "The damned stuff is way past its sell-by date and not suitable for drinking. I'm afraid my once famous pink gin has turned."

She inhaled, paused, and then sniffed.

"A decidedly iffy smell, both bitter and lingering. Hell in a glass if you ask me," she said, laughing.

Boudie crinkled up her nose. "I agree. Let's try again, shall we? I can recommend a glass of sweet heaven instead."

She bounced over to the bar and pulled a bottle of Premier Cru, by Louis Roderer, from the fridge. "I knew I would open this one day for an exceptional celebration." She settled the bottle into a silver bucket already filled with ice.

He stood waiting until Boudie returned and sat with them again.

"Florence, I shall not accept any excuses," said Boudie. "You simply must stay more than a night."

Bryce's heart melted on seeing Boudie place a loving hand on Florence's arm.

"You are part of the family now, my good man," she said, nodding at him. "I cordially extend the same invitation to you. Such wedding plans we can make together." Her eyes misted.

He ignored Mrs Cornell's grunting and snorting, for she remained oblivious to his and Florence's good news. Instead, he soaked up an atmosphere of excitement in the room.

CHAPTER 36

JAMIE TOOK ANOTHER COOL SHOWER, CHANGED his clothes, and remade the bed. Time to level up, he thought, contact Poppy, and ask her all the "whys" he'd been stacking up since she had walked out on him. He reached for his mobile and typed a text.

> *I felt shocked and angry when I saw you at the cafe earlier, with your secret of a baby and that you are living in Little Shore. You never thought to let me know about the child. She resembles my mother, Molly. We need to talk. Let me know when you are free.*

He sent another two text messages, lay on top of the bed, and considered whether he would go downstairs.

• • •

Downstairs in the conservatory, Boudie observed Mrs Cornell sitting at the dinner table, her head nodding back and forth, her snorting sounds growing louder. To block out the noise, Boudie picked up the handset and turned up the volume of the Adagio music.

To her surprise, a bleary-eyed Jamie appeared in the doorway.

"Ah, there you are, darling boy," Boudie greeted him. "I did not expect you to join us. How is that migraine of yours? Do the honours, will you, and pop the champagne? Let's fill our glasses. We have an important toast to make." She moved to where Jamie stood, pulled him to the bar and oversaw him opening the bottle. He filled the long-stemmed champagne glasses and Boudie served her guests. Once back in her chair, she beckoned him to sit next to her and poured him a glass of water. After a few seconds, she stood up. "To the happy couple." She raised her glass, as did Jamie. Glowing with the excitement of her sister's news, she watched Florence and Colonel Bryce Beckwith kiss each other.

Boudie nudged Jamie and they disappeared into the kitchen to plate up dinner. Following everyone being served, she patted Mrs Cornell on the shoulder. "Time to eat Mrs Cornell." She patiently waited while the woman opened her startled-looking eyes. "What's happening? Where am I?"

"You are at The Belleview."

"Is that so? I remember eating fish and chips today with mushy peas, on a seat that had been turned the wrong way around." She chortled and her false teeth became loose in her mouth. She clicked her tongue and Boudie watched her push her dentures with one finger back onto her gums. The woman scanned the table, her eyes shiny. "Who are you?" She stared at Jamie.

"Ah, this is my grandson. Remember? He drove you

here this morning," Boudie told Mrs Cornell.

The woman's eyes squeezed into slits as she continued to glare at Jamie. "This is not how I remember you." She lifted her fork to point at him. "The person who drove me this morning was the spit of my Cassie with long, dark hair and big earrings."

With a nod from Boudie, Jamie apologised to Mrs Cornell. "The wig is part of a theatre costume. I am the lead actor in a production of *Pirates of the Caribbean*."

Boudie looked at the blue-eyed young man. She recalled when he appeared a lost and vulnerable soul, standing on her doorstep in need of a room three years ago.

She changed the subject, for she realised the fragile woman was clearly still confused. "Mrs Cornell, you missed my older sister Florence's and Colonel Bryce Beckwith's glorious news. They are engaged to be married. That is why we are drinking champagne."

Boudie watched as the old woman's jaw dropped. Indistinct words tumbled out, but it was obvious nobody could understand her. "Bout bloody time, too," she eventually sputtered. "Skirting around each other, living side-by-side, like kindly neighbours. My Stanley would often say, 'Those two were made for each other.' We always knew twas a match made in heaven." Mrs Cornell slid her tongue around the inside of her mouth. "So, are me and my Stanley invited to the wedding?" She scratched around her plate and gathered a spoonful of food, shoved it into her mouth, and chewed incessantly. That followed with her head swaying from side to side. Then she closed her eyes and vanished into another world.

Boudie sat back in her chair, glad Jamie had reached out to shake Florence's and Colonel Bryce Beckwith's hands in congratulations.

"Bryce, I hope you plan to put a ring on Florence's finger? Have you considered where you might buy my sister's engagement ring? We have exceptional jewellers in Little Shore. I am happy to make any necessary introductions." She looked at her sister. "Of course, Florence, we have our family's inherited rings to consider. Do you remember, as children, we would open the boxes belonging to our mother? Circular shapes, festooned in gold and pink silk and inside a treasure trove of sparkly jewels awaited us."

Boudie smiled at the memory of Florence and herself sitting on the floor in their mother's bedroom in India, squealing in anticipation as they tried on their mother's and grandmother's rings. After their parents died, they eventually sold the house in Belgravia. The remaining heirlooms were locked away in a bank vault in the city of London.

Boudie turned to address Florence. "Perhaps you could make a formal announcement in the *Times* for our late father's and mother's sake?"

"I know you like drama and excitement, Boudie, but we are not aristocracy, nor do we plan to have a grandiose wedding." Florence spoke firmly and reminded Boudie their parents were long dead. "What would we achieve by placing a notice in the *Times*? I shall say this before making any arrangements for our wedding day. I understand your passion for seeking attention, planning events, your love of bright colours, and wearing glittery shoes with fancy buckles. They are your personal statements to the world, but they will never be mine." She turned to Bryce. "We shall be happy to celebrate our wedding day with a small gathering, and please, no fuss."

When Boudie started to say something, Florence put her hand up in protest at any further discussion.

"You can rest assured it will be a wedding to remember. On that note, will you be my maid of honour? Once Bryce and I decide upon a date, and our venue is booked, you and I can discuss a simple dress code. I will not wear anything lavish on my wedding day. I trust you understand that I am not interested in your kind of bling and sparkle."

Boudie nodded as Florence put her hand to her chignon and resettled herself in her chair.

"All my life I've sought refuge in simple, practical wear, nothing outrageous."

Boudie, undaunted by her sister's firm words, pranced around the table. "At last, I have a reason to buy a suitable hat and wear a dress that will complement you, my darling girl."

Boudie listened while her sister shared the idea of an early summer wedding.

"Bryce," said Florence, "do paint a picture of our street covered in foliage and blossoms at that time of year and the natural arc the trees will make. And perhaps you might also draw up plans for the lawns and garden outside the church."

"I hope to plant and display your favourite sweet-smelling roses," said Bryce. "And I know Reverend Horatio Jones will agree to officiate our wedding ceremony."

Bryce's cheeks turned bright red.

She so wanted to intercede with her ideas, but Florence quickly interjected. "My fiancé knows well of my feelings about vicars, churches, and services. And please, no confetti. Can't abide the stuff." Florence shot her a warning look. "It seems proper to ask Molly Mulligan to give me away. She is the one who changed our lives for the better. Old Lulabelle can be our ring bearer if she is able to stand upright for the duration."

"I'm concerned for Molly," Bryce piped up. "She'll worry without news from us. Would you kindly call her and pass on a message? We shall stay for another day or so, and Lulabelle will need her care until our return."

"Leave it to me, Bryce," said Boudie. She excused herself, but before she stepped into the kitchen to make the call, she heard Mrs Cornell and Florence giggle. She watched them walk out to the reception area.

• • •

Excitement and the amount of consumed alcohol made Bryce stagger slightly. He linked his arm in Mrs Cornell's and unsteadily assisted her up the stairs.

Once he'd escorted the woman to her bedroom, he wandered towards Florence's room and knocked on her door.

After a few seconds, the door opened. She appeared in what he thought to be a most fetching white cotton and lace negligee. Her hair sat loosely around her shoulders. Bryce took her in his arms and smelled the perfume of her hair brushing against his face. He could not wait a moment longer and delicately traced her lips with his. Intoxicated with champagne and passion, he kissed her as he had never kissed a woman before. He fought against lifting her up and carrying her to the bed, but hesitated at that thought that might appear too presumptuous. His pulse raced, his heart soared, as did his ardour. Sorely tempted, he wondered if he should insist on sharing her bed on this momentous night. After all, it was the twenty-first century. On the other hand, he decided, perhaps it would be better to wait until they were married.

"I shall never tire of your kisses and intend to kiss you every day for the rest of our lives." He squeezed out ideas of a romantic night together. “Our youth may have faded, and time has robbed us, but when we kiss, I am back as we once were, innocent and free in India.” Reluctantly, he pulled away, but not before kissing both of Florence’s hands. To his pleasure, Florence kissed him on the cheek, and he bade her a good night’s sleep.

CHAPTER 37

JAMIE BEGAN TO CLEAR AWAY AND TIDY THE conservatory and kitchen in readiness for breakfast service the following morning. Boudie appeared, and he noticed a look of contentment spread across her face. "So much for a day of bonding with my sister! It was more a day of astonishing revelations and surprise visitors."

Over the course of the evening, he'd felt awkward at the dinner table. While the others chatted animatedly, he'd remained silent. *Like an armadillo, I could have curled myself into a tight ball, unexposed to what's going on around me,* he thought. Taking a seat at the table in the conservatory, he pulled out a chair for Boudie to sit next to him.

"Spill it," Boudie said. "What else have you to share with me?"

Moving closer to her, he told her about his departure earlier when he'd taken a Belleview bike and cycled towards St. Clements Bay. "I needed headspace and a break from cycling when I glimpsed a cafe sign and decided to stop. I sat outside, hoping to quiet my aching brain. Unprepared, I asked myself, 'Am I being haunted by insecurity?' because opposite me, a tangible Poppy La Grange took a seat. I realise Poppy and I were not about love, but my obsessive fixation. My naivety allowed that bloody woman to crush my heart."

He apologised again to Boudie, then said, "I've been such a fool. I got swept away by lust and a woman who made endless promises. Ones she'd never intended to keep."

Weighed down, feeling smothered by what he'd run away from, he didn't have a clue how to free himself from the pile of emotional rubble. "This afternoon I got another almighty punch. Not only did my ex appear at the table, but she had a child with her." His eyes felt like they'd flipped inside their sockets with an unbearable burning sensation. "I believe I am the father of this child. Her name is Melina. What do I do now? I need your help."

His adopted grandmother remained quiet. He watched her mull over this update. A deafening silence filled the room. Agitated, he walked into the kitchen, boiled a kettle of water, made two mugs of chamomile tea, and served them back in the conservatory.

Boudie stood and hugged him hard. "Rest assured, dear boy, I shall not desert you." She sat back, sipped the scalding tea, her eyes radiating a bubble of reassurance towards him.

"We've all done things we are not proud of. Most importantly, are you willing to take responsibility if DNA tests prove you are the father of this child? Whatever the outcome, you must face the truth. No more secrets or pretending. Is that a deal?"

"Whatever it takes. That is a promise."

• • •

Boudie brought the hot liquid to her lips and heard the clock at reception chime the midnight hour. "Right, young man, I have formulated Plan A. Here's our first step. We will go on a journey, one that will change your life again, but one that will provide an opportunity to make amends. To do that, we shall depart early tomorrow morning." She spotted the smallest of smiles creasing his mouth. "Here's Plan B. Let's set up a meeting with this Poppy woman. You need to hear the truth and get on with your life. I'll act as a mediator if you would like support." She yawned. Her eyelids felt heavy, and sleepiness was overtaking her. "I'm bushed. You best lock up, and for heaven's sake, get some sleep."

Padding into the kitchen, she boiled another kettle of water and prepared two mugs of hot chocolate. She placed the nightcaps on an embellished tray and made her way upstairs.

She first checked on Mrs Cornell, who appeared mummified as she lay on her back, mouth slack, swathed in a sheet and a duvet cover. Boudie felt empathy as she observed the woman's pale features and her wisps of hair across the goose-down pillow. Her glasses peeked out above the duvet cover, the reading light still on. After removing and placing the glasses on the bedside table, she switched off the lamp and left the room. She walked further down the corridor.

When she tapped on Colonel Bryce Beckwith's door, he swept it open. He wore a striped silk dressing gown.

"Ah, what an excellent service you provide." He thanked her and grasped the mug of hot chocolate.

"Promise you'll look after my sister. Love one another

a little more each day, for time has the habit of slipping by easily."

He nodded.

Close to tears, she bade him goodnight.

Knocking on Florence's door, she heard her sister's laboured voice. "It's late. Go away. I need my sleep."

"It's only me, darling girl, come to say goodnight and offer you a nightcap." She stepped into the room, sat on the edge of the bed, and observed Florence. Her face seemed quite flushed.

"Remember when we were little, and nanny or Mother would bring us hot chocolate in bed and read to us?" She set down the mug on Florence's bedside table. Her sister sat up in bed, and Boudie carried on talking.

"You shall make the loveliest of brides. After my years of designing glamourous kaftans for famous English and American actresses in the seventies, I can be your fairy godmother. Knowing the fabrics and colours that rest kindly against your skin, place complete trust in me, and you shall wear a most resplendent wedding outfit. We can make the necessary alterations, fittings with nips and tucks in all the right places." She flung her arms around Florence and wished her sweet dreams.

"I will not wear frills, nor do I not want any fuss. Are you listening to me?"

Boudie had already slipped out and then popped her head back around the door.

"Thrilled for you, darling girl. Sleep tight. I'll see you and your fiancé for breakfast."

She headed to the basement, which had the smallest bedroom in the house, and collapsed onto the single bed.

CHAPTER 38

JAMIE SWITCHED OFF THE KITCHEN LIGHTS AND went to double lock the entrance door. A cream envelope lay on the mat, his name marked clearly in calligraphy upon it. He picked up the piece of post and climbed the stairs to his room. Once settled in bed, he opened the envelope and read aloud.

Hey, Jamie,

I was as shocked as you were today. Seeing you alone and looking rather miserable, I decided to put my side of the story in writing.

I am truly sorry for the heartache I've caused. I thought I was doing the right thing, giving you creative freedom, allowing you to become the actor you were born to be.

I didn't mean to leave abruptly, but hey, there is never the right way of saying goodbye, is there?

I found out I was pregnant by my ex-boyfriend a few weeks before I resigned. I panicked. I would never have given you that responsibility.

Of course, I fancied you. Who wouldn't? You stood out on the day we met in college, unsure of yourself, mingling with some of the more confident students. I am ten years your senior. I was around long before you got past wearing white socks and shorts.

I realise what I did was out of line. You must believe I was more than fond of you. Really!

As it happens, my ex was once a professor at your College of Performing Arts. He claimed he was a free spirit and didn't relish any form of commitment. Nor did he want to get tied down by me and a baby. Sure, I chased you initially, but Melina is not yours.

My ex and I got back together when I moved to Little Shore to have our daughter.

Everything changes, doesn't it? Sometimes, we are given a second chance, as I have been with my partner and our beautiful Melina.

I would like to think we can move on.

Be happy and don't be afraid to love again. I hope you will go back to college and complete your degree. You don't belong in Little Shore. London and New York are waiting to discover you and your talent.

Best we do not contact each other again.

Please remember you will always have a special place in my heart. Great memories of our secret affair.

Poppy

Jamie let out a sigh. Poppy had sought him out for her selfish reasons. Time to dump his anger. What would he do with the next stage of his life? He had no idea, but he knew he could not waste another minute. First things first. He needed to sleep.

He switched off the night light and immediately crashed out and dreamt of taking several encores on an international stage to the sound of continuous applause.

CHAPTER 39

THE NEXT MORNING, BOUDIE STOOD ON THE steps of The Belleview and waved at her guests as they left. Walking through to reception, she heard animated voices and spied Florence and Bryce sitting side by side in the conservatory. They giggled as they held hands and ate breakfast. She moved into the room and again observed how Florence's skin glowed. Her sister had always been the serious one, hesitant to fully live life. Boudie believed with Bryce by her side Florence's new circumstances would bring her the happiness she deserved. Approaching the breakfast table, she placed her hands on both Florence's and Bryce's shoulders.

"I am handing over complete responsibility for The Belleview to you two lovebirds for the next few days. That said, dear sister, we will not be sharing precious time together. I feel duty bound to sort out a particular family dilemma and am driving Mrs Cornell home. Jamie shall accompany me. I'd like to stay at your house, Florence, until bridges are built with my adopted grandson," she said, taking a seat opposite them.

Florence gave Boudie a radiant smile. "I cannot think of a family situation that needs solving. Unless, of course, you wish to take care of my Lulabelle while I remain here? Whatever the mystery, of course you must stay at my home. Do remember to pack antihistamine tablets. You'll need protection against Lulabelle's long, hairy coat. Your business is in safe hands." Florence placed a kiss on Bryce's cheek.

Boudie, bursting with happiness for the engaged couple, said, "You can enjoy some peaceful days. I have no bookings until a week from Monday. You'll have a chance to brainstorm your impending nuptials in quiet." Boudie winked at Florence, stepped out of the conservatory, and headed upstairs to pack a bag and wake Jamie.

She'd telephoned Molly the night before and confirmed both her sister and Colonel Bryce Beckwith had arrived safely. She and Molly chatted amicably. Boudie told Molly the two tearaways had agreed to stay at The Belleview for a few days. She said she would drive Mrs Cornell home the following morning.

About to knock on Jamie's bedroom door, it swung open. An animated Jamie flung himself at her. "Guess what landed on the doormat last night?" He pushed a letter into Boudie's hands. "Before anything, please read my awesome news." They both stood on the landing while Boudie read the contents.

"Whoop, whoop," she shrieked on refolding the written pages and handed them back to Jamie. "My darling boy, now you can get on with your life and I believe more good news awaits you.

We really need to step on it and drive Mrs Cornell

home. Are you packed and ready? We can talk more in the car."

He nodded, picked up his bag, and raced down the stairs.

Boudie hastened down the corridor to check on Mrs Cornell.

• • •

Molly lay awake. The reflective green arms of the ticking clock glowed in the dark. Some of her concerns had dissipated following Boudie's call the night before. Her mobile vibrated on the bedside table. The whisperings of the night fast fading, she sat up in bed to read a text message.

Hey Ma,

Sorry it's taken so long. I've made a mess of things and I plan to make it up to you sooner than you think.

Love, Jamie

Molly re-read the message. Was this some sick joke? Someone who knew of her last three years of torment? She noted the telephone number wasn't Jamie's. Her hands shook. She sent a text.

Jamie, is this really you? For the love of God, please call me. Let me hear your voice so I know you are safe. Your ma has missed you.

Mobile in hand, she got out of bed, walked over to the bedroom window, and opened the curtains. Peering out, she felt ripples of excitement as she observed tinges of blue and pink suspended in the cold morning sky. She opened the bedroom window and whispered, "Can I finally divulge the secrets of my old life with my neighbours? Reveal how my life changed when my husband went off to live in France, after which, my only son opted out just as we were about to start over?" She came to a firm conclusion. Honesty would set her free, like a fog dissipating to reveal brighter days ahead. She checked the message again and dialled the number. No one answered.

"Could this really be my Jamie?" she wondered aloud as she walked into the bathroom.

Following her shower and getting dressed, she padded into the kitchen to make tea. Her thoughts bubbled. Clasping the hot mug of tea, she put it to her lips. The message from Jamie spun around in her head.

She grabbed her coat, wrapped a scarf around her neck, and left the apartment to walk across the road. She unlocked Florence's front door, and a waggy-tailed Lulabelle greeted her in the hallway. Putting Lulabelle on a leash, she walked down the path. She spotted a robin hopping territorially across Colonel Bryce Beckwith's lawn. "May you bring me the good luck I need today," she called to the bird.

As she closed the gate, she spotted Stanley waving from his usual vantage point. After ambling around the streets with Lulabelle for a bit, she headed to Stanley's house and walked through the open front door. Lulabelle padded over to Stanley and stretched her long body at his feet.

"Morning, Stanley. Hope you slept well. Time to prepare your breakfast." She'd placed the ingredients in the fridge the night before.

"What happened to you overnight, Ms. Mulligan? You seem more animated than usual."

Molly put one finger to her nose and tapped it. "Your food will be served shortly is all I can say for now." She stepped into the kitchen and set about frying two eggs and grilling some Irish bacon along with a few jumbo sausages bursting with meat. She realised the meal would not be complete for Stanley unless she made him a stack of hot buttered toast with marmalade, accompanied by tea.

"You've never lost your Irish touch. You know how best to feed a man. Fit for a king, this is." He nearly drooled when she placed the tray in front of him. He shovelled forkfuls of food into his mouth. What a cacophony, she thought, as he slurped the tea noisily from his mug.

"Stanley, there is no need to rush. You'll give yourself indigestion. I need you to be well for my yoga class later."

He nodded, but didn't look at her. "Sure, thing. Let's go do yoga."

She spied melted butter from the toast dribbling down his chin and onto his red-chequered shirt.

"I'm in heaven. This is the best breakfast I've enjoyed in a long while. Ta love. Do me a favour? Don't tell Rita what I've eaten. She would only worry about me cholesterol." Stanley winked at her.

Buoyed by renewed hope, she fast walked out of the front door, and left him and Lulabelle together while she went to change for her class.

• • •

Once she'd retrieved the odd pair of yoga students, Lulabelle on her lead and Stanley in his wheelchair, they headed up the path. In the church hall, she prepared and waited for the group to arrive. Her mobile on silent, she placed it on a nearby chair. Lulabelle flopped down on her squishy bed in the corner. She looked unimpressed by the meditative music, *One Step at a Time*, by Mitten. The sound flowed through the room.

With only minutes to go before the class began, an out of breath Reverend Horatio Jones and his wife, Gabriella, hurried into the hall. They each shook her hand. She watched them inhale the jasmine incense that puffed cloud-like and rose to the dome-shaped ceiling. Taking their places, they laid down on yoga mats.

After taking a few deep breaths, Molly said, "Welcome, everyone. As we breathe in, let us close our eyes and take a moment to get centred. Allow all outside thoughts to fall away. Let's continue to focus on our breath." Placing her hands in front of her chest in prayer, her yoga and stretch class began.

CHAPTER 40

IT WAS ALMOST NOON. THROUGH THE MEDITATIVE silence, Molly instructed Reverend Horatio Jones and his wife, Gabriella, to sit cross-legged on their yoga mats. The rest of the group formed a circle, sitting on chairs around her.

"For those sitting, plant your feet firmly on the floor and let us turn our palms toward the ceiling," she said, leading them into the last salutations and breathing exercises. "Stanley, relax your jaw." She watched him visibly relax. "Good man."

Following the final reflection, the squeak of the hall door broke the calm. She heard a heavy shuffling sound and the tapping of a stick hitting the floor. Cool air swept across Molly's face.

Opening her eyes, she spotted Mrs Cornell walking towards Stanley. On reaching him, she gave her husband a look of tenderness and flopped onto a nearby chair.

Beyond where Mrs Cornell sat, two people had

entered the room and sat in the shadowy light at the back of the hall.

With a bow of her head, Molly called out, "Namaste."

After one-and-a-half hours of being in deep contemplation together, the class clapped their hands in gratitude. The soporiferous music stopped playing, and she thanked her students for their participation, adding, "Excellent. Well done."

She glimpsed Stanley turning in his chair towards his beloved wife. He rubbed her hand. The woman seemed lost in some dream.

From the back of the room, a petite woman stood up and walked towards her. "At last, we meet. Boudie Scott-Thomas; Florence's younger sister," the woman said as she reached her. "As you can see, Mrs Cornell is back, safe and well." She swept her hand over to where Molly's neighbour now dozed. Florence's sister turned to the man who sat near Rita. "You must be Stanley. You have a devoted wife who clearly adores you. What a blessing that love still blossoms between you after your many years of marriage." Boudie shook Stanley's hand firmly.

"Thanks for taking care of the missus." Stanley shook his wife's shoulder.

Mrs Cornell opened her eyes. "Am I home now?"

"Indeed, you are home, Rita love, all down to this good lady." He turned back to Boudie. "I can see she looks well. A day away and a sleepover must have done her good. Thank you for your kindness and hospitality. Yer welcome to come across the road and have a cuppa while you're here," said Stanley.

Molly turned away, searching the back of the hall to see who had accompanied Florence's sister. A young man stood waiting.

Boudie beckoned to him to come forward. "I believe this is someone you know. Another lost traveller who is returning home." She stepped away from Molly.

Molly immediately recognised her son. She saw a glint in his eyes as he walked, concentrating only on her.

"Hey, Ma. I promised I'd come back. Didn't know Boudie had a plan when I sent my text last night."

Molly froze, her bare feet stuck to the spot on the floor. Jamie drew closer, towering over her.

"Is it really you? Tell me I am not dreaming." She clutched her hammering heart.

"Yeah, it's really me." Without warning, he swept her up in his arms and spun her around several times.

"Oh, my dearest Jamie." Molly stroked her son's face. Melting into his arms, she held him tight and felt him squeeze her close as he eased her down.

She heard the class members stacking chairs against one of the walls. Gathering their coats and bags, they trickled out the door. She nodded in thanks to Reverend Horatio Jones and Gabriella. They ushered the yoga students, along with Mrs Cornell and Stanley, out of the hall.

Locking eyes on Jamie, the steel vise that had pressed into her head for three long years, finally released itself. They both wept.

Jamie's face reddened. "I'll make it up to you, Ma, even if it takes me the rest of my life. I'm sorry for the hurt and grief I've caused."

"I felt racked with guilt and couldn't understand why the abrupt departure. I thought I'd let you down as a mother. You were my light, my reason to carry on after your father went away. This nightmare is finally over, and you are home." Pure love trickled into her whole being. Anguish fell away, and she stopped trembling. She looked up and saw Boudie starting toward the door.

Jamie had noticed her glance and said, "Hey, Boudie, hold on." He walked over and took Boudie's hand, bringing her back over to where Molly stood. "Ma, if not for this woman, I don't know where I would have ended up. She's been my shining light, guiding and taking care of me."

Molly felt another stir of emotion as Jamie wrapped an arm around both hers and Boudie's shoulders. He bent down and kissed each of them on the cheek.

"Boudie, please join us back at my apartment," Molly said. "We can talk there."

Boudie shook her head. "Thanks, but I think it best you have time together to fill in the many blank pages. We have lots of days to make plans and as I'm staying at Florence's, I need to acquaint myself with Lulabelle."

Molly watched Boudie fetch the dog from the squishy bed. Lulabelle kept her head low, ears pricked back, and they walked in tandem towards the exit.

• • •

Boudie did not look back at Molly and Jamie, but the atmosphere in the hall felt wrought with emotion. *Finally, the woman's tormented years are over, and they'll forge a new kind of relationship. With Kit gone, does this mean Jamie is also lost to me?*

A sharpness tore at her heart, but once outside, her heart lifted at what might be. "Lead on, Lulabelle. Point me in the direction of your mistress's house." The dog wagged her tail and gazed into Boudie's eyes, as if to say, *Okay, I'm ready to go home.*

CHAPTER 41

MOLLY MADE A COMPLETE CIRCLE AROUND the empty hall. Silently, she watched Jamie collect the yoga mats and place them in a cupboard. With a nod from her, he packed the portable audio system, along with the incense sticks and their wooden holders, into her tote bag. "I'm at a loss over where to begin, Ma," he eventually said. "But I need your forgiveness."

"What do you say that we take it nice and slow? Just you and me. You are not the same boy who left home in his first year at college. You're a mature adult now. One I plan to get to know. Life and what's happened has changed both of us." The pain of three lost years shot through her like a crack of lightning, then just as quickly vanished. "As long as you assure me you really are back, I know we can work out the rest." She could see the remorse etched across Jamie's face.

"I've been a jerk, Ma."

"There is no blame. My worries are over." She moved close to him. "I never gave up and did my best to find you. I've never stopped loving you and believing you would return." Speaking of how the last years cut her deeply, she said, "Every drop of blood in my body ran almost dry. Sometimes, I thought I'd lost my mind, trying to get through the endless hours. Thankfully, the nightmare is over. We've been given a second chance."

Molly forced herself to breathe. "My community, my studies, and yoga classes re-enforced my resolve to carry on and keep my sanity. Yet, these friends and neighbours knew nothing of my old life and the secrets I'd hidden until today."

She grasped both of his hands. "Promise me this—no matter what you decide to do with your life, no more withholding feelings. Please don't take off without talking things through, eh?"

"That's two things, and I promise I will." He hugged her.

They linked arms, headed out the door and walked in step down the road to her apartment.

The following morning, while Jamie slept, Molly left him a note on the kitchen table.

> *I'll be at Florence's place just across the road. Time to get to know the woman who watched out for my son these last years. Back soon. Love, your ma.*

She slipped across to meet Boudie. They sat in Florence's kitchen and drank coffee. Lulabelle stretched out at their feet, fast asleep.

Within the hour, she returned, but there was no sign of her son. She sneaked upstairs, gently opening his bedroom door. He lay cradled in the duvet, deep in slumber. She noted his steady breath. Grateful for the gift of his return, she stared at his sweet and handsome face. Back in the kitchen, she hummed a song and danced nimbly, her feet barely touching the floor.

She would spoil him by preparing a feast. The aroma wafting around the house of fresh coffee, bacon grilling, and bread toasting would tempt her son to appear. They would eat breakfast together again. The thought elated her.

CHAPTER 42

BEFORE THE FIERY GLOW OF THE SUMMER'S DAY appeared, Colonel Bryce Beckwith paced up and down the path to the church gates. Dressed in dungarees, holding a water mister in one hand and a set of shears in the other, he inspected the results of his handiwork. The street glowed in the morning light. Heart-shaped pink bunting, entwined with garlands of fresh-scented roses in the shade of buttermilk, adorned the route from Florence's house to where the wedding service would take place. He'd also grown sweet peas in the palest of lilac and pink. They rested on newly painted white pillars outside St. Johns, tied in bundles of satin ribbon. He inhaled the perfumed air, feeling satisfied with the results of his endeavours. He'd fulfilled a promise to his bride. With a great sense of pride, he gazed around the lush green gardens. High in the trees, birds sang in unison. "Indeed, this is a glorious day," he called out.

His heart felt jittery. Would Florence approve? Thinking about her bluntness, he knew she would not hesitate to say so if the colours of his plant designs did not meet her expectations.

Following an earlier ritual of a close shave, he'd trimmed his moustache, followed with a moisturiser of shea butter and ginger. The ingredients gave him a refreshing glow, he thought. He was ready for his first kiss as Florence's husband.

Bringing himself back to what lay ahead, he looked to the church steeple and the view across the Kent countryside. A wren flew past and into the foliage, singing her song. A single white feather floated in front of him, landing at his feet. He bent down to pick up the curling feather. It must be a symbol, he thought. Perhaps an angel was watching over him and the wedding service and the reception would be a well-ordered event.

He headed back to his house. As a mark of respect for Florence's and his birth and heritage in India, he hoped his baking would impress her, too. He placed the two trays of vol-au-vents he'd prepared earlier into the oven. The smell of the thimble-sized coronation chicken and Indian spiced salmon with spinach canapés filled the tiny kitchen. Locally brewed cider, beer, and refined sparkling wine from the chalky Kent plains sat in the shade outside the kitchen door, immersed in buckets of ice.

He recalled the day Florence and he had agreed to a wedding reception. As the groom, he felt responsible; this wedding affair would be best, overseen by him. Molly and Boudie suggested a street party and confirmed they could deliver a memorable reception with a local team of caterers.

He remembered Florence's insistence that he not become involved with the setting and dressing of trestle tables, or the setup of the overhead awning for shade. He realised people would soon arrive, and he began to visualise the wedding scene.

He'd been taken off guard by the buzz within the community. "We've never seen such activity," neighbours told him. Some students from Molly's yoga class had insisted on providing food and wedding decorations. Florence had approved.

He checked his watch. In two-and-a-half hours he would take his vows. He said a prayer, then whispered into the morning sunshine, "Florence, please don't change your mind. It's all set. Don't back out now."

• • •

Propped up in bed, Florence sipped her morning tea. Her stomach fluttered, and she understood what other brides meant when they talked of having butterflies on their wedding day. In equal measures, a headiness enveloped her. What would today and their married years be like? She assured herself that life with Bryce would be the happiest of adventures.

Florence knew overdue words were required between her and Boudie. Since the marriage announcement at The Belleview, she'd repeatedly cautioned her sister, saying, "Surprises regarding my wedding dress are strictly off the menu. On my wedding day, I want to look in the mirror and recognise myself as a bride, not some version of how you think I should look."

Downstairs, she could hear Boudie clattering about. Preparing breakfast, Florence assumed. Her sister sang along, although out of tune, to *You Can't Hurry Love* by Phil Collins as it played on the radio.

Boudie appeared at the open bedroom door, holding a tray. Lulabelle stood behind her.

"Rise and shine, my darling girl. I have made us a hearty breakfast." Boudie carried in a tray filled with plates of fresh grapefruit segments, poached eggs, Florence's favourite raspberry conserve, and croissants. She laid the food out on a table by the bay window. Sniffing the air, she left the room for a moment, then reappeared. "Dear, oh dear. I'm afraid in Colonel Bryce Beckwith's zealousness to impress you, the aromas of his baking are currently filling your kitchen. Luckily, I found a fan and have closed the back door."

In one hand, Boudie held a cafetiere of fresh coffee. In the other, she held a single pink rose in a slim crystal vase with a note attached. "The rose and note are from your loved one. He couldn't help himself and knocked on the front door earlier." Boudie set the vase, note, and coffee down.

• • •

Florence complied with the summons to get out of bed, sit with her sister, and eat at the table.

Quite taken by the fragrance of the rose, she tentatively opened the envelope.

"Oh, do share," Boudie said.

Florence obliged and read the contents aloud.

My dearest Florence,

I know it is tradition that I must not see my bride until you and I stand side by side at the altar today.

With this rose, I wanted to tell you I sincerely love you. I also know that as husband and wife we shall enjoy an exceptionally happy life together.

Tenderly CBB x

"The path of true love has finally found its way into your heart," Boudie said.

Florence felt a lump form in her throat.

The two sisters ate breakfast and drank coffee. Florence noticed Boudie had sneaked in a chilled snipe of champagne that she had diluted with orange juice to kick-start the day. They raised their glasses in a toast. Florence caught Boudie's arm. "I owe you an apology, one I put to the back of my mind for many years. But it needs to be said."

"And pray, what is that?" Frowning in concern, Boudie leaned across to pull wisps of hair from her sister's face.

"You once asked my advice, desperate to free yourself from the constraints set by our parents. You felt trapped, you said, by Mother and Father meddling in our lives. They placed far too much pressure on us to play by the same rules they had been brought up with. They wanted you to take life more seriously, I remember, and marry a man of immense standing. You were single-minded and wanted to make your own decisions, whatever the outcome."

She looked at Boudie.

A ghostly tension filled the room.

"You needed help with ideas to set up a design and tailoring business in London to include bespoke kaftans. You asked if I thought your idea would work."

Florence had chastised herself over the years for never giving Boudie the time and support. Especially these last few years, such unkindness towards her sister had gnawed at her.

"I grieved, and continued to feel anger at Bryce's betrayal," Florence explained. "You, whose beauty and charisma I could never match, lived with mother in India and once you came to London, you were hailed as the toast of the town. I read about you in the social columns in father's paper."

Florence paused. The time had come to clear the air before she married Bryce.

"I suppose your intention had been to seek my acceptance. Back then, I looked plain and stuffy, the daughter who always did her father's bidding. First on the farm in the wilds of Tamshire, then later I obliged him by working at the War Office in London."

"Oh dear," said Boudie. "The truth of the matter is this. In the early seventies and with times changing, I'd probably not have heeded your advice. Determined to be independent, your words would have been wasted. I was petulant and did exactly what suited me," Boudie declared.

"In any case, I chose to ignore any of your grand plans. I suppose deep down I knew you'd find your own imitable way. And you have," Florence added, wiping away a tear. "Can you forgive this soppy old fool who has waited until now to make amends?" She accepted a linen handkerchief from Boudie and blew her nose before continuing.

"I'm proud of you, your tenacity and what you have accomplished, even your talent in redesigning one of your kaftans into my wedding dress." Florence's eyes darted across the room to where Boudie's handiwork hung. On the outside of her mirrored wardrobe, the grandest of dresses awaited her. She even approved of the well-placed handstitched beading that reflected through the window and shined like a burst of sunshine.

Boudie reached across and Florence let her wipe her tears.

"As it happened, without help from the family, I opened my business in tailoring and design. A Common Trade is what mother named my business. Father never understood why I refused to content myself and marry a titled man. Look here, darling girl, this is no time to dig up the past on your happy day. There's no need to reproach yourself. We were young. What did we know then? We both struggled to find out who we were and who we'd become," Boudie said softly.

Florence sniffled. "Well, thank you. On a good note, I am about to marry the man I love, and you and I are reunited as sisters."

"There you are. See? That's a start." Boudie hugged and kissed her on each cheek.

Florence quickly gathered herself back to her no-nonsense, practical self. "This does not give you a license to play havoc with my grooming or makeup. As the bride to be, I must insist again, please, no fuss or shocks." Florence enjoyed hearing herself use the word *bride*. "Not too much of anything. A little colour on my lips and cheeks shall do me just fine."

"You will look positively beautiful, and I can promise Bryce shall not be disappointed. Time to get ready and escort you to St John's, along with my new friends, Molly and Lulabelle. You and Bryce have some serious vows to take. Before I forget, I have a vital piece of information to share before you two depart on your honeymoon."

CHAPTER 43

Colonel Bryce Beckwith had dressed in an army uniform of dark green. A gold-plaited cord decorated one shoulder, and three shiny medals hung on the left-hand side of the jacket. His freshly steamed colonel's hat was trimmed with red ribbon and sat in position on his head. Black laced-up shoes, buffed to a high shine, caught the morning light. He almost marched through the main entrance towards the open door of St. John's church.

Reverend Horatio Jones greeted him, wearing his celebratory vestments. They shook hands, stepped together into the main aisle, and headed towards the nave. Strains of a potent rhythm caught Bryce's attention.

"Bryce, I hope you don't mind, but I thought we'd begin with an upbeat song, *Marry Me* by Bruno Mars, allowing the congregation to soak up the atmosphere of love."

Flustered, Bryce stood where he would take his vows, believing this modern music to be completely unacceptable, especially for a man who'd once held the position of colonel.

His voice rose in panic as he said, "Reverend, this is not the music Florence and I agreed to. Everything must be perfect on this sacred day. My bride is due to arrive any minute. I insist we have our chosen music playing when Molly and Boudie enter the church." He looked around the empty pews, glimpsing the reverend's daughter, Grace, and Molly's son, Jamie, who waited near the entrance for their cue to head inside.

About to have more words with the reverend, to his relief, he spotted Gabriella, Grace's mother, and she immediately went to switch off the sound of Bruno Mars. After doing so, she nodded to her husband. He said to Bryce, "My dear fellow, there is no need to fret. All is in hand. Please excuse me for a few minutes. I see Gabriella wishes to speak with me."

Bryce watched the vicar walk towards the vestry.

• • •

Hands in his pockets, head down, Jamie kicked the shingle stones with his new patent-leather shoes and flicked a self-conscious look at Grace. He wore a morning suit, and his jacket was decorated with buds of pink roses pinned to the lapel. "Think it's fair to say we are the youngest new things at this wedding ceremony," he joked.

"My mother mentioned you attended The Performing Arts College," Grace said.

"Yeah."

"Just wondered, as I haven't seen you around before today."

"That's because I was away being someone else for a while." He tried to laugh. "Oops, I've turned bright red, I fear. I sometimes get prickly heat." He rubbed his face and continued to kick the shingle.

"Probably best if we head inside," said Grace. "My father gets carried away with wedding ceremonies. Unfortunately for the bride and groom, he doesn't always listen to what music they may have requested. I think Colonel Bryce Beckwith is looking for support." Grace grinned and pointed to where Bryce stood alone by the altar.

Something about the reverend's daughter fascinated Jamie. Following the speeches and usual wedding formalities being executed, he hoped to spend more time in her company.

"Are you hanging around for the summer?" He caught himself staring at her sparkling sea-green eyes.

"Guess I could if there was a reason to."

He stretched out his arm. Grace nodded and linked hers through his. Stepping inside, they walked up the aisle together.

Standing next to Colonel Bryce Beckwith, he again observed Grace. He admired the dress she wore, a swirl of pink satin accessorised with a matching pink corsage. She daintily walked to a corner of the nave and sat at a piano. He continued to look in her direction while she opened the lid, watching her slim fingers glide over the keys. She began to sing the melody, *Morning Has Broken*. He found her angelic voice soothing.

He felt Colonel Bryce Beckwith nudge his elbow. "That's more like it," said the colonel.

Jamie looked at Grace and gave her a thumbs-up, then whispered in the colonel's ear, "This is your wedding day. Don't look so worried. I'm fully committed to the role of being your best man and taking care of you."

"Have you put the rings in a safe place, dear boy?" Bryce nervously asked.

"They are tied firmly onto Lulabelle's back on a velvet cushion, as Miss Scott Thomas directed."

"A risky business," Bryce muttered.

The purity of Grace's voice pulled at Jamie's heart. Turning around, he watched the procession of guests filter into their designated pews. He patted the colonel's arm and handed him a handkerchief to wipe the beads of perspiration from his brow.

CHAPTER 44

Boudie walked up the path to St John's with Lulabelle at her side. On reaching the arched entrance of the church, she noticed hand-cut carved letters on each stone. Perhaps, she thought, they marked a moment in history. High above the arch, she glimpsed an impressive sundial set in marble and brass.

She took time to observe Bryce's gardening skills. Climbing pink roses stood in dramatic pots on either side of the church door. Lulabelle pulled on the lead, trying to sniff at their perfume.

Boudie, dressed in shades of lilac to complement Florence's wedding outfit, wore a wide-brimmed hat with a sweeping cream feather that curled around on one side. In her opinion, this seemed a discreet homage to the excitement of the day and would be acceptable to Florence.

Lulabelle wore three matching lilac plumes. Boudie

had stitched them onto a purple velvet cushion and secured the cushion onto the dog's back. Florence's and Bryce's wedding rings sat in the centre, tied with a ribbon of the same colour.

"Good girl," she said, patting the dog.

She sneaked a peek through the main door and spied Bryce's well-placed array of flowers in vases the size of roman urns on either side of the altar. Always drawn to colour, her eyes drifted to the red, orange, and yellow stained-glass windows rising high above and behind the altar.

Turning, she watched Florence and Molly, arm in arm, deep in conversation.

She'd taken great pleasure in remodelling one of her kaftans for Florence. She gazed proudly at the wedding outfit skimming her sister's waist and the scalloped hem brushing Florence's ankles. Boudie had patiently pinned and dressed Florence's hair into a chignon and created a circle of pink rosebuds meshed into a gold band, now positioned on her head. Both sisters held bouquets of lavender, delicate sweet pea, and fragrant ivory roses threaded and held together with satin ribbon. She and Molly had designed the bouquets.

Molly broke through her thoughts when she said, "I have to say the fragrance from Colonel Bryce Beckwith's flowers and aromatic herbs would lift anyone's spirits."

She felt delighted with the bond Molly and she had formed over the past months as they prepared for the wedding event. Their closeness had been helped by a shared love for Jamie and Florence. They exchanged smiles and moved to stand on either side of Florence.

"Darling girl, you are quite the radiant bride. You are about to take Colonel Bryce Beckwith's breath away," Boudie whispered to her sister.

• • •

Following the emotional return of Jamie, a different kind of contentment filled Molly's heart. Touched by the respect and care he'd bestowed on her, she felt heartened by the steps he'd also taken to renew contact with his father. She prayed father and son would form a close relationship.

Over the last months, Brandon O'Neill and she had enjoyed candlelight dinners. To her delight, Jamie approved.

"Ma, as long as you are happy and Brandon looks out for you, you'll have no issues with me," he'd said.

On hearing she had a man in her life, Florence and Colonel Bryce Beckwith insisted she invite Brandon to their wedding.

Lost in dreams of an all-around brighter future, she heard Florence whisper, "We best get on with the ceremony."

Molly apologised for her lack of concentration and took one of Florence's hands in hers. "Are you ready?"

"Too late for second thoughts now. I've been waiting for a fairy-tale ending since I was twelve years of age."

Molly gazed at her neighbour's animated face. The entrance music, *Let the Bright Seraphim* by Handel, began to play.

She inspected Florence from the top of her head to the tips of her toes and gave her approval. "Lulabelle, go walk by Boudie." She beckoned for Lulabelle and Boudie, an unusual pairing, to step forward. The maid of honour and the dog almost glided towards the altar. Florence and she followed behind them, arm in arm.

Molly's heart skipped a beat when she spied Brandon sitting at the back of the church. She took in his grandness and admired his suit of dark navy. It suited his handsome face and olive complexion.

At the front of the church, she spotted Bryce grasping his trembling hands together. As they drew close, she placed Florence's hand in his. She saw tears in his eyes as he turned to look at his bride. "May you treat each other with love, compassion, and kindness throughout your married life," she said. Stepping away to take a seat close to the altar, she heard Bryce say, "My dear, you look wonderful."

Molly locked eyes on Jamie and blew him a kiss.

Reverend Horatio Jones walked from the vestry to take up his position on the first step below the altar. He began. "Brethren, we are gathered here today for the union of two people."

The entrance doors to St John's crashed open.

"Are we late? Sorry, sorry. You see, my old wedding outfit doesn't fit anymore," Mrs Cornell shouted at the reverend and seated guests. "I had to search for something else to wear."

Molly looked towards Mrs Cornell, who wore a rather tight-fitting dove-grey two-piece suit. The woman huffed and puffed and pushed Stanley up the aisle.

"We see no reason why Colonel Bryce Beckwith and Florence Scott Thomas should not be joined in holy matrimony. Is that the right thing to say?" Mrs Cornell called out.

"Thank you, Mrs Cornell." Reverend Horatio Jones put his hand up and calmly asked someone near her to aid Mrs Cornell into a pew.

Molly pitied red-faced Stanley, who sat in his wheelchair next to his out-of-breath wife.

"Sorry, yer reverend," said Stanley.

Reverend Horatio Jones nodded and smiled down on Florence and Colonel Bryce Beckwith.

"Dearly beloved gathered here today, let us begin the

wedding ceremony for this couple who wish to take their solemn vows of matrimony."

CHAPTER 45

From the Monte Carlo airport, Molly and Jamie took a train. Within thirty-eight minutes, they found themselves, suitcases in hand, standing outside the station in Menton. The city's architecture, painted buildings, and the famous Côte d'Azur's skies immediately captured Molly's attention. With hardly a tourist in sight, she felt the city's uplifting energy and hoped Jamie felt the same.

"What do you say we take ourselves off to a beach? Go fill our lungs with Mediterranean Sea air, and paddle in crystal clear water. Then we can drive to your father's café," she suggested.

"Sure thing," he responded.

Looking to hail a cab, she spotted a statuesque young woman climbing out of a nearby sleek silver Mercedes. The woman was dressed in a chauffeur's uniform. She waved and walked towards them.

"Bonjour. My name is Patrice. Welcome to the

French Riviera. Rory Mulligan requested I drive you to his bistro."

Before she had a chance to thank Patrice, Molly heard Jamie speak in French. He must have conveyed their wish to head to the seashore, for Patrice said, "On this summer's day, why not?" Patrice picked up their suitcases.

"I'm impressed. I didn't know you spoke French." Molly felt proud of Jamie's efforts to make this trip work.

"After we agreed to travel and visit Pa, I decided to learn some basic French via audio. It seems I'm mastering the language." He opened the passenger door and assisted her into the back seat.

She watched him settle in the front while Patrice placed the two suitcases in the boot. "Your father is obviously trying to dazzle us, hiring a top-notch S-class Mercedes." Molly slowly stroked the leather interior of the seats. Jamie turned and nodded in agreement.

Patrice positioned herself behind the wheel and checked the wing mirror. "Let's go. Allons-y," she called out.

They drove through narrow streets, ending up on a promenade with the aqua-marine blue sea before them.

"Why so many pizza restaurants and ice cream cafes?" Molly asked.

"Menton is the nearest French city before crossing over to Italy. I believe it influences the food here," Patrice replied.

Molly inhaled the sea air and dipped her feet in the refreshing, sparkling water, while Jamie and their chauffeur chatted. An hour passed before they climbed back into the Mercedes. Patrice took them on a leisurely drive through more of the winding cobbled-stone streets that shone with rays of morning light. Molly squeezed Jamie's shoulder as they arrived at Rory's

Brasserie and Art Gallery.

She waited while Patrice jumped out and carried the cases from the boot to the entrance of the café/bistro. She emerged from the car, followed by Jamie. Not to be outdone by her son, she said, "Merci, Patrice. Bonne journée."

"Bonne vacance." Patrice shook Molly's hand and kissed Jamie on each cheek. Molly observed the bustle of French outdoor café life. Remembering Rory's friends describing this atmosphere, she noted the traditional French tightly woven wicker tables and chairs in green and red. Men, women, and children sat drinking coffee, fresh orange juice, or citron pressé accompanied by croissants and fruit-conserve.

A few scrappy looking dogs sat upright on their owners' laps and bowls of water and biscuit treats rested underneath the tables.

She looked at Jamie, who, like her, seemed excited by the interactive hub. Voices hummed and animated conversations grew louder. Molly noticed a few customers sitting alone, reading their morning papers and pulling heavily on cigarettes. A wiry-framed man appeared from the shadows of the open cafe doors. He walked eagerly towards them. Gone was his physical solidness, but she recognised Rory's spirit of times past. He'd grown a beard and grey touched his temples. She noted his facial features held deep lines, especially at the corners of his eyes. Red-framed glasses sat on the tip of his nose and a loose-knit blue jumper hung from his shoulders.

"Ah, would you look at you? Sure, you haven't changed one bit. As for those eyes, they still captivate me." Rory awkwardly took hold of her shoulders and kissed her on each cheek.

"Thank you for your kind compliments. I'll accept them." She laughed nervously. Recalling the love they'd once shared, she felt heartened by the efforts she'd made to re-establish a friendship with him, especially since Jamie's return. Watching her ex-husband go to their son, she willed the father/son knots to untie.

"Hi, Pa." Jamie stretched out his hand to shake his father's.

"Come here." Rory reached up and wrapped his sinewy arms around Jamie. "I'm sorry for the pain and suffering I've caused. I don't blame you if you've felt resentful."

"I was an angry teenager when you left, and Ma took the brunt of that rejection. But hey, we're here now." Jamie hugged his father, then pulled away.

She could feel a hush as customers stared at her and Jamie. They stood silently while Rory gathered himself.

"How about a café au lait and some breakfast?" he suggested.

"A black coffee for me," she replied.

"Me, too. Coffee would be great." Jamie nodded at his father and escorted her to an outside corner table.

To her left, she caught sight of her reflection in a mirrored glass window in Rory's art gallery. Next to the silhouette, she noticed an easel displayed in the centre of the window facing out to the street. She stared at the portrait of a young woman, recognising the painting; a replica of the one resting against Jamie's bedroom wall back at her apartment.

"And who might this beautiful young woman be?" Rory teased. He had followed them to their table, peering first towards the painting in the window, then at her.

"That's from a long time ago and we've both changed, haven't we? Thankfully, that chapter blessed us with our son." She rested her head against Jamie's shoulder. "They are well-read pages from another book. I would like to believe we have both moved on and formed a different love." Although she willed her voice to hold kindness for Rory, she noticed a dart of envy cross his face. Should she reach out to her ex-husband? But her heart no longer flipped at the sight of the man she'd once been so besotted over.

"Wonderful memories," Rory said, "and the portrait keeps my spirits alive. It's okay. I get it. Best bring the coffees." Rory stroked his beard, looking crestfallen. She watched him slink back through the entrance door.

Soaking up the heat of the sun, she became even more aware of the locals. They continued to stare in her and Jamie's direction. "I believe we are the morning's news as newly arrived foreigners," she whispered to Jamie. "Your father is not a bad man. For a long time, he'd been depressed. Thankfully, he's turned his life around and here's the proof of his success." She swept her hand toward the café building and gallery. "Forgiveness is key. Don't we all deserve happiness and another chance to get it right?" She placed a hand on Jamie's arm.

• • •

Jamie recalled his pa enclosing a photo of the three of them smiling at the camera—the same photo Boudie found on his bedroom floor at The Belleview. He had to give his father credit for not giving up on him.

Whatever you may think of me, I will love you and your mother until the day I die.

He often said that, or something similar on postcards, sent to a younger Jamie at the old family home.

Filled with a new compassion for his father, Jamie decided to do his best to let go of any repressed anger. He hoped they could rebuild a strong relationship.

"I'm fine, Ma, really." He kissed her cheek. "After my behaviour, I can see everyone has stuff to go through."

"Remember, your father wants you here. It's only two weeks. See how it goes. Relax and have some fun. If you feel stifled, you can always walk away."

• • •

A few minutes later, Rory appeared at their table and served them coffee.

Molly glanced up and down the street. A taxi appeared and parked at the side of the pavement. She stood up when she saw Brandon O'Neill step out of the cab. She turned towards Rory. "I'm not staying."

Following Florence and Colonel Bryce Beckwith's wedding, she'd taken some brave steps. Brandon and she had enjoyed a closer relationship.

"Easy does it. I'll roll with you," Brandon had assured her. And he'd kept that promise. She mentally hugged herself in gratitude for embracing a second chance at finding love.

Brandon walked over. He blocked the space between her and Rory, who remained quiet.

"Hey, man, good to meet you again after all this time." Brandon slapped Rory on the back. "Are we set to go?" Brandon pulled her to him.

"Ah, come on, there's no need to rush off, is there?" said Rory.

She saw the disappointment in Rory's eyes, that glint of mischief long gone. Perhaps, she thought, he realises whatever his expectations were of us getting back together, it's not going to happen.

"After all this time apart, surely you can stay and enjoy a drink?" Rory added.

Molly looked at Jamie and then at Brandon.

"It's okay, Pa. Ma is not going anywhere until she drinks her coffee, and I'm with you for the next two weeks. There's no sweat."

She nodded in agreement, took Brandon's outstretched hand while Rory pulled up some chairs, and they all sat down together.

CHAPTER 46

Colonel Bryce Beckwith and Florence walked arm in arm, stopping for a while to check the newly manicured lawns. Set amongst a grassy bank leading to Florence's parents' house, banana and mango trees bowed down, heavy with fruit. Monkeys howled overhead, hiding in the branches.

The newlyweds turned and gazed into each other's eyes.

Following sunrise, Colonel Bryce Beckwith had stepped out to the garden and picked a fresh orchid with stripes of white and pink. Before sitting down to eat breakfast, he'd ceremoniously placed the flower into Florence's neatly set bun. Now, turning to his wife, he noticed the flower had disappeared. Must be the moisture and humidity in the air, he thought, for Florence's hair hung limply around her shoulders.

"My dear, to think I hesitated for all those years. I'm sorry I didn't stand up to my parents' disapproval when you were the woman I loved. I am a better man for marrying you." Bryce's eyes followed the ripples of the river to his right. "Life is like this river, burbling and passing us by."

"Better late than never, my good man," said Florence. "Most importantly, we are where we belong. There will be no regrets while on our honeymoon."

Florence clutched a deed letter, still not believing her luck. On her wedding day, Boudie had revealed one of their mother's secrets, disclosing what she'd put in place before returning to England at their father's insistence.

"To think my mother foresaw that one of us would eventually return to our homeland. I'm still in shock." Florence waved the faded papers in the air. "Our mother left one box for me and another for Boudie, a copy of the deed letters in each, in case either of us returned."

Florence scrunched up her eyes and began to read aloud a few lines from the note her mother had written.

If you are reading this, you have returned. My heart broke the day you, my eldest daughter, had to depart from our life in India. This is your home for as long as you live out your days. I pray you will be happy back where you belong.

Florence touched her husband's perspiring face. Her hands shook as she placed the letter and deed in the top pocket of his shirt. She recalled the day Bryce and Boudie proposed that Florence and Bryce celebrate their honeymoon in India.

"Imagine this as Boudie's and mother's wedding gift to us. I cannot believe my sister took on the project of tracking down the families of the original staff who worked for my mother, even engaging some of them to repaint and clean the interior of the house before our arrival."

The humidity remained high, and a warm wind blew around them. Even wearing another of Boudie's restructured kaftan creations in flowing linen with matching harem pants, she felt the clothes stick to her body.

Bryce had attired himself in cargo shorts and a linen shirt. The green fabric of the wide-brimmed hat she'd bought him to replace the ancient bowler had tilted to one side, covering one of his eyes. In her opinion, he had the stance of an adventurer on a mission to discover more about his family history.

A strong light sprung through the wide leaves of the nearby trees. They continued their stroll, accompanied by the gurgling music of the glassy green river that flowed over rocks and stones.

"I shall never forget our wedding day and the street party in our honour." Florence kissed Bryce's hand. "With your house for sale, we have little need to head back to England. Lulabelle has taken to Molly's son and as he is both house and dog sitting at mine, following his return from spending time with his father. We have no need to worry."

Florence leaned into Bryce. "What a happy ending for Molly, with Jamie's return. How did she manage to keep such an overwhelming secret? Alone, silently suffering, she never uttered a single word, not even to us."

"It's been a most confusing business." Bryce scratched the side of his head and pulled his hat back to the centre.

"Sheer fate," he said, "took him to Little Shore. It's something of a miracle that the boy found his way back to his mother."

Florence pondered on Jamie's adventure, which eventually brought everyone together.

"Thanks to Boudie and Molly, this sad affair is behind him."

She reflected on Boudie living alone, a woman who had been desperate for a family she could call her own. Florence now understood why her sister renamed Jamie "my adopted grandson." She admired Boudie's generosity, for Boudie had promised to hire transportation for Molly's yoga students, giving them the opportunity to stay at The Belleview for a weekend in late summer, free of charge. Florence laughed, realising she had become completely immersed in Boudie's never-ending ideas.

Bryce interrupted her musings by kissing her cheek.

Turning to observe the state of the house, she said, "Such good fortune to be here." She loved the outside of the regal building. Sun-scorched, unlike the interior, which was newly painted in shades of pale pink and cream, the family home still held a unique charm. Her eyes drifted across to the mosaic-tiled swimming pool, empty and damaged in places. Florence believed with the help Boudie had engaged, they could look forward to swimming after the pool's restoration to its former glory.

Noting the veranda, she glimpsed the ghost of her mother, Elisabeth, holding a glass in her hand, laughing, and gazing down to where she and Bryce stood. She remembered the tune her mother and her friends would sway and move to—*Love is the Sweetest Thing.* Recalling the music and songs that once echoed through the open windows and down to rolling lush gardens, she said, "We have found our way back home."

• • •

Bryce disturbed her thoughts of the past by guiding her to a metal love seat. Weathered and rusty in parts, moss and leaves stuck to the curls of iron at the back. He recalled the fireflies appearing, the burnt-coloured sun setting and how Florence's mother and father would sit in this same spot.

A lone monkey swung from a branch, panted hard, and scooped up his hat.

"Damn monkey." Florence jumped up, waving her hands to shoo the animal away. With a shrill scream, the animal disappeared, swinging through the trees with the hat.

"Time to head back to the house. Let's make lemonade, just as nanny would," Florence suggested. "We can bring it back out and sit in the shade of one of the trees on the lawn." She rose and walked away.

Bryce wiped his brow, stood up, and started to follow Florence. But his attention was drawn to loose threads of rope. He reached across and grabbed the rope. Pulling at some lumps of warped wood, he found dried out seats nestled behind a tree. He recognised them; swings Florence's father had made for them using timber and thick-plaited rope. One, frayed and twisted, the other unbroken, still hung from gnarled overhead branches. Bryce decided the rough wood was strong enough to sit on. He called to Florence.

"Hold on a minute. Look what I've found." He pointed to the swings. "Remember when we held each other's hands and swung high into the air, innocent children, laughing and crying out 'higher, higher, faster . . .'" He thought of Florence's sweet mother, Elisabeth, admonishing them from a shaded veranda, "Be careful, children. Not so high."

He waited for Florence to walk down the grassy bank. Upon reaching him, she fell into his arms. "For old time's sake, come and sit on this sturdy swing," he said.

"You know perfectly well I am not a young girl." He watched her hesitate. "What if the swing won't support me?" With some persuasion, he assisted her to settle onto the swing and rock her body back and forth. "There we go." Building momentum, he pushed his wife into the air.

"Whee! I am free, just like the birds flying across the sky." She giggled as her footwear slipped off onto the ground below.

After a few minutes, Bryce slowed the swing and helped Florence stand. He knelt, picked up the sandals, and placed them on her feet. "My dearest wife." He looked into her eyes. "Seems we have found our lost chapter." He held her close. Hand in hand, they headed for the main kitchen, where a young housekeeper greeted them. She carried a tray with a jug of lemonade and some crystal glasses. On a china plate, to his delight, sweet Indian treats of Jalebi and Modak were temptingly displayed. Another plate held English biscuits, custard creams, and chocolate digestives.

Bryce guided Florence to sit under a coconut tree, where a table had already been set. Clapping their hands in joy, they sat together, raising their glasses to a new life and their happy place.

FROM THE AUTHOR

Thank you for reading *Second Chances*. I hope you enjoyed this story. I would be delighted if you would leave a review. This helps me so much as an author and encourages me to write more stories for you.

A bonus story about Boudie can be found here: www.thepublishingcircle.com/Boudie.

SOCIAL MEDIA LINKS

Follow Miriam at
www.MiriamMcGuirk.com

Miriam McGuirk Author
@Miriam_McGuirk
miriammcguirk1
Miriam McGuirk
Miriam McGuirk

ABOUT THE AUTHOR

Born in Dublin, there has been a constant thread of writing and storytelling running through Miriam's life. She proudly nurtures her ability to tell stories, thanks to her Irish heritage.

Miriam lives in the historical town of Rye, East Sussex with her husband, Chris, spending time in her writing cave where only her characters join her. When not writing, Miriam enjoys reading, cooking, sea swimming, and walking along the healing coast.

www.ingramcontent.com/pod-product-compliance
Lightning Source LLC
Chambersburg PA
CBHW030606310726
48979CB00003B/595

* 9 7 8 1 9 5 5 0 1 8 2 8 9 *